The Thrice Named Man

Part XV

Avenger

The Thrice Named Man

Part XV

Avenger

by

Hector Miller

www.HectorMillerBooks.com

The Thrice Named Man

Part XV

Avenger

All characters and events in this publication, other than those clearly in the public domain, are fictitious and any resemblance to real persons, living or dead, is purely coincidental.

Author: Hector Miller

Proofreading: Kira Miller

First edition, 2024, Hector Miller

Part XV in the book series The Thrice Named Man

ISBN: 9798327733657

Text copyright © 2024 CJ Muller

All rights reserved.

No part of this publication may be reproduced, stored in a retrieval system, or transmitted, in any form or by any means, without the prior permission in writing of the author. Publications are exempt in the case of brief quotations in critical reviews or articles.

Contents

Chapter 1 – Moneta (October 270 AD) 1
Chapter 2 – Ravenna 23
Chapter 3 – Semnones 37
Chapter 4 – Quadi 48
Chapter 5 – Ferryman 61
Chapter 6 – Grain 72
Chapter 7 – Boar (February 271 AD) 81
Chapter 8 – Hunt 90
Chapter 9 – Fortuna (March 271 AD) 105
Chapter 10 – Horse 117
Chapter 11 – Moccus 125
Chapter 12 – Nordstau 134
Chapter 13 – Perchta 142
Chapter 14 – Scout 153
Chapter 15 – Trebia (April 271 AD) 167
Chapter 16 – Turn of the Tide 182
Chapter 17 – Pyre 194
Chapter 18 – Onion 203
Chapter 19 – Attrition 211
Chapter 20 – Rites (May 271 AD) 222

Contents (continued)

Chapter 21 – Metaurus 235
Chapter 22 – Trade 248
Chapter 23 – Deception 256
Chapter 24 – Ticinum 267
Chapter 25 – Passes (June 271 AD) 279
Chapter 26 – Advice 295
Chapter 27 – Road to Rome (July 271 AD) 303
Chapter 28 – Posca 314
Chapter 29 – Reward 323
Chapter 30 – Legions 333
Chapter 31 – Honour and Virtue (August 271 AD) 348
Chapter 32 – Caelian Hill 363
Chapter 33 – Peace 387
Historical Note – Main characters 396
Historical Note – Avenger storyline 400
Historical Note – Random items 403
Historical Note – Place names 410

Chapter 1 – Moneta (October 270 AD)

Rome, the Eternal City.

It was not yet the end of the first watch of the morning, but already people were flocking up the hill along the Via Sacra. Some were on their way to the Senate House, while others were bound to pay obeisance at the sanctuaries of the three gods whom Romans revered most.

Aurelius Felicissimus was heading to the Temple of Juno Moneta for reasons that could not have been further removed from the spiritual.

Only one of the two narrow bands of Tyrian purple adorning his tunic was displayed to passersby. The other stripe was concealed by a crimson toga cut in the short style. It was not only the quality of the wool or the pattern of the weave that ensured that the garment remained in place, but also the meticulous way in which it had been folded. It marked him as a man who liked things neat and tidy - a man in charge of his own destiny who left little to the fickle hand of fate.

"Greetings *procurator*", a man said from inside a litter balanced on the shoulders of six strapping Germani slaves. In their wake strolled four hard-looking men, no doubt the occupant's guards.

'They may be toughs straight from the Subura, but in a scrap my coin will be on Praximus', Felicissimus thought as he slowed his pace to fall in beside the transport. He stole a quick glance over his shoulder and noticed that the unimposing, sinewy man who trailed twenty paces behind, had also shortened his step. *'That's why I freed you from the ludus, Celt. It's rare to find a killer with a head on his shoulders.'*

"I will send you the details of the craftsman who builds these", the corpulent occupant said while running sausage-like fingers along the ornately carved wood inlaid with gold leaf and ivory. "And I am willing to discuss a loan", he added, smiling amicably to show that his words were in jest.

Although Felicissimus was of the equestrian class - not the new military order introduced by Augustus, but from an old and respected family - he was wealthier than most who wore the broad-striped toga. "Not a bad suggestion, neighbour", he replied. "Just decide how much you wish to loan from me."

The grey-haired patrician roared with laughter and leaned out to playfully slap the *procurator's* shoulder. "You are long overdue for elevation to the senatorial class, Aurelius", he said. "If you wish, I will personally argue your case."

"But then I will have to rise earlier because litters are so slow", Felicissimus replied with a friendly grin.

The senator reciprocated and waved a hand to show that the equestrian should go about his business. "Carry on then, an important functionary like you must have much on his plate. Besides", he added, and indicated the dark clouds gathering above, "you might get wet if you do not get under roof soon."

Felicissimus quickened his step to ensure that his neighbour did not catch a glimpse of his grin morphing into a self-satisfied smirk. *'You just wish to be my sponsor, you decrepit old fool'*, he thought. *'Little do you know that my ascension is assured as I have already come to an arrangement with a man much more powerful than you.'*

The remnants of the smirk vanished when he noticed that, up ahead, a group of well-dressed men were congregating in front of the Rostra, close to the carved stone reliefs of Emperor Traianus. Most of the men were nodding their agreement as a grey-haired patrician spoke animatedly, slapping a palm with a balled fist to emphasise his words. Although his back was turned to Felicissimus, the *procurator* immediately recognised his noble benefactor by the way he asserted himself. His sponsor remained adamant not to make public their relationship, so, during the hours of daylight at least, he avoided the senator whenever possible.

"By the gods, I'm late as it is", he cursed out loud, and turned left onto Etruscan Street that passed between the Temple of the Divine Twins and the towering Basilica Julia. To his right, on the marble steps of Caesar's law court, the complainants whose cases were scheduled to be heard, were already lining up, waiting for the judges to summon them.

Again, he quickened his pace to reach the next intersection before a procession of chanting priests who were on their way from the cattle market. The holy men drove half a dozen pure white oxen destined to be sacrificed on the stone altar at the Temple of Jupiter Optimus Maximus.

Having skirted the basilica, Felicissimus slowed down to catch his breath just as the first heavy drops splattered onto the paving stones. He turned right onto the road that ran along the ridge and paused under the Arch of Tiberius to allow the worst of the shower to pass.

When the rain eased off, he noticed that the steps which led up the hill were unoccupied, and he thanked the gods that the executions were yet to commence. Passing by the stark grey walls of the Mamertine Prison, he could faintly hear the wailing of the men suffering inside. He skipped up the

Gemonian stairs, not so much to get out of the drizzle, but to steer clear of the pleas of the condemned.

Winded by the second flight of steps, he paused to rest and admire the view. From the corner of his eye, he caught movement amongst the shrubs of the overgrown field that abutted the temple complex. All knew that the summit of the Capitoline Hill had since time immemorial been dedicated to the cult that divined the will of the gods. As a leading citizen, it was his duty to expel the trespasser.

"Nothing is sacred anymore", Felicissimus muttered to himself as he waded through the shrubbery to chase away what could only be a vagrant, who, by his mere presence, was defiling holy ground. His mood soured when the drizzle intensified.

Strolling closer, he spied a hooded figure sitting cross-legged in the centre of a clearing. His eyes were closed and, seemingly unaffected by the downpour, the black-robed man swayed forward and back while he hissed an incantation in a forgotten tongue, his gnarled fingers wrapped around a spiralled staff that lay across his lap.

Although it was expected of the holders of high office to take the auspices before major events, the rites had become little more than a formality. The *college of augers*, like most other organisations in Rome, had not been immune to the rot of corruption. In exchange for a donation of gold, diviners all but guaranteed a positive outcome. Nevertheless, Felicissimus was not aware of any impending actions of the magnitude that required divine guidance.

He was about to call the man out as a charlatan when he noticed the ring of stones surrounding the black-robed oldster. He had read about the square pieces of marble that were worn smooth from centuries of use, but never laid eyes on them. Each one bore the markings of the ancient cult that was as old as Rome itself. It was rumoured that Romulus's own hands had chiselled the cubes from the monolith that birthed the Black Stone.

To disturb an auger was to doom one's shade to wandering the darkness for eternity. Instinctively Felicissimus retreated a step, and his right hand fumbled beneath his tunic. He uttered a muted curse when he realised that he must have left his amulet beside the washbasin in his chamber.

Just then, the holy man opened his eyes and seemed to stare directly at him, his lips moving silently. Feeling naked without his talisman, Felicissimus was overcome by a sensation of unease. He prayed to Fortuna that the priest was not cursing him, but rather mouthing the hidden name of

Rome, or mayhap reciting an invocation to the unnamed guardian spirit of the city, as required by the sacred rites.

Four vultures, running before the worst of the storm, glided overhead. The priest came to his feet and moved a sacred stone to mark their passing. A nesting pair of large black woodpeckers, spooked by the vultures, fluttered down from their perch high up in the canopy of a nearby pine. Again, the bearded man repositioned a stone to note the path of their flight.

Spellbound by the spectacle, and ignoring the pouring rain, Felicissimus remained rooted to the spot, watching intently while the priest recorded the signs of the heavens with the stones. Involuntarily, he ducked as a lightning bolt lit up the sky around him. Moments later, a clap of thunder echoed across the seven hills of the Eternal City.

With a sombre expression, the priest moved the seventeenth stone into place. Rather than returning to his seat, the robed figure approached at a shuffle.

Felicissimus had the clarity of mind to raise a closed fist - a signal to his tame gladiator, who was no doubt watching from the shadows, to keep his distance.

The oldster, bent with age, came to a halt when less than a pace separated them. Leaning on his crooked staff for support, the priest studied the *procurator* while the rain continued unabated, rivulets of water running from the hair and robes of both men.

"Have a care, mint master", the priest croaked. "I am bound by duty and honour to inform you that you have angered the gods."

"I… I did not request your services", Felicissimus stammered. "In fact, I… I regularly contribute handsomely towards the college."

"Mars has passed judgement on you and on this city", came the reply.

"I… I will amend my ways", Felicissimus stuttered.

For a span of heartbeats, the old priest regarded him as a viper would a mouse. Then his thin lips parted into a humourless smile and the *procurator's* gaze was drawn to purple-black gums that must have been devoid of teeth for years.

The oldster indicated the pattern of the stones in a sweeping gesture. "The gods have given their judgement through the sacred stones. It is too late to repent - the die is cast."

"I will sacrifice a dozen red bulls", Felicissimus replied. "Mars will be appeased."

"Mayhap he will", the oldster shrugged, "but the god has already dispatched his messenger. He will fall on the corrupt like a flood tide and the streets of Rome will run red with the blood of the wicked."

* * *

When Felicissimus sat down in his office in the Roman Mint, he gestured for his slave to pour him a cup. "Make it neat", he commanded.

"As you wish, master", the Greek replied, averting his eyes as he presented a jewel-inlaid gold goblet on an ornate silver tray.

The mint master chugged the contents and breathed a sigh as he surrendered to Bacchus's comforting embrace. The wine almost immediately drove away the dark thoughts, and his eyes settled on the bondsman standing near the door. Although the slave had only been in his possession for a month, Felicissimus had already come to rely heavily on the man whose talents seemed to be without limit. The mint master could not help but ponder how he had managed to get by without him.

"Draft a message to the head of the *college of augers*", he snapped. "I wish to know if one of theirs was on the summit today. I will put my seal on the missive. Do not dare return without a reply."

The procurator was sipping on his second goblet of wine when the Greek presented him with a scroll. He read the concise message, silently marvelling at the quality of the writing. Yet, it was not his way to give praise to mere slaves. It was common knowledge that such a practice would soon cause the lowest of men to get ideas above their station. "Acceptable", he snapped, and pressed his seal ring into the blob of molten red bitumen. "And do not drag your feet on the way back or I will have you whipped."

"Yes, master", the slave replied dutifully, his head bowed in supplication.

His nerves calmed and the missive dispatched, Felicissimus decided to take a stroll through his domain. He made his way to where the process started, the melting shop on the upper level. He climbed the stairs while Praximus, who led the way, callously shoved aside the slaves struggling under the weight of heavy bags of charcoal that were needed to feed the insatiable fires.

Although the large shutters of the workshop were wide open, the furnaces were already warming the building to an uncomfortable level. Clerks seated at strategic points kept tally of the ingots of silver, tin and bronze that were being melted down to produce the silver coins needed to pay the legions. Not that much silver remained in the coins of Rome, but in an effort to reverse the slow collapse of the fiscus, Emperor Claudius Gothicus had decreed that the minimum amount of silver in the *antoninianus* was to be one in twenty parts.

Just then, a foreman shouted a warning. All except a slave wearing a thick wool tunic, and armed with a long iron rod, stepped away from the furnace. The man inserted the rod into a slot in the dam stone and pried out the stopper to release the molten metal from inside the crucible.

Even though the mint master was twenty paces from the furnace, the heat accompanying the pour was almost unbearable. He shielded his face with a forearm while the slave, whose tunic had started to smoulder, struggled to replace the stopper. Eventually he succeeded, but afterwards collapsed from exertion. "Them dam stone slaves never last more than a month, master", Praximus remarked as the man was dragged away. "Vulcan's breath got this one proper. He ain't comin' back."

When the worst of the heat had receded and the molten metal had run along the channels into the coin moulds, dozens of tong-wielding workers rushed to remove the trays of flans to where teams of *monetarii* were waiting.

Felicissimus watched the closest group with interest.

A man with thick leather gloves plucked a blank from the tray and expertly placed the hot metal disc onto a die. Another positioned a punch containing the reverse die on top of the flan and held it securely in place. A third worker, a large man with the meaty forearms of a blacksmith, wielded a heavy forge hammer. Twice he struck the punch cleanly, setting the image of the emperor into the coin.

Moments later, the whole of the workshop reverberated with hammer strikes as the well-oiled machine that was the Roman Mint churned out coin after coin.

The dies and hammers of the moneyers had hardly devoured the hundreds of hot flans when again a warning echoed across the floor.

The dam stone slave appeared two heartbeats later.

Felicissimus fixed his guard with a sidelong glance. "You were right, Praximus", he said, raising an eyebrow. "I believe that's a new one."

* * *

At dusk, the head clerk presented the daily report to the master of the mint.

Felicissimus's mood had darkened as the day progressed because his Greek slave was yet to return with a reply from the *college of augers*. "Give me the gist of it", Felicissimus snapped at his subordinate.

"Today, forty-eight thousand two-hundred and ninety coins were minted, *procurator*", the functionary said. "We used four hundred and fifty-eight *libra* of metal ingots, of which twenty-two were silver."

The mint master had not gained his position because he was a fool.

"Your figures do not add up", he said. "You have produced too many coins." He looked the clerk straight in the eye while tapping the index finger of his right hand on his desk to show his impatience.

"The balance was made up of yesterday's *corrodere*", the clerk replied, "which was exactly three *libra*."

After minting, the rough edges of the coins were clipped and shaved. These shavings, or *corrodere*, which could be substantial, were collected and reintroduced into the furnaces.

"Very well, then", Felicissimus muttered. "How much clippings were produced today?"

The clerk consulted his records. "Five *libra*, procurator", he replied.

"I will confirm the weight of the *corrodere* and sew up the bag", he said. "You may go home."

"Thank you, lord", the man said, inclined his head, and did as he was told.

Once the clerk had gone, the mint master addressed his guard standing at the door. "Any word of the Greek slave?"

"No, lord", the Celt replied.

"Make sure that everyone has gone home", he instructed Praximus, and sent him on his way with a wave of a hand.

The guard nodded and walked out the office to do his master's bidding.

Having the whole mint to himself, Felicissimus strolled down to the strongroom where the precious metals and coins were stored. Meticulous records were kept of the number of coins minted while the raw metals used were reconciled per weight, leaving little room for fraud or theft. But the mint master was a clever and resourceful man and he had long before discovered a loophole in the system. Because the *corrodere* was easy to steal, he insisted that every evening, he personally, in his official capacity as the mint master, seals the bag containing the offcuts. The following day the bag's weight would be confirmed and, while still closed, committed to the furnace. Whenever circumstances forced others to be around, he made a show of meticulously testing, weighing, documenting and sealing the canvas bag. When he was alone, which was most of the time, Felicissimus got up to mischief. He replaced the contents of the bag with cheap lead, iron or zinc shavings and delivered the valuable offcuts to his sponsor who processed it into coins with the dies that the mint master had provided. Apart from his sponsor, only Praximus was aware of his ongoing fraud.

As he emptied the fine silver shavings into a leather pouch that Praximus normally concealed beneath his cloak, Felicissimus's thoughts dwelled on the encounter with the auger. So preoccupied was he that he failed to notice that the Greek bondsman had arrived at the door.

When he had finished his dark toil, he turned to leave and came face to face with the slave. Caught red-handed, the blood drained from the mint master's face. He did well not to gasp in shock, and collected himself within the space of a heartbeat. "What are you doing here?" he barked.

The Greek nervously rummaged through a pouch and presented a small scroll. "I apologise for my tardiness, master. I had to wait for the reply of the head of the *college of augers*", he said, making sure to avert his eyes to avoid being struck for insubordination.

"Wait in my office", the mint master said, dismissing his bondsman.

When the Greek had gone, Felicissimus slumped down on a stack of ingots and buried his head in his hands. Slowly and deliberately, he drew half a dozen deep breaths to steady himself. '*Damn it. Damn it. I was careless*', he thought. '*The slave saw it all.*'

There was only one solution to the predicament the mint master found himself in. He would sorely miss the slave, but it was a small price to pay for peace of mind.

Just then, he realised that he was still holding the long-awaited reply from the *college of augers* and unrolled the scroll.

Procurator Felicissimus. Greetings from Gaius Cerialis.

The man you encountered upon the Capitoline was an imposter. The stones of Romulus are undoubtedly forgeries as years ago they were interred with one of our order.

Sadly, charlatans posing as augers are becoming an everyday occurrence.

Felicissimus issued a sigh and thanked the gods that the man he had stumbled upon earlier in the day was a fraud. He was sure that the reply was a sign that the gods favoured him.

It was time to deal with the issue at hand.

He strolled to where his guard was waiting at the bolted door that provided the only access into the mint. "Why did you allow the Greek slave to enter?" he snapped.

"You have been waiting on the scroll, lord", Praximus replied sheepishly.

His words were met by a frown from the mint master.

"I apologise for my lack of judgement, *procurator*", the guards said.

"Very well", Felicissimus sighed, placated by the submissive tone. He beckoned the ex-gladiator closer, "I will allow you to right your mistake."

When he had finished giving instructions, the mint master added, "Do not allow him to speak with anyone and make it clean and discreet. There is no need to make him suffer."

"As you wish, lord", Praximus replied, but judging by the look in his eye, Felicissimus suspected that the death of the slave would not be quick.

* * *

"Thank you for escorting me home", the slave said meekly after he and the guard had been on the road for nearly a sixth of a watch. "The neighbourhoods at the bottom of the hill are no longer safe after dark."

Praximus resented the slave's fear. The guard did not wish to engage in idle chatter and issued a grunt that was open to interpretation.

After a hundred heartbeats had passed, he fixed his companion with a sidelong glance. To his amusement, he noticed that the bondsman walked with a gait that was unusual for his kind. He had seen it before, but only in the arena when he faced men who knew how to wield a blade. He remained unconcerned because he was confident that the Greek had never even gripped a weapon, never mind wielded one in anger.

Praximus waited patiently until he and the slave were the only ones walking down a poorly-lit alley between two warehouses. Slowly his hand moved to the hilt of his dagger. He had wished to strap on his shortsword instead, but his master had been adamant, that to avoid drawing unwanted attention, he should use the weapon favoured by the gangs of the Subura.

The Celt's fist tightened around the leather grip as he waited for the perfect moment. He closed his eyes, visualising the iron entering the side of the Greek's neck, near its base, and suppressed a smile as he imagined the look of utter surprise on his victim's face.

As soon as they were in the darkest part of the alleyway, Praximus struck with the speed of a viper. But rather than finding soft flesh, his dagger was deflected by iron. Years on the sand of the arena had honed his reflexes, and he skipped out of the way of a counterstrike, but too late to avoid the burn of a sweeping blade cutting deep into his forearm.

The guard stumbled backwards, only coming to a halt where an oil lamp was recessed into the stone.

Praximus squinted into the night and noticed the slave calmly strolling towards him. In his fist glinted the blade of a dagger the likes of which the ex-gladiator had never seen before. His first thought was to turn around and run, but he managed to suppress his fear. "What blade is that?" he asked, shocked at the sudden tremble in his voice.

"Leave your weapon on the ground", the slave said, ignoring his words. "In return, I will give you your life."

The Celt recognised the iron in the man's voice. He knew that he was not facing a mere slave, but someone accustomed to the power of command. The urge to cast aside his dagger was almost overwhelming, but he drew confidence from his countless victories.

The Greek stopped two paces away, adroitly twirling the dagger in his fist. "Make your choice", he said.

In answer, Praximus lunged.

He would never know how his opponent managed to dodge the strike, but his dagger met only air and he felt the bite of a honed blade sliding deep into his flesh at the base of his neck. His vision blurred, his legs gave way, and he collapsed facedown, dead before he hit the cobbles.

Diocles bent over at the waist, heaved the corpse onto its back, and wiggled the *akinakes* from the body. He proceeded to wipe the iron on the dead man's cloak, moving closer to the dim light to inspect the blade. Carefully he ran the back of a nail along the edge and uttered a curse in his native Greek when he felt the nick. "The Hun is going to kill me", he mumbled, and quickly moved back into the shadows when he noticed movement at the far end of the alley.

A bear of a man lumbered closer. He came to a halt three paces from the corpse and prodded the dead man with a boot. "My man didn't see you leave the mint, Master Diocles", he said. "But I wasn't worried 'cause I know that Umbra's taught you good and proper. All I need to do is doll up this one for the city guard."

The big man reached down, and with his own blade cut the throat of the dead man.

"That's better", he said. "That's how them gangs of the Subura like to do business."

"Thank you, Ursa", Diocles said.

"No need", the big man replied, waving away the Greek's words. "I owe Umbra more than I can repay in a lifetime."

Ursa turned around and beckoned for the Greek to follow him. "Come. Let's get you out the gates and on a horse before someone starts asking questions."

Chapter 2 – Ravenna

The inn of Hortensius in Siscia. Two weeks later.

As soon as I laid eyes on Diocles, I ordered him to the baths. The Greek had no doubt ridden hard to reach Siscia in good time, and it showed.

"But I bring urgent tidings, Lord Emperor", he protested. "I have spent two weeks in the saddle."

"Sixteen days!" Hostilius exclaimed. "Were you trotting all the way or did you get lost in the passes?"

Diocles rolled his eyes. "Fourteen days, centurion", he said, correcting the Primus Pilus.

Hostilius possessed little tolerance for the culture of the Sasanians and Greeks, no matter how insignificant or harmless the ways of the Easterners appeared. "How many times must I tell you that a week's got eight days", he snapped. "First they cajole you into adopting the small things, and before you know it you're darkening your eyes with that hideous grease paint. Next you'll be wearing jewellery like a woman and pretty soon you'll be too meek to go to war."

I waved Diocles away to put a stop to the argument.

Two-thirds of a watch later my aide returned, refreshed by the warm water and the ministrations of strigil-wielding slaves. He poured himself a cup and joined Gordas, Hostilius and me where we reclined on couches, sipping wine. Once he had recounted what he had learned in Rome, he reached underneath his cloak, drew a blade, and handed it hilt-first to Gordas.

My barbarian friend accepted the dagger with a nod and lovingly wiped the honed edge with an oiled cloth while turning it over in his hand. "I don't remember this nick being here", he said, his gaze fixed on the grey iron.

"Your dagger saved my life", Diocles revealed. "It turned the blade of an assassin."

The Hun frowned at my aide's words, as all in our inner circle knew that parrying a dagger strike edge to edge was a mistake expected of a novice.

"Cut him some slack", Hostilius said, waving away Gordas's words. "I owe you a favour, Greek, and I'll repay it by commissioning a new *akinakes* for the Hun."

Gordas stopped drawing the oiled stone along the razor edge and gently touched it to his cheek. Immediately a thin red line appeared. A heartbeat later a crimson droplet trickled down his tattooed, scarred flesh. "No need", he growled, issuing a wolflike grimace. "This blade is special to me. It has sentimental value."

"Why do you owe me a favour, tribune?" Diocles asked, skilfully changing the subject.

"This arrived yesterday", the Primus Pilus replied while holding aloft a scroll. "The legate based at Castra Regina confirmed the deployment of the new recruits. Maximian and Nidada are both part of a vexillation of two centuries that has been sent to bolster the garrison at Abusina, a fort on the Raetian *limes* just a few miles west of the legionary fortress."

"If my memory serves me correctly, the *cohors III Britannorum* is stationed at the fort", Diocles said.

Hostilius nodded. "Those Brit auxiliaries are tough as nails", he said. "It'll take more than what's left of the Alemanni army to breach the stone walls of Abusina, especially if two centuries of legionaries are fighting by their side."

"I don't believe it will come to that", I said. "The Alemanni will take many seasons to recover from the defeat they suffered on the shores of Lake Benacus."

"I agree", Hostilius said. "Now that I know that my two boys are doing just fine, I can't wait to get to Rome and deal with the bastards who ordered Marcus to be poisoned. We'll ask Gordas to get a few names from the mint master and work our way up the ladder, if you know what I mean."

The Hun, who was concentrating on polishing the last remnants of the nick from his blade, issued a grin to show that he had indeed been listening and was keen to render his aid.

Just then Vibius was shown in by the duty tribune and he joined us on the couches.

"Any news from the Eternal City?" he asked, and accepted a cup from Diocles.

"The Greek caught the master of the mint red-handed. He is bleeding the treasury dry", Hostilius summarised. "And it looks like the thief is in cahoots with a few senators. It wouldn't surprise me if it's the same men who conspired against Marcus."

"What do you plan to do, Lucius?" Vibius asked.

"I suggest we head west with the Illyrians and the two Raetian legions that are camped outside the walls of Siscia", I said. "When we arrive at the gates of Rome, I will investigate the fraud and act in accordance with the Laws of the Twelve Tables."

"I say we skip the formalities", Hostilius replied. "And go straight to the part where they get shoved off the Tarpeian Rock. That way, we don't give them time to fight back. Don't be fooled to think that we're not marching to war, Domitius. We're heading into battle, alright. You, for one, should know that in war, the element of surprise carries much weight."

"The last thing I want to do is cause a bloodbath in the Eternal City by being rash", I said. "I will take the risk and deal with the culprits in a civilised manner."

Hostilius shrugged. "Have it your way, Domitius", he said. "As always, I'll be watching your back, but don't say I didn't warn you. Those patrician bastards are more dangerous than savages."

* * *

The following morning just after practising bladework with Cai, serving slaves arrived from the kitchen with cloches heaped with grilled fish, fresh baked bread, cheese and fruit.

The servants were still arranging the food on a low table when Hostilius and Gordas walked in.

I popped a nugget of white fish into my mouth, gestured for my friends to join me on the couches, and offered the plate to Hostilius. The Primus Pilus passed the fish to the Hun, leaned forward, and instead took a fresh loaf from a serving dish. He tore off a piece, which he dipped in his cup of wine. It was the way of peasants, who used sour wine to soften old, stale bread.

"My *ava* couldn't afford fresh fish", Hostilius said. "So I never got used to breaking my fast with it." He motioned to Gordas who seemed intent on devouring the whole plate of cheese. "See, the Hun also sticks to what he knows."

I was about to comment when Diocles arrived, a scroll bearing the mark of the Roman Senate in his fist. "A delegation from the Senate wishes to meet with you, Lord Emperor", my aide announced.

"Where?" I enquired, and selected a ripe fig from amongst the chilled fruit.

"Ravenna", he replied.

"Why in hades would a bunch of senators want to come all the way to Ravenna?" the Primus Pilus asked. "From what I've seen, most of them don't even want to venture more than a day's ride from their heated baths and stocked wine cellars."

"They fear that you have uncovered their corruption, Lord Emperor", Diocles ventured. "And they know that you are not a merciful man."

"I agree with the Greek. They want to see whether you are on the war path, Domitius", Hostilius said. "If they believe that you pose a threat, they will either try to kill you or prevent you from going to Rome."

"Mayhap they have a plan to turn your face away from their mischief", Gordas said.

"Ravenna is on our way", I shrugged. "We might as well hear what they have to say. Besides, there is nothing that the conscript fathers can do that will keep me from going to Rome."

* * *

Without rising from my seat I extended my right hand, which prompted Pomponius Bassus, who led the senatorial delegation, to bow low and press his moist lips against the iron signet ring adorning my little finger. He held the position for a heartbeat too long, which tainted the gesture of obeisance with a mocking quality. "Lord Emperor", he said, the hint of a smile playing at the corners of his mouth. "It is an honour to meet the man who has subjugated so many of Rome's enemies."

"The enemies of Rome are numerous indeed", I replied, and indicated for Bassus and his two companions to take seats on the couches arranged within the pavilion that had been pitched inside the legionary marching camp.

"Would it not be better to meet inside the walls of Ravenna where we are able to offer you hospitality more suited to your status?" Bassus suggested in an effort to ascertain whether I could be swayed by the lure of pleasures of the flesh.

"I am a soldier, senator", I replied. "And my place is with my men."

With much satisfaction I noticed that Bassus's eyes kept darting to Gordas, whom I had brought to the meeting with the sole intent of intimidating my honoured visitors.

"As long as you keep your voice down and refrain from making any threatening moves, you will be quite safe from my guard", I said, and issued a pleasant smile.

"Of course", Bassus replied, swallowed, and wetted his lips with his fleshy tongue before accepting a cup of wine from a pouring slave.

"I could not help but notice that two of the Empire's legions are camped outside the walls", the senator on Bassus's right observed. "Some would think that it is posturing meant to intimidate."

"Is that what you believe it is - posturing?" I asked.

Gordas's hand dropped to the hilt of his blade and he fixed the speaker with a leer.

"Not at all", the senator replied, emphasising his words with a vigorous shake of the head. "I meant that others might get that impression."

"Good", I said, and took a long, slow swig from my cup.

Bassus leaned in closer and lowered his voice. "The reason why we have come all the way to Ravenna is to inform you of a case of corruption that has recently come to our attention", he said. "We have discovered that the newly-minted silver coinage is being debased by the addition of cheap iron and lead."

"The *head count* noticed it too", the third senator interjected. "Neither they nor the traders want to accept these *antoniniani*. The coins carry your likeness, Lord Emperor, which is most unfortunate as it has also tainted your image in the eyes of the populace."

"What remedy do you propose?" I asked.

"Allow us to investigate this despicable act of corruption, Lord Emperor", Bassus suggested. "By the time you arrive in the Eternal City, the heads of the perpetrators will decorate the arch above the gates."

For a span of heartbeats I sipped on my wine, supposedly weighing up his words in my mind.

"No", I said.

Almost identical frowns wrinkled the brows of the three senators.

"I wish to deal with the guilty men myself", I said. "Even if a small part of a festering limb is allowed to remain, the rot soon spreads. I plan to cut out the corruption with my own hand to save the Empire - and be warned", I added, "I will cut as deep as I have to."

"May I offer you a word of advice, lord", Bassus replied with an insincere smile.

"Of course", I said.

"Use gold to settle internal disputes, and reserve the use of iron for the enemies of Rome", he replied.

* * *

"I think you might have kicked a hornets' nest, Lucius", Vibius said later that evening. "Word is that the delegation boarded a galley at the Classis Harbour less than a third of a watch after your meeting. The ship departed immediately even though the wind was unfavourable."

"They are in a hurry to return to Rome", Diocles said.

"Those three senators are trouble, especially Bassus", Hostilius said. "I wouldn't be surprised if he's the ringleader."

"Well, we have two full legions and ten thousand horsemen at our back", I said. "It is time to confront the enemy lurking within and settle this matter once and for all. Marcus's murder must be avenged."

I noticed that Cai, who normally cautioned against rash action, just sipped his wine and refrained from making a comment.

* * *

Early the following morning while Cai was helping to fit my armour, there was a knock at the door. A heartbeat later Diocles entered. Behind him, I caught a glimpse of a large tribesman flanked by four praetorians.

"The barbarian carries a message from Belimar, the king of the Quadi", Diocles said. "He refuses to speak with anyone but you, Lord Emperor."

While Cai tied my breastplate at the back, I gestured for the man to enter my chambers.

Unlike the Romans, the tribes north of the Danube and Rhine did not commit their messages to writing. "Speak the words of your king", I commanded in the tongue of the Germani.

The warrior showed his respect by bowing deeply and repeated the message he had learned by heart.

"The ancient enemies of the Quadi, the Semnones, are stirring in the woods of the North. For a change, the clans are not

gathering to come east, but rather to cross the Danube and raid the lands of Rome. Travellers speak of a priestess conducting blood rites in the holy groves, summoning Wodanaz, their terrible god of war. Some say that her name is Braduhenna, the war-witch of the Alemanni. I am calling my warriors to arms to come to your aid should you so desire."

Years before, in the time of Gallienus, I had assisted the Quadi and their allies to repel an invasion of the northern Germani tribes. The Semnones, or Juthungi as some called them, were no insignificant threat, but a warlike people, fierce and numerous.

"Tell your king that I thank him for the warning", I replied to the messenger in his native tongue. "If the Semnones cross the Danube I will accept his offer of assistance. Rome will not forget their friends and neither will I."

He inclined his head. "I will do as you command, Lord Eochar."

"What was that all about?" a dripping wet Hostilius said as he pushed past the praetorians escorting the warrior from my chambers.

"Belimar believes that the Semnones are preparing for war", I explained.

"So he's asking for our help?" the Primus Pilus asked while he dried his face with a linen rag.

"No, he is offering us assistance", I said. "The rumour north of the river is that the Semnones plan to invade Roman lands. Apparently Braduhenna has a hand in it."

"I wouldn't put it past that bitch", he said. "Question is, are we still heading for Rome or will we go north to guard the border?"

"The Empire cannot be governed based on fear", I replied. "Our plans remain unchanged, although I will alert the garrisons manning the border fortifications."

"Well", he said, unclasped his cloak from his shoulders, and handed the soaked garment to a servant. "Even if you want to, we won't be going anywhere today. The scouts report that the road west is flooded. Unless you intend to break the boys' morale, I recommend you give them more firewood and an extra wine ration and allow them to warm themselves around the cooking fires until the weather clears."

Chapter 3 – Semnones

Hostilius drained the last drops from his cup while staring at the storm raging outside the pavilion. "It's been seven bloody days", he sighed, "and the weather hasn't improved one bit. Truth is, it's getting worse. If I didn't know any better, I'd think that the gods don't want us to go to Rome."

I had been plagued by the same thought so I offered no counter argument.

"Why would the gods bring us as far as Ravenna if they don't wish us to go all the way to the capital?" Vibius mused.

Diocles arrived with the answer to the question. Following close behind my aide was a soldier dressed in the garb of a Syrian auxiliary. Judging by the expression on Diocles's face, the man was not the bearer of good tidings.

"Lord Emperor", the messenger said, inclining his head. "Hanicus Ababunis, decurion of the *ala Ituraeorum sagittariorum*, reporting as ordered."

"Speak, decurion", I commanded.

"The Germani have invaded Raetia", he said. "Five days ago, a horde crossed the Danube near the stronghold of Castra Regina."

"Which tribe?" Hostilius asked.

"Semnones, tribune", the decurion replied.

I shared a look with Hostilius before I asked the obvious question. "How many?"

"Our scouts talk of fifty thousand, lord."

I felt my throat constrict at the answer, but tried my best not to show concern. "Does the legionary fortress still stand?" I asked once I had calmed myself.

"They came in the middle hour of the night, lord", the Syrian decurion replied. "Thousands threw themselves at the walls, but we managed to beat back their attacks."

I noticed that Hostilius had turned pale. "And Abusina, the fort that lies to the west of Castra Regina?"

"I heard that the men who garrisoned Abusina fought valiantly, tribune, but they were overwhelmed by the barbarians' numbers."

"Any survivors?" Hostilius croaked, his words laced with desperation.

The cavalry officer averted his eyes. "The soldiers who died fighting are the fortunate ones", he said. "The survivors must have been taken by the Germani to serve them as slaves."

"Are the invaders on their way to Italia?" I asked, and noticed that Hostilius had lowered himself onto a couch, his head buried in his hands.

"No, Lord Emperor", the messenger said. "All indications are that they have no intention of remaining in Roman lands for long. The savages are not raiding deep into our territory, but are moving east along the Danube, through Noricum and Raetia towards Pannonia."

"Why is that?" I asked, as it was rare for invaders to turn away from the prospect of loot, even if their carts were already filled with spoils.

"Our scouts trapped a few of the savages", the messenger replied. "When they applied iron and fire the Germani told them that they had no wish to share the fate of the Alemanni who invaded Italia last year. They plan to take their loot across the river at the ford near Carnuntum."

"Ready the legions", I said to Vibius when the man had been escorted from the pavilion. "Tomorrow at first light, we will lead the army north."

Hostilius raised his head from his hands and it was clear that he was sick with grief over the fate of his boys who were amongst the soldiers who had garrisoned the fort at Abusina. "The savages fear you, Domitius", he said. "Their scouts will tell them of the legions' approach and they will flee across the Danube into the dark forests before we can get within ten miles. Even if Maximian and Nidada still live, we will not see them again in this life."

I walked closer and laid a hand on Hostilius's shoulder. "That, my friend, is why we are going to speak with Belimar."

* * *

The following morning we were greeted by clear skies and sunshine. Judging by the way the men jested with one another, the pleasant weather served to improve the spirit of the legionaries who had been wallowing in the muddy streets of the camp for days.

"I believe that it was Arash who kept us from travelling all the way to Rome", Gordas ventured.

"I hope you're right", Hostilius said, the set of his jaw showing that the shock of the previous day had been replaced by a steely determination.

Although the ground bordering the road was a mire, the cobbled surface was dry. From experience I knew that the cool, dry conditions would enable the legions to march farther than the expected twenty miles. Still, it would take the infantry a minimum of three weeks to reach the Raetian border. By that time, the barbarians would have retreated into the near-impenetrable forests that covered most of the lands north of the river.

"How long before the invaders cross the Danube and return to their lands?" I asked Gordas.

"It is not easy to drag wolves away from a fresh kill", he replied. "The war leaders of the Semnones will take at least ten days to round up the warbands who had ventured too far south." The Hun rubbed a palm over the scars adorning a cheek - a sign that he was deep in thought. "Add two more days for the chiefs to execute those who defy their orders, and another seven to heave their laden carts across the ford."

Few men knew the ways of barbarians as intimately as my savage friend.

I mumbled to myself as I calculated our route.

"Did you say something, Domitius?" Hostilius asked.

"We have to reach the stronghold of the Quadi within two weeks", I replied. "While the legions march for Carnuntum, we will head for Brigetio on the Danube, which lies seventy miles to the east. The fort borders the territory of the Quadi."

I noticed Hostilius and Diocles share a look. To avoid the inevitable argument, I added, "But thirteen days would be better", removing any ambiguity.

"Who's the 'we' you're talking about?" the Primus Pilus asked.

"You, Gordas, Cai and me", I replied, my words drawing a frown from my aide.

I beckoned them closer, lowered my voice, and explained what needed to be done.

* * *

The Danube near Brigetio. Two weeks later.

Although I was sure that he meant no disrespect, the praetorian tribune stared at me like one would at a child who failed to grasp the enormity of a situation. "Lord Emperor, I have sworn an oath to protect you", he whispered, indicating the flat-bottomed barge in the shallows behind him. "Which means that I have no choice but to accompany you if you decide to cross the river."

I was about to remind him of his oath of unquestioning obedience but decided on another strategy. "I am bound for a secret meeting with the king of the Quadi", I said in a manner that suggested I was taking him into my confidence. "My spies fear that the jealous Marcomanni king have sent a handful of chosen men to ambush us near the river on our return. While I venture into the hinterland, I need you and your unit to remain on the northern bank of the Danube to make sure that their plans are foiled."

Convinced that he was performing an important task, the tribune inclined his head. "I understand, Lord Emperor, and I will obey", he said, and signalled for his thirty men to board the riverboat.

Not long after, I stood on the deck holding Kasirga's reins while the barge silently glided over the dark water, cleaving the layer of early-morning mist that would obscure our arrival from anyone watching from beyond the river. Eventually the captain directed the stern towards the far bank where the transport parted the bull rushes, slid across the mud, and shuddered to a halt.

While the men of the imperial guard reconnoitred the woods bordering the river, Hostilius, Gordas and I dressed in the garb of Germani nobles. As soon as we were done, the officer of the guard signalled that all was well and we led our horses onto solid ground.

"He seems the eager type", Hostilius said once we were out of earshot of our escort. "How did you convince him to stay with the transport?"

"He is guarding against a Marcomanni ambush", I replied.

Hostilius raised an eyebrow. "There probably hasn't been a Marcomanni in these woods since the time of Marcus Aurelius", he said.

"Probably", I grinned in agreement. "But one can never be too careful, eh?"

Gordas issued a grunt and nudged his mare to a canter. "It is good that you left them behind, Eochar", he said in the tongue of the Sea of Grass. "I have seen them ride - they would have been a burden."

We thundered along the muddy forest tracks, watering and changing horses regularly. The farther north we ventured, the more often we spied small farms and pastures which the Germani had cleared with axe and hoe. For the peasant farmers it was the time of year to prepare for the cold season. Some were busy gathering late crops of spring barley, emmer, einkorn and oats, while others stared at us wide-eyed, their arms stained red up to the elbows with the blood of goats and pigs whose smoked meat would sustain them during the coming winter.

Disregarding the occasional plough horse that toiled in the peasants' fields, only the nobles of the tribe owned horses fit for riding. The locals had learned the hard way that it is preferred to avoid their social betters rather than run the risk of a confrontation with mounted warriors. Apart from an occasional rustle of leaves on the side of the road, we found the paths deserted as whoever used the tracks melted into the greenwood at the first sign of approaching horsemen.

Mid-afternoon, we arrived at the stronghold of the Quadi - a sizeable settlement of wooden dwellings built on the summit of a low hill. The village was protected by a ring wall of packed stone topped with a palisade of sharpened logs that were lashed together with braided rope.

At least twenty Quadi warriors guarded the entrance to the town. Two of the spearmen crossed their weapons when we rode up to the stout gates. "We do not know you, lord", one of the guards said, his tone cold but respectful, no doubt careful to offend an important noble.

"I am Prince Eochar of the Roxolani", I said. "I seek an urgent audience with my friend, King Belimar."

The guard nodded and indicated that we should wait outside the gates.

"My *ava* always said that one shouldn't trust Germani. Even though they may not try to be devious, the wickedness has been bred into them, so they can't help themselves, you see", Hostilius reflected. "Be on your guard, Domitius, especially when they appear friendly."

"Best is never trust new friend or old enemy", Cai said. "Belimar both."

"Yet, in our darkest hour, Belimar and his Quadi came to Rome's aid", I countered. "Without them, we surely would have been defeated by the great army of the Goths."

Hostilius scowled in reply, while Cai's face remained expressionless.

I was about to offer a retort when the guard returned. "Follow me, Lord Eochar", he said, and inclined his head in respect. "The king will see you immediately."

The residence of the Quadi ruler was even grander than I remembered. Belimar, his black beard streaked with grey, met us at the top of the wooden steps leading up to his great hall. "It is good to see you all", he said, embraced me like a long-lost brother, and clasped arms with Hostilius before inclining his head to Gordas and Cai. "Come", he said, "tonight we will feast our friendship."

I could not help but notice Hostilius raise an eyebrow, giving me his I-told-you-so look.

Chapter 4 – Quadi

Despite Hostilius's concerns, the hospitality provided by the Quadi king could not be faulted.

While slaves fed the flames of the great hearth with thick beech logs, kitchen servants stacked food on the table. Unlike the peasants who sustained themselves on a thin gruel of coarsely ground oats, Belimar's table creaked under the strain of platters heaped with spitted boar, grilled beef, smoked pork, soft cheese and berries fresh from the surrounding forests.

"The Semnones have grown much in power", Belimar said, and took a swallow of mead from his ornate drinking horn. "They regularly raid our northern lands, but pickings in the territory of the Quadi are slim at best. Now, instigated by the war-witch of the Alemanni, they have turned their gaze to Rome."

"The last time I encountered the tribe, they had many warriors who fought from the saddle", I said. "I am told that the invaders are footmen."

"They are a numerous and ancient race", Belimar replied. "Some of their eastern clans use horses to make war, but those chieftains have not joined their brethren in the invasion of Roman lands."

I nodded to show that I accepted his explanation. "I wish to bring my horsemen across the river at Brigetio and travel west along the northern bank all the way to Carnuntum", I said, and reached for another chunk of boar. "North of the river we will lay an ambush for the Semnones where they least expect it."

"How many of your warriors will traverse my lands?" Belimar asked.

"Ten thousand of the ones you call *black riders*", I replied.

"Your horsemen are feared in our lands, but they are too few to destroy a force of fifty times a thousand", Belimar said. "Besides, too many of the Semnones will escape into the forest where your cavalry cannot pursue. There, they will regroup and overwhelm you with a counter attack."

Belimar was right, of course.

"What do you propose?" Gordas asked while tearing into a juicy cut of beef.

"I have eight thousand warriors straining at the leash", the king said. "They are all footmen who know the ways of the forest and are keen to avenge years of incessant raids."

"At what price?" Hostilius asked, and swallowed down another piece of pork with a gulp of ale.

A smile split Belimar's bearded lips. "The Quadi will share in the loot equally", he said.

"One quarter", I countered.

"We will be travelling through the southern domains of the Marcomanni", Belimar pointed out. "Although their king is a friend, I will have to part with much coin for him to allow a Roman force to pass through his lands. Allow me to claim one third of the loot, and I will ensure that your men and their mounts are fed while they are north of the river", he suggested.

I extended my arm.

Belimar reciprocated, gripping my forearm in the way of the warrior, thereby sealing the arrangement.

Then the king raised his horn in a toast. "I thank you all. For the first time in many seasons I have something to look forward to, now that the destruction of my enemies is all but assured." He pressed the vessel to his lips and thirstily slurped the contents while two golden rivulets spilled from the corners of his mouth, streamed down his beard, and dripped onto the rushes.

Just then I noticed a number of scrolls scattered amongst furs in the corner of his hall. "I did not know that you are interested in the writings of the Romans", I said.

"When I was a slave in the *ludus*, I learned to read the words that the Romans draw", he said.

"You never fail to surprise me, my friend", I replied, duly impressed with his skills. "What are you reading about?"

The great General Hannibal", he said, and took another swig from his horn.

* * *

On the morrow, escorted by twenty of the Quadi king's oathsworn, we made our way to where we had left the *turma* of imperial guardsmen. A mile north of the river, the tribune and six of his men rode out to meet us.

"Lord Emperor", he greeted, inclining his head.

"Anything to report?" I asked.

A look of disappointment flashed across his clean-shaven face. "Although we combed the area, we could not find any sign of a Marcomanni ambush", he said.

"You must have scared the savages off", Hostilius suggested drily, which seemed to appease the young officer.

"Nothing else?" I asked.

"And the Illyrian horsemen have arrived at Brigetio", he added sheepishly. "Tribune Diocles has assembled a fleet of troop transports and will commence ferrying the men and their horses across the river at your signal, lord."

Not long after, I stood beside Gordas at the water's edge as he launched pitch-smeared fire arrows high into the sky, the missiles leaving a trail of smoke that was impossible to miss. He had hardly released his third shaft, when from the other side of the grey water I heard the shrill note of a *buccina*. In response, a handful of military barges pushed off from the far bank.

Their progress was painstakingly slow as it took close on a sixth of a watch for the first vessel to glide onto the muddy northern bank. Diocles led his horse off the timber deck and joined Hostilius, Gordas and me where we were watching the spectacle. "Ideally we should have used fifty barges", he said as he watched another boat unload its cargo of thirty horsemen together with their mounts. "But the river fleet is not what it used to be", he sighed. "For years, destroyed or damaged vessels have not been repaired or replaced because of the shortage of coin in the treasury. I managed to commission twenty-two. I have inspected them, and it is a miracle of the gods that half of the boats still float."

"Gallienus and his cronies always had enough gold to dine on lark tongues and host extravagant games", Hostilius grunted.

Before I could add my support to the Primus Pilus's statement we were distracted by shouts of alarm. Gordas pointed to the middle of the river where a barge was leaning to one side at a precarious angle, half of its deck already submerged. Fortunately the stricken vessel had been making its way back to the far bank with only the ship's master and half a dozen crew on board. We watched as the men abandoned the doomed ship and splashed towards the nearest vessel.

"Make that twenty-one", Diocles sighed.

The remainder of the day, as well as most of the following, was spent ferrying the Illyrians across the Danube. By the time that the last of the horsemen led their mounts onto dry ground, only seventeen barges remained afloat, the other five having found a final resting place at the bottom of the river.

Late afternoon, while the Illyrians were setting up camp, Belimar and two of his ringmen arrived at our fire under escort of a dozen praetorians. I stood to show my respect for the Quadi king. "You are welcome at my hearth", I said, and gestured for my friend to take a seat on the furs beside the fire.

"I have brought my army south as promised", he said. "Eight thousand of my best men are camped but two miles to the west." He indicated the surrounding forests. "We know this land, so tomorrow my warriors and I will lead your horsemen west."

* * *

Initially I was concerned that Belimar's infantry would significantly impede the Roman horsemen and keep them from reaching Carnuntum in time. But the Quadi, who were accustomed to the narrow muddy tracks winding through the forest, made excellent progress. The same conditions slowed the Illyrians to such an extent that we struggled to keep up with the barbarians, who were encumbered by little more than furs, spears, waterskins and small pouches filled with cheese or smoked meat.

We continued our advance west for ten days, hardly progressing thirty miles on a good day.

Hostilius, who rode in the vanguard beside Diocles, reined in at the bottom of yet another muddy incline and carefully guided his gelding along the left edge of the path where the underfoot conditions appeared to be less treacherous. He pointed at the trailing Quadi footmen who were jogging up the last steep section with ease before they disappeared over the crest. "Just like bloody animals", he muttered.

Kasirga, in whose veins flowed the blood of the sure-footed horses of the Sea of Grass, effortlessly powered up the slope. Gordas, who rode beside me on a Scythian mare, had no difficulty matching my pace.

"I remember a time when I would never have been able to keep up with him", the Hun said, indicating my mount.

In my heart I knew that it was time for Kasirga to retire to a life of ease. Truth be told, my stallion was past his prime, but to me he was more than just a horse - he was a friend who had saved my life on more occasions than I cared to remember. I stroked his muscular neck and he whinnied in reply.

"That must be Gerulata", I heard Diocles say from behind me as we descended the far side of the hill. I twisted in the saddle and noticed my aide pointing across the river at the blackened remains of a Roman fort situated on an embankment overlooking the Danube. "I heard that the Alemanni overran the garrison last year and burned it to the ground."

Diocles's comment must have reminded Hostilius of the unknown fate of Maximian and Nidada, his expression suddenly turning serious. "If that is Gerulata, it means that Carnuntum lies but fifteen miles to the west. I don't know about you, Domitius", he growled, "but I've had enough of struggling through the mud churned up by Belimar's band of savages. I say we leave the Illyrians to keep an eye on the Quadi, and we ride west."

Gordas squinted up at the clear morning sky. "Without the Germani and the black riders we will be there a watch before sunset", the Hun said, throwing his weight in behind the Primus Pilus.

"We need guide", Cai pointed out.

"I will ask Belimar for a scout who rides well", I suggested.

"Just make sure he doesn't give us one who blabbers all the time", Hostilius said. "I'm fed up with the savages' incessant chatter as it is."

We made our way up the column with our spare horses in tow, the Quadi parting to allow us to reach Belimar and his escort of mounted warriors.

"We wish to ride ahead and scout the position of the enemy", I said as I reined in beside the king. "We need a man to be our guide, one who rides well and knows the tracks."

"Bojos!" the king called out, which prompted a ruddy-bearded rider to steer his horse closer. The warrior inclined his head when he reached his lord's side. "Guide Lord Eochar and his men to the ford in the Mother River."

Again, Bojos bowed his head without a word, which earned him a grunt of approval from the Primus Pilus.

Our guide signalled for us to follow, then nudged his horse to a canter.

"I like him already", Hostilius grinned as we fell in behind the Germani.

It was evident from the onset that Bojos not only knew the lay of the land, but he was also a decent horseman. Having said that, our progress left much to be desired. A sixth of a watch after breaking away from the Quadi column, Gordas fell in abreast of me and indicated the scout. "It's his horse", the Hun said. "We should give him one of the spare mounts when we change."

Three or four miles down the track we stopped to water the horses. I extended the reins of a magnificent roan gelding to Bojos. He accepted the reins, his expression incredulous.

"It is a gift", I said in the tongue of the Germani. "Guide us well and you may keep it."

In the lands north of the river not even chieftains or kings could afford a horse the likes of which I had gifted to Bojos. His gaze alternated between me and the horse, a deep frown on his brow. Then he seemed to accept the fact that it was not a jest at his expense and bowed deeply before gaining the saddle.

"It seems that our guide is truly a man of few words", Hostilius said as he mounted his own horse.

Gordas's assessment was accurate. By the end of the first watch after noon, Bojos led us off the track, eventually reining in on a forested embankment overlooking the river.

To our left, on the far bank, the dark stone walls of Carnuntum towered over the surrounding landscape. Two massive stake-lined, V-shaped ditches surrounded the stronghold. Of the sprawling civilian settlement that had flourished outside the battlements, only smouldering ruins remained.

Hostilius pointed at the distant walls where spear-wielding soldiers patrolled the rampart. "It's the improved fortifications that you ordered built that saved them, Domitius", he said. "You see those black dots in the ditches? They're rotting Germani corpses impaled on stakes."

Diocles was the one who had drafted my orders and he recalled the specifications. "The inner ditch is ten paces wide and six feet deep", he said. "The outer trench is the same width, but two feet deeper."

On the far side of the tower-studded walls, a long line of Germani ox-wagons were slowly making their way through the ford in the Danube. Hundreds of carts, heaped with plunder, were still waiting their turn on the Roman bank. Even from far away the shouts of the drovers could be heard as they jostled to be the next to guide their carts into the water to gain the perceived safety of the northern bank.

"The garrison must have used up all the bolts of their *ballistae* fending off the attack", I ventured. "Else they would be targeting the wagons."

Behind the wagons waiting to cross, thousands of Semnones warriors were congregating. They blocked the approach from the south, the hafts of their spears swaying like barley stalks in a breeze.

"They're expecting trouble", Hostilius said. "The legions must be closing in and the savages have gotten wind of it."

"Look", Diocles said, and pointed at a few hundred fettered captives still on the far bank. "I wonder if Maximian and Nidada are amongst them."

I turned to face Hostilius. "They will be", I said. "And once we spring the trap, freeing your sons will be a priority."

Chapter 5 – Ferryman

Having taken stock of the situation, I waved Diocles closer. "Take Cai with you and return to the Illyrians. Bojos will guide you", I said. "Set up camp no closer than five miles east of where the invaders are crossing. Make sure to speak with Belimar, no fires must be lit. Be ready for battle when the sun rises tomorrow."

"I understand and I will obey", my aide replied.

I turned towards Gordas and explained what I needed of him.

While Diocles and the Hun went about their business, Hostilius and I watched as the Semnones toiled at the ford.

"Most of them own little else than a rusty spear and the lice-ridden furs they wrap around their shoulders", the Primus Pilus reflected. "Because they have nothing to lose apart from their pathetic existence, the chieftains have no trouble persuading them to raid south of the river." He pointed at the many wagons still arrayed on the far bank. "But now that they are rich in loot, they fear losing that which they have gained by the blade. They will first take their booty across the river before they, themselves, cross."

Gordas returned at dusk.

"Come", he said. "I have found a fisher and persuaded him to take us to the southern bank."

Although I did not ask, I was sure that my friend had not convinced the poor man with honeyed words or the lure of coin.

We followed the Hun down game paths until we arrived at the Danube where a skiff had been pulled onto the mud. In the boat, a peasant lay on his back, his hands and feet bound and a crude gag stuffed into his mouth. Judging by the man's appearance, he was Roman.

Gordas and I climbed into the skiff and sat down on either side of the trussed creature. Hostilius shoved the vessel into the water and nimbly hopped in without getting his boots wet. While the Hun and I negotiated with the owner of the boat, the Primus Pilus pulled at the oars.

"Do you understand my words?" I asked our captive once we were out of earshot of the bank.

The terrified fisher nodded his head, his wide eyes unblinking.

"Untie his bonds and remove the gag", I said, and added for good measure, "but slit his throat if he so much as issues a peep."

To show that I meant what I said, Gordas kept the blade of his dagger at the man's throat.

Long before, I had learned that news travels faster than an army on the march. "Where are the legions?" I asked.

The man's eyes grew wider, clearly concerned that providing the answer would result in his throat being opened.

I indicated for Gordas to remove the honed edge from the man's neck. "Speak", I commanded.

"The legions have built their camp three miles up the road, lord", the peasant said, and pointed south. "I came to catch fish 'cause I want to help our good soldiers, I do", he added, and gestured to a woven basket filled with a dozen or so pike and redfish. "Only the best for the brave men of Rome, at no charge of course."

It was common practice for the locals to try and sell their produce to the legions at exorbitant prices. There was no reason to believe that our guest was any different. "I will pay you two silvers for the lot", I suggested.

Although I had offered double what his catch was worth, the peasant had obviously planned to vend it at an even higher price. When an immediate acceptance was not forthcoming, Gordas pressed his blade to the man's jugular.

"Th.. Th… Thank you, lord", the fisher stammered. "You are most generous."

Two hundred heartbeats later, Hostilius guided us into the shallows, jumped onto the bank and dragged the skiff onto the grass. I harboured no doubt that the only thing that kept the man from darting into the undergrowth was the promise of two silvers.

"Bring the fish", the Primus Pilus snapped. "Or do you want me to carry it for you?"

Most men would not dare disobey a command from Hostilius. The fisher was no exception. He picked up the basket and followed us into the shrubbery.

* * *

"Who goes there?" the guard officer at the main gate of the legionary camp growled. He squinted into the low light, the sentries beside him already drawing back their *pila*.

"I wish to speak with Legate Vibius Marcellinus", I said.

"Who in hades do you think you are?" the centurion barked.

"Is that the way to speak to your emperor?" Hostilius growled in reply. Arguably, the Primus Pilus's voice was even more recognisable than his face, and the centurion obeyed instantly.

"Open the gates!" the officer barked, and hurried down from the rampart.

"Forgive me, Lord Emperor", he said, and bowed deeply.

I extended my hand and gripped his forearm in the way of the legions. "You did well, centurion", I said. "Now take me to the legate."

I paused to look over my shoulder and noticed that the fisher was still there, an incredulous expression plastered on his pock-marked face while he kept on repeating the same words, "They will never believe me. They will never believe me."

"And make sure that the fish is taken to the kitchens", I commanded. "I am famished."

* * *

"The redfish is excellent", Vibius said, and took a morsel from the bed of crispy fried onions.

"I prefer the pike", Hostilius replied, and scooped another generous helping of fish from the rich white wine sauce flavoured with lovage, oregano and crushed black pepper.

"I have but fifteen thousand legionaries under my command", Vibius said, "and that includes the auxiliary infantry. The odds will be three to one at best. I have my doubts whether we will be able to withstand a determined onslaught from the enemy."

"The Semnones will not have their hearts in the fight because their loot will be on the other side of the river", Gordas said, and helped himself to a piece of soft cheese that he swallowed down with a gulp of wine. "Men who are constantly looking over their shoulders do not fight well."

"Tomorrow morning, make sure that the legions are drawn up for battle outside the camp", I said. "Do not advance until you hear the call of the *buccina*."

"I understand and I will obey", Vibius confirmed. "But how are you going to get back to the northern bank?"

"I still owe the ferryman two silvers", I replied, and savoured the last swallow from my cup.

"Just make sure you don't pay him until you get to the other side", my friend advised.

* * *

The following morning at the grey hour of the wolf, the invaders resumed carting their spoils across the ford. Once the exhausted oxen had dragged the last of the wagons onto the northern bank, we abandoned our position on the hill and made our way to the nearest dirt track. Gordas led us east, back to where the Illyrians and the Quadi were waiting.

"The Semnones have brought almost all their wagons to this side of the river", I said, and noticed that a greedy leer appeared on Belimar's face. "As we speak, the invaders will be bringing their warriors across."

"The ford at Carnuntum has been in use since the time of the ancients", I said. "For centuries traders have camped at the side of the track and harvested wood for wagons or fires. Their passage has left swathes of ground devoid of growth on both sides of the track."

"Which makes it ideal for the Illyrian horsemen", Diocles surmised.

I nodded. "The open ground is bordered by forests of oak and beech. King Belimar was right when he said that the invaders will melt into the trees if we do nothing to prevent it", I said, and acknowledged the Quadi king with a nod. "I asked him to array his warriors in the shadows of the greenwood bordering the battlefield."

Belimar nodded his agreement with my words. "I will do as you ask", he replied. "The Quadi will silently make their way through the forest while Bojos guides you and your horsemen to the place of ambush."

"Come. It is time", I said, and followed the guide west.

A sixth of a watch later, Bojos reined in where the path emerged onto a broad track. He used his chin to gesture to the left and raised three fingers.

"I'm starting to think that the savage can't speak", Hostilius mumbled. "If I were a gambling man, I would guess he means we are three miles north of the ford."

"The river crossing lies three miles to the south", Gordas confirmed.

I led the Illyrians into the open. Behind me, the well-trained riders deployed in closed formation across the width of the four-hundred-pace-wide track of open ground.

"Signal to the legions south of the Danube to advance", I said.

The signifer drew a deep breath and the shrill notes of the *buccina* made their way over the open ground and across the river, no doubt also alerting the Semnones that there was a hostile force to the north.

For effect, I raised my blade to the heavens and allowed Kasirga to rear up onto his hind legs as the *draconarius* of the Illyrians lifted the standard high into the air to signal the charge. A deafening roar escaped from the ranks as ten thousand black riders spurred their warhorses to a gallop.

There was no doubt in my mind that the invaders became aware of our presence as soon as the *buccinator* had touched his lips to the war trumpet. It was not an error in judgement, it was a deliberate strategy. I have heard men claim that in war, total surprise must be achieved in order to overwhelm an adversary, especially if the foe is superior in numbers.

They are wrong.

When an army is ambushed without warning, it is not the element of surprise that brings about their destruction. It is the fear and panic that sets in afterwards that takes them to their doom.

By the time the enemy detected us, about ten thousand had managed to cross to the northern bank, leaving close to forty thousand men south of the river. Realising that the precious loot that they had bled for over the last weeks was on the other side of the wide water, thousands of Semnones on the southern bank surged into the river to reach the northern bank and protect that which they held dearest.

The warriors who found themselves on the northern bank had only a span of heartbeats to react. When they laid eyes on the thousands of iron-clad riders thundering down upon them, fear got the better of their greed. They turned tail and sprinted towards the ford and the safety of the bulk of their army.

The Illyrian signifer tilted the wolf head standard, causing a shrill wail to escape from its iron maw. I lowered my lance, but did not waste the spear by driving it into the back of a fleeing tribesman, and simply ran him over. My gaze settled on another fur-clad warrior. Having learnt from the fate of his kinsman, he jumped onto the platform of an ox-wagon and drew back his weapon. The iron head of my armour-piercing lance skewered his torso, the momentum lifting him high up into the air before the haft gave way and the corpse disappeared amongst the hooves. All around I heard the cries as Semnones fell to the lances of the black riders.

Many of the fleeing Germani must have realised the folly of running back the way they had come, and sprinted for the cover of the trees on either side of the track. When the first of them were but a few paces from salvation, Belimar's Quadi stepped from the shadows and cast their throwing spears at the mob trying to find refuge in the greenwood. In desperation, the survivors joined their brethren running towards the river.

The wall of Roman horsemen flowed around the abandoned wagons, driving the Semnones before them like Scythians herding sheep across the steppes. Eager to get to safety, the warriors of the foe jumped into the river, struggling through the waist-high water. Halfway along the ford, the routed foes fleeing south met the horde surging towards the northern bank. In the ensuing confusion, hundreds lost their footing and were swept away by the powerful river.

I reined in on the bank and gestured for the signifer to issue the command. Each horsemen unclipped two lead-weighted darts from the inside of his shield. Thousands of lethal missiles arced into the sky and rained down on the exhausted men battling the current. Hundreds were injured by the barbed war darts, and the ones too weak were swept to their deaths.

Chapter 6 – Grain

On the southern bank of the river there had been no clash of arms, which, to me, came as no surprise. My orders to Vibius were to approach the enemy, but to refrain from engaging. Under normal circumstances the barbarians would have relished the opportunity to give battle. But with the hostile force appearing north of the river, the chiefs must have been debating what the best course of action was, their indecisiveness giving rise to inaction.

While the Semnones argued amongst themselves, Vibius and his legions were far from idle, the rear ranks toiling with shovel and mattock. On my orders, they dug a trench across the open ground and used the spoil to construct an earthen rampart. By the time the invaders relinquished their plans to recover their lost loot, the legions had retreated behind their fortifications.

The Semnones must have realised the precariousness of their position. Although they had lost only one in twenty of their fighters, they were stranded on the southern bank of the Danube with little provisions, hemmed in by the river to the north and the Roman defences to the south. But the Germani were a proud people and I suspected that they would sooner die fighting than beg for mercy.

"Bring me a leafy green branch", I commanded the nearest Illyrian, who immediately galloped off to do my bidding.

"You've got the Semnones right where you want them, Domitius", Hostilius said. "Why in hades do you need a branch of truce?"

"In the coming months Rome will need her legions", I said. "I do not wish to waste the lives of my soldiers on that which can be resolved with words."

I leaned closer to the Primus Pilus and lowered my voice. "Maximian and Nidada are most probably in the enemy camp", I said. "They are a vicious breed, and will not leave their captives alive if we attack."

Judging by his expression, it was clear that my reason for clemency appealed to the Primus Pilus.

Just then the horseman returned with a substantial branch.

"Here, let me carry it, Lord Emperor", Hostilius sighed, and took the branch in his fist.

* * *

Belimar had chosen not to be party to the parley, because, as he had explained, the Semnones loathed the Quadi even more than they despised Rome. Although the king would not attend, he counselled that the Semnones, for all their bravado, would not be opposed to accepting an arrangement of peace. For that reason, it was only Gordas, Hostilius, Diocles and me who watched as four mounted nobles approached, allowing their horses to pick their own way across the rock-strewn ford. Like most Germani, they were tall men, broad in the shoulders and muscular. Their beards were thick and unruly, their lank hair fastened in a variety of knots and braids. Although their horses were of reasonable stock, their leather *braccae* were worn and their furs had seen better days. Iron or bronze helmets dangled from their saddles, but only one of the warriors was encased in scale and chain.

"Seems like the Semnones have fallen on hard times", Hostilius whispered while the delegation was still out of earshot. "Maybe raiding is not as good a business as it used to be."

"It is peculiar", Diocles said. "The Semnones are supposed to be the most aggressive and numerous of the Germani race. I have heard that other less warlike tribes pay tribute to keep these feared warriors from raiding their lands."

I noticed that a deep frown creased Gordas's brow. "They seem little different from the Alemanni", he said.

"They all look the same to me", Hostilius grunted. "Big, clumsy savages with oily beards and filthy hair crawling with vermin."

The warriors reined in when ten paces separated us.

"We have come to offer terms", the big, blonde-bearded noble wearing scale said. "If you return the loot, we will not destroy you, but go back to our lands."

"Although you seem confident of victory, remember that the gods alone decide the outcome of battle", I replied in the tongue of the Germani. "Have you not heard that we defeated the Goths and vanquished the Alemanni?"

"If they wish, the clans of the Semnones can field eighty thousand footmen and double that number of horsemen", the scaled man boasted. He extended his right arm and slowly closed his fist until the veins bulged on his forearm. "We trust in our gods and the strength of our spear-arms, Roman. And we will crush your iron legions with the help of Wodanaz, the lord of the raging horde."

"If the slaves you have taken are returned unharmed, I will allow you to cross the river and return to your lands with your weapons strapped to your belts so that your honour remains intact", I said.

I noticed a flicker of uncertainty in the Semnones's eyes.

"Return to your warriors, speak with them around the cooking fires, and give me an answer when you are ready", I said. "You have ten days to make up your minds."

* * *

Come evening, we all congregated around a fire outside my pavilion in the centre of the Illyrian camp.

"If the savages decide to fight to the death, it will be a bloody affair", Hostilius cautioned, and took a swig of wine. "We caught them off-guard today, but now they know that they outnumber us and they will be prepared."

Just then Belimar arrived, escorted by four hulking axemen.

I stood and motioned for the praetorians to allow the Quadi king to approach. "You are welcome at my hearth", I said, inviting him to take a seat on the furs beside the fire.

"I do not believe that there will be a battle", Belimar concluded after we had voiced our concerns. "Wait three days until the Semnones are hungry. Invite their chiefs to a feast and when they return to their camp, provide them with wagons heaped with freshly slaughtered beef and good wine, enough for every man in their camp. It is dishonourable for Germani to draw a blade against someone who has shown them hospitality."

Gordas grunted his agreement. "Sometimes it is better to bribe hungry warriors with meat and wine than to offer them gold", he said. "A wolf with a bulging belly is meeker than a hungry one."

Not long after Belimar had departed for his own camp, there was another disturbance. I was surprised to notice Vibius approach. In his hand he carried a scroll bearing the seal of the Roman Senate. My friend, who was of a jovial disposition, wore the look of a paid mourner in a funeral procession.

"I have read it", he said, and passed the scroll to Diocles. "It was the only way to know if the missive was important."

"Tell us", I said, already tasting the bitter bile associated with bad news.

"There is trouble in Aegypt", Vibius sighed.

"By the gods, please don't tell me that Zenobia is up to her usual tricks", Hostilius said.

A year before, while we had been battling the Goths at Naissus, Marcus was informed about Zenobia's capture of Alexandria, the capital of Aegypt. I was present when the previous emperor had issued orders for the governor to assemble his forces to reclaim the city. Just two months before, we had received the good tidings that the garrison of the Palmyrene army had been defeated and that Aegypt was under the control of the Empire once again.

"Zenobia's main army returned and attacked Alexandria three weeks ago", Vibius announced.

"Surely the governor repelled the attack", Diocles said.

"I agree with the Greek", Hostilius said. "Zenobia's army is mostly cavalry. Horsemen have little chance to unseat defenders fighting from atop a stone wall."

"A commander of the local militia betrayed the governor and opened the gates to Zenobia's forces", Vibius explained. "The governor managed to extract most of his army from the city. They marched south and took up a strong position on high ground, but somehow Zenobia's army managed to fall upon the rear of the legion. The forces of the governor were scattered and, rather than live with the humiliation, he opened his own veins."

Hostilius nodded, no doubt condoning the governor's honourable actions.

"There is more", Vibius replied. "A letter from Zenobia arrived in Rome. If she is not acknowledged as the joint ruler of Aegypt, she threatens to halt the supply of grain."

"If the grain supply from Aegypt is suspended, it will lead to massive riots in the capital", Diocles said. "It will be a disaster if the Senate is left to their own devices. We will have to travel to Rome."

"We can go to Rome once we're done with the Semnones", Hostilius suggested. "It will be over in a week, maybe sooner."

I felt my throat constrict as I was overcome with the familiar sensation that the three *parcae* were toiling at the spindle, shaping our destinies. As often before, I was left with little choice but to submit to their power which cowered even the gods. "I will depart for Rome tomorrow morning", I heard myself say. "Diocles, Gordas and Cai will accompany me."

"I'm going with you", Hostilius said. "You need someone to watch your back in that nest of vipers."

Although I wanted Hostilius by my side, I could not ask my friend to abandon Maximian and Nidada in their hour of need, so I steeled myself. "Tribune Proculus", I said, and met Hostilius's gaze. "You will remain to assist Legate Vibius Marcellinus in concluding the campaign against the invaders."

The Primus Pilus remained silent for a span of heartbeats. Eventually he issued a curt nod. "I understand, Lord Emperor, and I will obey", he replied.

He turned around to leave, but paused at the flap of the pavilion. "Thank you, Domitius", he said, and stomped off into the night.

Chapter 7 – Boar (February 271 AD)

A thick, dark fog slowly trickled through the canopy and settled on the forest floor, enveloping all in its gloomy, moist embrace.

I moved at a crouch through the greenwood. My right fist was clamped around the pommel of my blade, so I used my dagger hand to part the undergrowth. Near where the gnarled trunk of a massive linden erupted from the carpet of rotting leaves, three women sat on furs beside a blazing wood fire.

The nearest hag looked up from her toil of twirling wool around a spindle. "Sit", she snapped, offering me a gap-toothed grimace.

I did as I was told and noticed that her distaff was no ordinary peasant's tool but an ornate spear, the haft and iron blade still shiny with bright blood. The gore had not only tainted the combed wool, but also the thread that she was winding around her spindle.

"What did you expect, mortal?" she snickered. "A thread as pure and white as a Vestal Virgin's?"

The second hag was measuring the spun wool with an ivory rod, a deep frown etched on her brow. The third, her features hidden by a hooded cloak, leaned over the measurer's shoulder, the gleaming blades of her shears hovering close to the thin, blood-stained thread.

"Even if you beg, you cannot change your fate, mortal", the third sister hissed from underneath her hood. "Even the gods tremble at the mention of our names."

She had hardly spoken the words when a bright streak cleft the air and a silver arrow thudded into the moss-covered trunk of the ancient linden. Moments later, a hulking warrior stepped into the open, a silver bow slung across his broad shoulders and his hand on the pommel of a mighty sword.

As one, the three sisters issued a gasp.

"I alone decide the mortal's fate", the god replied. "You should not have interfered."

"You have no business here, violent one", the third sister spat, her breath frosting the air from underneath her hood. "You cannot harm us, you must bend to our will", she chided, and moved her shears closer to the thread.

"I am Arash the Destroyer", the god of war growled, his voice as powerful as rumbling thunder. "Relent, or you will soon find out that you are not immune to the blade of the lord of the field of blood."

"Lord Emperor", Diocles said, and cleared his throat in a way that confirmed my suspicion that it was not his first attempt at waking me.

I sat up and relinquished my grip on the dagger that I kept underneath the furs. "What time is it?" I asked.

"It is the start of the last watch of the night", my aide replied.

"Are you so eager to travel to the capital?" I jested, knowing full well that Diocles would not bother me unless it was urgent.

"The Vandali reneged on their oath", he said. "They have crossed the Danube and are ravaging our lands."

"Convene a council of war", I said. "Then help me don my armour."

Just then Hostilius pushed past Diocles. "The Greek's one step ahead of you, Domitius", he said, and lifted my scale vest from the rack. "We'll talk while you get dressed."

* * *

"My daughter has concluded her campaign against the mountain tribes north of the great plain of the Roxolani", I said. "Her horse warriors patrol the flatlands north of the Mother River. It is almost inconceivable that the Vandali would risk being caught on the plains where the Scythians would slaughter them to a man."

"The reports are clear", Diocles confirmed. I could not help but notice that he avoided making eye contact with the Quadi king who was seated opposite him. "The invaders crossed the river at Aquincum and are pillaging Pannonia Inferior, the lands west of the Danube."

"So the Vandali invaded Roman lands by moving through the lands of the Quadi", Hostilius said, fixing Belimar with an accusatory glare.

"The Vandali must have gotten wind of the absence of my army", the king replied. "They probably pillaged and raped their way through Quadi lands while I was doing Rome's dirty work."

Belimar stood to leave. "I have no choice but to return to my lands and destroy the invaders", he said. "I cannot allow them to raid my domain with impunity."

"More than anything, I need the Quadi to ensure that the Semnones do not escape our trap by traversing the forest paths", Vibius said. "Your men have proven themselves not only as woodsmen, but also as warriors of renown, lord king."

I gestured for Belimar to retake his seat. "I agree with Vibius", I said. "Besides", I added, "the Vandali have broken their oath, so they will not be returning the way they have come."

A deep frown wrinkled the king's brow. "How can you be so sure, Eochar?" he said. "They have broken their oath once. They might do so again."

"Dead men do not break oaths", I replied. "Neither do corpses cross rivers."

"How in hades will you manage to defeat them?" Hostilius asked. "We don't have enough soldiers as it is. If you take men to campaign against the Vandali, the Semnones will not accept your offer of peace, but fight their way out of the trap."

"I plan to take five thousand Illyrians to counter the new threat", I said.

"The remaining five thousand horsemen, the legions and the Quadi might not be enough to fend off a concerted effort of the Semnones to break out", the Primus Pilus insisted.

"I know", I said. "But if you promise not to tell their war leaders that I have taken half the cavalry east, neither will I."

* * *

On the morrow, Cai and I rode from camp at the head of five thousand black-clad horsemen. I was intent on crossing the Danube at Vindobona, the legionary fort twenty-five miles to the west. The detour would add two days to our travelling time, but there was no way we could ford the Danube at Carnuntum without alerting the Semnones.

Gordas and Diocles departed at the same time. The Hun, leading three spare horses, cantered north and east, carrying a message for the queen of the Roxolani. My aide, armed with the gold-inlaid ivory baton of imperial authority and a pouch of orders carrying my seal, was escorted south, to Rome, by the most trustworthy men amongst my mounted guard.

Belimar, Hostilius and Vibius remained at Carnuntum to conclude the campaign against the Semnones, confident that the invaders would soon accept the proffered terms of peace.

After spending the night inside the stone walls of Vindobona, I led the Illyrians east along the *limes* road, heading for Aquincum, the capital of Pannonia Inferior, where the Vandali had breached the border fortifications only days before. The undulating countryside bordering the river was heavily forested. On occasion the monotony of seemingly never-ending forests was interrupted by a cleared field or pastureland. Only a handful of hardy peasant farmers possessed the determination to keep the woods at bay while braving the incursions from hostile tribes north of the river.

Although it would take days to reach Aquincum, I erred on the side of caution and my outriders scouted far and wide for any signs of the enemy.

Late morning, three days after setting foot on the southern bank, we approached the stone walls of a minor fort built on an embankment overlooking the river.

"Cirpi, Lord Emperor", our local guide said. "It is where the river changes course and thunders south towards the fertile plains. Aquincum lies but twenty miles downriver."

I had not visited the area for years and wished to know the lay of the land. "Do the woods continue far south of the capital?" I asked.

"To the south of Aquincum lie mostly flatlands covered with fields of oats, barley and nard", he said. "The local barley makes the best *sabaia*", he added, and tapped a palm on the skin hanging from his saddle.

I extended a hand.

Cautiously he unstrapped the skin and passed it to me.

I accepted it with a nod and took a long swig, savouring the surprising richness of the dark brew. "It is good", I replied, and handed the skin back to him.

"It is best enjoyed after hunting boar, lord", he replied with a grin. "But you need good dogs if you wish to flush out the prey."

For a fleeting moment I felt the presence of the god.

"Repeat what you said," I commanded the guide, whose jovial expression immediately changed to one of concern.

"I am sorry, lord", he whispered. "I meant no disrespect."

"Repeat your words", I said.

"One needs good dogs if you wish to flush out the prey", he said in a quivering voice.

"Tell me how you hunt boar in these lands?" I asked.

The guide slowly released his breath when he realised that he had after all not offended the ruler of the known world. "We make tar from the fatwood of young beech trees, lord", he said, eager to please. "We mix the tar with oats, stuff it in a linen pouch and hang it from a branch. The pigs can smell it for miles."

"And then?" I asked.

"When they come, we set the dogs on 'em", he said. "To drive 'em onto our spears."

I took a gold coin from my purse and flicked it to the guide, who caught it adroitly.

"Lord?" he asked, not sure why he was being rewarded.

"Thank you for the advice", I said, and pulled on Kasirga's reins so that I could draw level with Cai.

Chapter 8 – Hunt

Come afternoon, a fresh breeze picked up. The icy blow drew in heavy clouds from the northeast and the temperature dropped. Five miles north of Aquincum I called a halt, just as the first white flakes floated down from the heavens.

Once they had lit a wood fire, I dismissed my guards, sat down opposite Cai on the soft furs, and pulled my oiled sagum tight around my shoulders.

South of the capital, between the dark woods to the west and the Mother River to the east, lay a strip of rich farmland studded with villas. My scouts had reported that the Vandali main camp was situated inside the greenwood on the western edge of the plain. By day their warbands raided Roman farms, returning in the evening to the familiar cover of the forest.

"I was the one who advised Marcus to be merciful to the Vandali", I reflected from the other side of the cooking fire. "Now they have broken their oath. My words resulted in many Romans being killed or taken as slaves."

"Yes", Cai replied.

Ten heartbeats later he asked, "Do you believe that it mistake, Lucius of Da Qin?"

I filled two cups with purple-red *basarangian* while I reflected on the Easterner's question.

"It was a harsh winter on the Sea of Grass", I replied. "Two young jackals were out scavenging when they noticed a fresh kill outside the entrance of a wolf's den. Driven by hunger, they approached, each grabbing a large chunk of meat. One scampered away to the right, the other to the left. Hardly had they claimed their prizes when the vicious wolf emerged from its lair. He chased down one of the jackals, ripping it apart in a most brutal fashion. The other scavenger escaped, the rich meat allowing it to regain its strength and survive the winter."

"The dead jackal made a mistake, some would say, while others would praise the survivor for its boldness", I said. "Yet, their actions were identical."

I shrugged.

"The people of the Sea of Grass believe that mistakes and successes are illusions", I said. "There are only choices - some the gods bless with a favourable outcome, others they curse with failure."

A thin smile split the Easterner's lips. "You have learned much, Lucius of Da Qin."

"I have come to the conclusion that the gods do not wish for me to be merciful towards the Vandali", I said. "They have chosen to enter the lair of the wolf. If it is the will of Arash, they are about to be ripped limb from limb."

* * *

"Mid-morning on the morrow, Gordas returned from his mission to the hinterland north of the Danube.

"The queen has answered your call, Eochar", he said, and accepted a cup of neat wine from a servant. "She is leading her warriors in person. They should arrive at the ford in the river before dark."

Gordas could predict the speed of a moving body of horsemen with great accuracy, which made me suspect there were other things at play. "What is holding her up?" I asked, already knowing the answer.

"Queen Aritê is travelling with three hundred archers, all mounted on good mares", the Hun said. "But Naulobates insisted on accompanying her with the same number of his men. His footmen are slowing the horsemen down", he added with a sigh.

"We will need the wolf warriors of the Heruli", I said. "We are outnumbered more than two to one."

"What is your plan, Eochar?" Gordas asked. "How will we defeat the Vandali?"

"We will hunt them in the same way that the locals hunt wild boar", I replied. "But first we need to lure the invaders to their doom. Tell me", I added, "how do the people of the horse entice their prey out into the open?"

A savage grin split the Hun's scarred lips and his hand came to a rest on the hilt of his blade.

"The Vandali are like bears", Gordas said. "They are big, lumbering men who prefer the confines of the forest."

I nodded to show my agreement.

"Bears are not easily lured from the shadows of the greenwood", he continued. "I have tried to bait them with fresh carcasses of deer and sheep, but they are clever and suspicious by nature."

"So what do you do?" I asked.

"There is one thing no bear can resist", he replied, and took another swig from his cup. "Bears usually avoid wolves because they hunt in large packs. But if a bear comes across a lone wolf it will go out of its way to kill it."

"Many times have I seen a bear lured onto the plains when an injured wolf is tied to a post. It cannot resist the urge to kill its arch enemy", he said, and tapped his chest with a fist. "It is the way that the gods have made them."

"If the Vandali are the bears, who are the wolves?" I asked.

"Who do they despise more than any other?" Gordas asked.

"They have no love for us" I replied. "But the ones they truly hate are the Scythians, the horse lords of the plains."

* * *

The following morning at sunrise, I watched from the cover of the greenwood. Behind me, five thousand black-clad riders waited in silence, the hafts of their iron-tipped lances grounded on the forest floor.

From a meandering track, my daughter led a small band of Scythians down onto the flatland south of Aquincum. Five hundred paces to their right, the forests loomed dark and foreboding. On her far side I could make out the western bank of the Mother River. The three hundred Roxolani warriors accompanying her moved no faster than walking pace, escorting seven ox wagons heaped with the most valuable commodity I could find inside the walls of the capital of Pannonia Inferior.

"It is unnecessary, the Vandali won't even notice the salt", Gordas growled. "All the dirt eaters will see is the queen of the tribe that is their nemesis. Her presence will blind them to the riches on the wagons."

From the far side of the Hun I heard a grunt of agreement from Naulobates, my son-in-law. He had reluctantly remained behind to command the wolf warriors of the Heruli.

The salt convoy had progressed less than two miles down the road when the axle of one of the transports broke, causing the cart to veer from the track. The wagon tipped over, depositing the priceless bags of salt into the ditch bordering the cobbles.

Almost half a watch passed while the Roxolani struggled to mend the wagon.

"Maybe the invaders have other things on their minds, or they suspect a trap?" I eventually said, indicating my daughter's party where they were toiling about a mile east of the treeline.

"They will come", Gordas replied confidently. "The enemy is in the greenwood, salivating at the prospect of shedding Scythian blood. But the Vandali fear the wolfpack. They are gathering their numbers to overcome the queen."

A watch before noon, Gordas's prediction came true.

The Scythians had hardly finished repairing their wagon when the wail of a Germani war horn rolled over the plain. Moments later, seven hundred spear-wielding warriors jogged from the cover of the trees, eager to come to grips with the seemingly disorganized Scythians who were feverishly trying to load the spilled salt back onto the cart.

Earlier I had attempted to convince my daughter to refrain from getting her hands dirty, or rather bloody, but to Gordas and Naulobates's obvious delight, I had failed dismally. Aritê had undoubtedly selected her best fighters, all eager to take Vandali scalps.

Below us on the flat ground, the Roxolani vaulted onto their horses, almost immediately transforming from an unorganised mob to the band of mounted killers they were. The riders wheeled towards the approaching Vandali, stringing their horn bows while in the saddle. Two heartbeats later, a dressed line of archers thundered down on the Germani, whose pace had slowed noticeably.

The Scythians dropped their reins, took arrows in their draw hands, and released. When the first volley of shafts rained down on the Vandali, three more had already left the sinew strings of the recurve bows.

But the Germani had been skirmishing with the horsemen of the plains for centuries. They halted their charge, went down onto one knee, and angled their shields to receive the brunt of the storm. When the worst had passed, all but a handful regained their feet to continue the charge.

The Roxolani line wheeled about seamlessly. At my daughter's command, three volleys were released in as many heartbeats, the shafts rising almost vertically. The horsemen slowed down to a trot, allowing their pursuers to gain on them. When the footmen once again kneeled to receive the missiles, they had no choice but to raise their shields above their heads.

Only fifty paces separated the Scythians from the Vandali front rank when the horsemen twisted in their saddles and drew back the strings past their ears. In quick succession, three heavy tamarisk shafts, travelling almost horizontally, fishtailed over each horse's rump. The wood and sinew bows, reinforced with strips of horn, endowed the arrows with incredible velocity. Many of the Vandali were too slow to slam the laminated wood into the earth, while others chose to shield themselves from the rain of missiles from above. Hundreds of cries of agony rose from the ranks of the foe as the wicked barbed tips, smeared with the most terrible of poisons, thudded into flesh and bone.

The Scythians wheeled again, raking the survivors with volley upon volley.

The Vandali wisely closed their ranks, overlapping their shields to present a near impenetrable wall of wood.

Aritê screeched a command and the Scythian horsemen divided into two groups to form counter-rotating circles, the hooves of the mares kicking up clouds of dust that swirled to the heavens.

I raised an eyebrow and stole Gordas a glance.

The Hun looked down on the unfolding spectacle, his expression akin to that of a proud father. "I taught her that", he said, his gaze unmoving. "The Vandali have never faced it before."

Spellbound, we watched as my daughter unleashed the feared arrow storm of the Huns on the unsuspecting foe. When their shield wall had been obliterated, the survivors turned tail and raced back to the cover of the trees. Only half of the original force reached the forest alive.

"The Vandali will be livid", Gordas growled. "They will not be content until their spears have tasted Scythian blood. The war leaders will be gathering the horde as we speak. They will come in numbers, and it will be soon."

*　*　*

At least a hundred of the queen's oathsworn remained in the saddle with arrows nocked. The remainder of her warband relieved the corpses of their scalps and anything else of value.

Like most savage races the world over, Scythians were usually quick and efficient at looting. Aritê took her time, knowing that the longer the Vandali were forced to watch the humiliation of their fallen, the sooner they would attack and the more likely they would be to throw caution to the wind.

Half a watch before sunset, the Roxolani had concluded their grim toil. They were loading their spoils onto wagons when the forest itself seemed to come to life and surge down the gentle slope towards the road.

"The war leaders have gathered the horde", Gordas said. "And they are eager for blood."

Aritê's warriors gained their saddles and charged towards the thousands of Germani bearing down on them.

From the corner of my eye, I noticed Gordas reach out and grab the reins of Naulobates's mare. The Herulian's horse, like its master, almost unable to restrain itself. "Wait", the Hun growled in the tongue of the Sea of Grass. "Be patient like the wolf who stalks the deer."

When the last of the rear ranks of the Vandali had cleared the forest, I nodded to the hulking warrior who commanded the Heruli.

To show his pleasure at being unleashed, Naulobates bared his filed teeth in a wolflike grin. "We relish to do your bidding, Lord Eochar", he growled, wrapped his wolfskin cloak around his shoulders, and swung down from the saddle. Three hundred wraiths followed him into the greenwood.

Below us on the plain, the Scythians were retreating before the onrushing horde.

Gordas pointed to the forest edge behind the ranks of the Vandali where two groups of mounted enemy spearmen, each numbering close to three hundred, were cantering from the treeline, thundering towards the flanks of their infantry.

"The Vandali are resourceful", the Hun said. "Their horsemen are screened by their footmen. By the time the queen sees them, it will be too late."

"It goes both ways", I replied. "Their horsemen will screen us from the eyes of the horde."

I raised my lance in the air, nodded to the signifer, and led the five thousand black riders down the hill. The Roman horsemen deployed in battle formation four ranks deep, their line stretching for almost a mile. So intent were the Vandali to envelop the Scythians in their trap, they failed to notice the wall of riders bearing down upon them from the north.

At that moment the Vandali sprang their trap. Their horsemen spilled around the edges of their footmen's flanks and spurred their mounts to a gallop to ensure that the Scythians would have no chance of escape.

The time for stealth had come to an end. I nodded to the *draconarius*, who tilted the iron maw of the wolf head standard into the wind. A high-pitched screech echoed across the plain, and in response the Illyrians kicked their massive warhorses to a gallop and lowered their long, thin lances.

I was fifty paces from the enemy cavalry when the wail of the standard alerted the foes to our presence. They twisted in their saddles and were confronted by the sight of a wall of spears and iron-encased horseflesh bearing down upon them.

The Vandali barring my way was too slow to react. It would have been a waste of a good spear so I angled the tip away from the rider's torso and allowed Kasirga to slam into the shoulder of his horse. The animal stumbled to the side and was engulfed by the wave of black riders.

Another noble, a big man with grey streaks in his ruddy beard, lowered his spear and nudged his horse to meet the threat head-on. I leaned forward, allowed the lance to slip through my fist, and felt the familiar thud of resistance as the forged tip parted the rings of his mail. Somehow the warrior managed to keep the tip of his spear trained on my heart. I twisted my torso to the right to place my oval shield in the way of the strike. The broad blade of what I believed was a hunting spear, slid off the layers of Spanish poplar. In the same movement I leaned further to the left and nudged the dying man from the saddle to rip the corpse from my lance.

The next in line of Vandali riders had had enough time to witness the encounters of their brethren with the black horsemen. They must have realised the futility of facing the heavily armoured riders, and as one they swerved to the right in a desperate attempt to escape their doom. The barbarian nobles crashed into the chanting mob of Vandali infantry who were sprinting over the flatland to come to grips with the Scythians. Fortunately for the Illyrians, the ranks of enemy footmen were spread out because they had been running for at least a hundred heartbeats. In their haste to escape their grim fate, the mounted nobles slammed into and trampled their own kind. Most of their mounts stumbled and went to ground, with only a handful proving skilful or fortunate enough to power their way clear of the mob.

The barbarian riders hurtling into their kin drew the attention of the horde away from Aritê and her oathsworn. Within heartbeats, the charging warriors baying for Scythian blood morphed into a confused, stationary mob.

Their inaction sealed their fate.

The thin ranks of tribesmen allowed the Illyrians to wash over the field of battle like a dark, unstoppable tide as there were no dense clusters of warriors to slow down the charge. Thousands of foes were killed as the first line of horsemen slammed into the savages. The second rank of riders crushed those who still drew breath, while the third trampled the broken bodies of the injured underneath the hooves.

Of the ten thousand Vandali, only one or two in ten managed to survive the charge of the Roman riders. With the Illyrians' warhorses spent, the fortunate amongst the barbarians who could still run, walk or hobble on one leg, made for the safety of the forest.

The queen of the Roxolani reined in beside Kasirga. "We can still kill half of the ones trying to escape", she said, champing at the bit to rid the earth of the Vandali.

I raised an eyebrow. "And rob Naulobates and his men of their fun?" I asked, which earned me a look.

No sooner had the survivors entered the treeline when blood-curdling howls emanated from the distant treeline as the wolves of the Heruli did that which they excelled at.

A sweet smile split my daughter's lips. "You are right, Father", she said. "I am fortunate to have a man like that, so I should learn to share."

Chapter 9 – Fortuna (March 271 AD)

Their grim toil completed, Naulobates and Aritê joined Gordas, Cai and me around a wood fire.

"Very few of the invaders escaped our blades", Naulobates said. "The Vandali will think twice before they cross the Mother River again."

"I have dispatched *turmae* of Illyrians into the countryside to hunt down the remaining bands of invaders", I said.

"You have done well, Father", my daughter reflected. "Not only have you crushed the Goths, but you destroyed the Alemanni and the Vandali. Even the mighty Semnones are at your mercy."

"The god of war favours you, Eochar", Gordas said, and lifted his cup.

I, too, raised my cup in support of the Hun's words.

Sometimes I wonder if that moment of hubris is to blame for what followed.

* * *

"Lord", the tribune of the guard said as he approached the fire, "a decurion of the Illyrian cavalry requests an audience."

"Has there been an incident with the division of the loot, or was one of our own killed during a wine-fuelled disagreement?" I sighed, expecting the usual unpleasantness that reared its head in the aftermath of a victory.

"The decurion is not attached to the divisions that fought today, Lord Emperor", the tribune replied. "He is carrying a message from Carnuntum."

"Bring him to me", I said, eager to receive confirmation that the Semnones had accepted my offer of peace.

Not long after, the cavalry officer was escorted into my presence.

"Lord Emperor", he said, and went down onto one knee.

I waved him to his feet. "Speak, decurion", I commanded.

When I saw the look in his eyes, I immediately knew that he was not a bearer of good tidings. "Lord", he said. "I bring dire news from Carnuntum."

I gestured for him to continue.

"Legate Marcellinus has sent me to inform you that the Semnones have broken out of the trap, lord", he said.

"How did the tribesmen manage to cross the ford without alerting the Illyrian cavalry?" I asked. "Was no watch posted?"

"They… They did not go north lord", the decurion stammered. "The barbarians are moving west at great speed."

I felt the dark fist of fate grip my heart, and imagined the three sisters at the base of the linden, cackling in glee.

"To the passes that lead into Italia?" I asked.

"Yes, lord", he confirmed, and took a scroll from a pouch attached to his belt. "Tribune Proculus ordered me to place this in your hand."

I nodded and the messenger handed the scroll to the tribune of the guard, who passed it to me.

Once I had dismissed them both, I read the letter out loud.

Greetings Domitius.

Do not assign any blame to Vibius. I am the one who failed miserably in my duty to you and to Rome.

During the middle hour of the night on the Ides of March, the Semnones managed to infiltrate the legionary fortifications. Many of our boys were slaughtered by a blade in the back.

The savages are heading west to Iuvavum at great speed. There, they will almost certainly enter the passes that lead to Italia.

Although the barbarians have abandoned their wagons, they still hold captive the slaves they have taken.

Vibius and I have decided to pursue the Germani with the legions as well as the Illyrian horsemen. The king of the Quadi has proven his loyalty by offering to fight by our side. If the gods will it, the savages can still be stopped before they ravage Italia and, may the gods help us, plunder Rome itself.

I am confident that you will soon add your forces to ours so that we may destroy the invaders together.

By my negligence I have not only endangered the Empire, but I have also placed my two boys in mortal danger. I doubt that my wife will ever forgive me, but pray that the gods will.

May Mars bless you.

"The scroll was written four days ago", I said. "If the Semnones are not encumbered by loot or heavy wagons they will advance thirty miles a day. In less than three days from now they will ascend the passes south of Iuvavum."

"We will not catch up with the enemy on this side of the great mountains, Eochar", Gordas said, his thin lips pursed in frustration. "It will take at least two days to gather the black riders that you have sent out to hunt the scattered remnants of the Vandali. If we ride well, another eight days will see us arrive at the passes."

I knew that Gordas was right. "Then we will join our friends in Iuvavum and together pursue the barbarians through the mountains", I said. "Once they are clear of the foothills of the Alps, we will destroy them on the flatlands north of the Po, just like we did with the Alemanni."

Later, alone in my tent between the furs, I pondered my sudden reversal of fortune. I was beset by a feeling that the god of war had turned his face from me.

But, like so many times before, I was wrong, which meant that I was about to find out what it really felt like to be abandoned by the gods.

* * *

The following morning at the hour of the wolf, I sent out riders far and wide with orders for the Illyrians to report to camp immediately. My daughter and Naulobates had agreed to remain south of the river for a few more days to finish the work that the black riders had started and eradicate any remaining invaders.

By the second watch of the day, all but two *turmae* of riders had returned. Many told of brief encounters with fleeing Vandali who were destroyed with relative ease. We were almost ready to depart when, by the first watch of the afternoon, the last *turma* of cavalry cantered in from the south.

Gordas and I, surrounded by my guards, rode out to meet them.

It was immediately apparent that the unit had been involved in a hard fight. At least ten of the riders nurtured wounds of some sort, and three corpses were draped over the backs of warhorses.

"Lord Emperor", the decurion said, and saluted in the required manner.

"Tell me", I said.

"We stumbled upon a Vandali warband of about a hundred footmen, lord", the officer replied. "They were heading for a ford a few miles south of here. The barbarians were well-armed and armoured, and it turned out to be a proper fight, lord."

"And those people?" I asked, pointing at a number of civilians mounted double on what appeared to be spare horses.

"Slaves that we captured from the Germani", he said with a grin, as it meant that he and his men would receive a generous portion of the spoils.

One of the male slaves, a dishevelled creature who sat atop a horse with an equally filthy young female, started to struggle against his bonds. He issued a series of muffled screams as they were bound and gagged.

The nearest rider lashed out and the young slave tumbled from the saddle, hitting the ground with a dull thud, winding and silencing him instantaneously.

"My apologies, lord", the decurion said.

"Why are they gagged?" I asked.

"They've lost their senses, lord", he said. "They insist that they know you, and no amount of beating seems to help." He drew his dagger. "Mad slaves don't sell, so I might as well silence them proper."

His words brought to mind something that Hostilius had said a few months before. "Stay your hand and bring the slave to me", I commanded.

The officer ordered one of his men to drag the slave closer.

Although his hair was lank and his face covered with dried blood and dirt, I recognised him immediately.

I retrieved a purse with twenty gold coins from my saddlebag and the tribune passed it to the wide-eyed decurion. "They are now my property", I said. "Untie them, allow them to bathe and give them good clothes from the loot. Feed them, mount them on two of your best horses, and report back to me with haste. Ensure that they are not harmed in any way."

"Do you understand, decurion?" I added to ensure his full compliance.

"I understand, Lord Emperor", the decurion replied. "And I will obey."

* * *

Less than a third of a watch passed before my two new slaves were escorted into my presence where I waited in the vanguard of the Illyrian column.

"It is good to see you and Ganna again, Secundus", I said once the young Roman and his Semnones bride had joined Gordas, Cai and me.

"Thank you, Lord Emperor", he said, and his woman inclined her head to show her respect.

"We will talk while we ride", I said, and indicated for the column to advance.

"Tell me all", I said once we were on our way.

"After you saved Ganna and me from the Alemanni, we did as we had intended, lord", Secundus said. "We went north, crossed the Danube and journeyed to the hinterland that is the domain of the Semnones."

"The Germani are nothing like I imagined them to be", Secundus said. "Ganna's father, a noble of the tribe, welcomed me into their home. When he heard our tale, he gave his blessing for us to wed."

I could not help but smile, as I, too, experienced only heartfelt hospitality from my wife's people who I had earlier regarded as the basest of savages.

"All went well and I started to realise that there was opportunity for trade with Rome", he said. "Trade goods that the Semnones do not place much value on fetch high prices inside the borders of the Empire, and *vice versa*, of course. But few dare to venture so deep into the territory of the Germani."

His words came as no surprise as I had long before realised that Secundus was far from a dullard.

"Soon, trade was blossoming and I earned much gold", he said.

"And then the witch and her allies arrived", Ganna hissed in her native tongue, confirming the rumours that somehow Braduhenna had a hand in the invasion of the Semnones. "Braduhenna told the council of elders that Rome was weak after the Alemanni had decimated its legions. She promised my people an easy victory and that they would return from the south with wagons heaped with gold and silver."

"My father sat on the council", she continued. "Secundus had opened his eyes to the benefits of trade, so he objected against following the path of spears. The elders called a *thing*, a meeting of the leaders from across the land, to decide the issue. But while they were gathering, my father fell ill and he crossed the bridge of stars."

"Poison?" I asked.

"The witch cursed or poisoned him for sure", Secundus said. "But it could not be proven."

"Braduhenna's honeyed words and beauty convinced the old men to take up the sword against Rome", Ganna said. "She said that the new emperor served the dark lord himself. Once the evil emperor had gathered his legions, he would invade the forests of the north like Rome's caesars did in times of old. She proclaimed that victory would belong to him who strikes first."

"The war-witch was the one who put forward the plan on how to defeat your legions", Ganna said. "It is not the way of honour, but a plan based on betrayal and deceit."

I felt my stomach churn at her words and exchanged a glance with Gordas, whose expression mirrored mine.

"Both Secundus and I owe you a life, Lord Emperor", Ganna said. "We decided to come south, to warn you of what is to come. Because we feared the spies of the witch, we first travelled north, then east, before we came south and crossed the Mother River."

"Fortuna frowned on us", Secundus said. "After we crossed the river, we fell into the hands of the Vandali, who took us as slaves. Again, you saved us."

"Tell me of the war matron's plan", I said.

"First, many warriors of the Alemanni and Semnones, the old, ill-equipped and injured, were to cross into Roman lands to draw the legions east", Secundus said.

"Once that happened, the main Semnones force, forty thousand horse warriors, would cross the river north of Iuvavum to join the others who had escaped your trap after the Vandali invaded."

"It is improbable for Braduhenna to have conceived that I would offer peace to the invaders, and close to impossible for her to have engineered the escape of the Semnones as well as the invasion of the Vandali", I said.

"No, lord", Ganna said. "It was not the war-witch who suggested it, it was her companion, King Belimar of the Quadi, who assured the counsel that it could be done."

Chapter 10 – Horse

Caesar Augustus had introduced a messaging system that allowed for news and imperial missives to travel up to two hundred and fifty miles per day. But mismanagement during the times of civil strife and the interminable wars that continued to plague the Empire had reduced the horse relay system to a shadow of its former self. The recent invasions had rendered many way stations abandoned or destroyed, effectively disabling relay communication all along the *limes* in Pannonia and Noricum.

Secundus had hardly spoken the words when Gordas volunteered. "I will go, Eochar", he said.

"And I will go with you", I replied.

"Who will command the black riders?" the Hun asked.

I twisted in the saddle and motioned for the officer of the mounted praetorians to approach. "Tribune", I said. "Effective immediately, you are the acting prefect of the Illyrian cavalry."

"What are your orders, Lord Emperor?" he asked, the confusion clear on his face.

"Make sure you get the black riders to Iuvavum in the shortest time possible", I replied, just as Gordas returned leading twelve horses.

I raised an eyebrow.

"Four for each of us", he clarified.

"Friends in trouble", Cai said, and fell in behind the Hun. "I go too."

The Hun dismounted and lifted the saddle from the back of his favourite mare. "Leave Kasirga with the column", he growled. "Unless you are willing to ride him until he collapses."

I obeyed Gordas's command and handed my horse's reins to the tribune. "Look after him", I said, and dug my heels into the Scythian gelding's flanks to catch up with Gordas and Cai.

* * *

Half a watch later, we stopped at a stream to water the tired horses.

"Tonight we must sleep at Brigetio to have any hope of reaching the main Roman force in time", Gordas said while gently stroking the neck of a gelding. "There, we will be able to source fresh horses."

Although I heard his words, they failed to penetrate the dark thoughts that had plagued me during the ride west. "Belimar has betrayed us and colluded with our enemies", I said. "He must have been planning Rome's downfall for years, since before he fought at our side against the Goths."

It is one thing to bend to the will of the darkness on the spur of the moment. To plant and nurture the seeds of evil over months and years until it bears its vile fruit is something entirely different. I felt the presence of Arash the Avenger, drew my sword from the scabbard, and rammed the iron into the soil. I went down onto one knee, gripped the blade with my left hand and bowed my head to the lord of the field of blood. "I will extinguish the evil that Belimar has become", I vowed as my blood ran down the honed edge and disappeared into the earth.

Cai and Gordas waited patiently until I plucked the sword from the ground, wiped it on my cloak, and thrust it back into its sheath. "Come", I said. "I have an oath to honour."

An hour after dark we reined in before the stone walls of Brigetio.

Once we had gained entry, the commanding officer, a senior tribune called Pius Salamallianus, met us inside the gates. The officer was of an age with Hostilius and it was immediately clear that he was cut from the same cloth. He did not present any excuses, nor did he waste our time with trivial questions. "Lord Emperor", he said, and saluted in the way of the legions. "What are your orders?"

"Make sure twelve of your best horses are ready to ride a watch before sunrise on the morrow", I said. "Me and my companions wish for an amphora of wine, hot pottage and a place to sleep."

"I know you have the blood of the horse warriors, Lord Emperor", he said as he took us towards the *praetorium*. "We can take a shortcut through the stables so you may choose the animals you want."

Gordas nodded and the tribune led the way.

"Legate Marcellinus and Tribune Proculus passed through here a few days ago", Salamallianus said while we made our way through the immaculately kept stables. "They told me that you would come, but I did not expect you so soon, Lord Emperor."

"Did the Germani horde come past here?" I asked.

"They did, lord", he confirmed. "Although we have only a cohort inside the fort, they did not even try to breach the walls. Truth is, they were in such a hurry they did not spare us a second glance."

To my right I noticed a magnificent roan gelding that must have been of Scythian stock.

"Eochar", Gordas growled, and approached the horse who whinnied in recognition. "It is the horse that you gifted the Quadi guide."

"How did you come about this horse, tribune?" I asked, suddenly intrigued.

"One day after the legions had passed through, we caught a savage not far outside the walls", he said. "The idiot must have lost his way because he was heading in the wrong direction. We couldn't get a word out of the dullard, though, even when we used irons."

"He lives?" I asked.

"We threw him in the hole, lord", he said. "He still breathes, we hear the moans at night."

"Clean him up, bind his wounds and bring him to me", I said, and made sure to meet the tribune's gaze. "You have one more guest for dinner."

I knew that what I suggested was unthinkable to a Roman, but the tribune proved his worth by issuing a salute. "I understand, Lord Emperor", he said. "And I will obey."

* * *

Bojos bowed deeply when he entered the room, winced as he righted himself, and pressed a palm to his side.

The torturer who practiced his trade at Brigetio must have been a skilled man. Apart from a few missing fingernails and a tooth or two, the guide's injuries were confined to the parts of his body covered by the undyed wool tunic.

"He is a mute, Lord Emperor", Salamallianus reminded us as he stepped from the room and pulled the door closed behind him.

I motioned for the guide to take a seat and partake in the wine and food.

Bojos ladled a generous helping of hearty meat and bean pottage into a bowl, and in a way that brought to mind a famished hound, greedily slurped up the contents. Only after his second bowl did he reach for the cup of wine that Cai had poured.

"Lord", the Quadi said in his native tongue. "I owe you my life."

I raised an eyebrow. "You are not mute?"

Bojos grinned like a fox. "It is the third time that it has saved my life, Lord Eochar", he replied in the tongue of the Germani. "I never enjoyed using words. Long ago I realised that others place an even higher value on men who cannot tell tales."

I motioned for him to continue.

"We had hardly departed from this stronghold when King Belimar ordered me to relinquish my horse to him", Bojos said.

"Did he give you coin in exchange?" I asked.

"Two silvers, which is hardly enough to buy a mule", he replied, the resentment clear on his face.

I knew that in the lands of the Germani the horse I had gifted Bojos was worth at least thirty gold coins.

"So you stole back the horse and escaped during the night?" I asked.

"King Belimar is not a good man", Bojos said. "He and the war matron told us that the man who rules the Romans serves the dark lord. We came south to safeguard our lands for our children and their children." He drew a deep breath and drank from his cup. "But now I believe that although you rule over an evil empire of stone and iron, you are a better man than our king. That, lord, is why I took the horse and abandoned the king."

"Why do you say that Belimar is a bad man?" I asked.

"I served the king's sister for many seasons", the guide said. "Two years ago, when the Roman envoy came, she overheard them planning dark deeds. Afterwards she and the king barely spoke. Then she suddenly fell ill. Why, no one knew."

Bojos's look said it all, but his words intrigued me even more.

"Romans?" I asked. "I know not of an envoy to the Quadi in the time of Claudius Gothicus."

"I know a Roman when I see one, lord", Bojos replied, and held two fingers against a shoulder. "I remember the old men well. They looked like jesters in their funny white robes with purple stripes."

Chapter 11 – Moccus

The following morning, two-thirds of a watch before sunrise, we exited our chambers to find the guide waiting outside the guarded door. I took the limping Quadi to the side. "You are injured and will hold us up", I said.

"Lord, I…" he started, but I raised a palm to silence his protest. "I want you to go east, to Aquincum, and take a message to the queen of the Roxolani", I said, and handed him a scroll carrying the imperial seal.

"I will ride to the edge of middle earth if I have to, lord", he replied, and turned around to do my bidding.

Mid-afternoon, after abandoning two spent horses along the way, we arrived at the gates of Carnuntum. All around the perimeter of the fort, legionaries were toiling. Teams of men were cleaning ditches while others hammered stakes into the earth.

By the time the officer of the guard had opened the gate, the commander of the fort had been summoned.

"I need twelve of your best horses without delay", I said before the tribune could waste time on decorum.

He bowed deeply before barking instructions to a centurion. "Lord", he said once the officer had gone. "We have lost many excellent mounts to the invaders, but we will provide to you the best we have."

I nodded my acceptance of his words. "I approve of the fact that you are strengthening Carnuntum's defences, tribune", I said. "Continue doing so. You may have need of them in the weeks to come."

* * *

At the cost of four more horses, we reached Vindobona at dusk.

I was too tired to do more than commandeer a hot meal and warm chambers, and fell asleep without removing my armour.

When I woke the following morning, I was as stiff as rusted chainmail, so much so that Gordas and Cai had to help me gain my feet. The fort was yet to stir, so we sat on couches in our chamber and broke our fast with the leftover pottage from the evening before.

Not long after, I bade farewell to the commander of the garrison and we continued our journey. This time headed for Lauriacum, nearly a hundred miles to the west.

The sun was low in the sky when we approached Arelape, almost twenty miles short of our intended destination. We were two hundred paces from the gate of the auxiliary fort when the horse Gordas rode issued a little whinny and summarily collapsed. The Hun managed to avoid being pinned, and crouched down beside the dying animal. He stroked the mare's neck and whispered words into its ears.

Cai and I dismounted and joined Gordas on foot.

"What you say to horse?" Cai asked while the three of us walked towards the stout stone walls.

"I made an oath of my own, Easterner", the Hun replied, and a savage leer split his scarred visage.

I did not dare imagine what awaited Belimar if he were to fall into Gordas's clutches.

"We should spend the night at the fort", Gordas advised, pointing at the hill country to the west. "We can get fresh horses, but we need to rest our bodies if we wish to have the strength to ride on the morrow."

I had hardly conceded to Gordas's sage advice when the gates creaked open. A stocky, barrel-chested officer, dressed in the garb of a commander of auxiliaries, exited and approached at a brisk walk. He came to a halt ten paces from us and saluted in the way of the legions. "Tribune Bellicius Sucessus at your service, Lord Emperor", he said jovially. "When I received the missive that you are travelling west along the *limes*, my men believed that you would prefer to stop over at Lauriacum, but I told them the hospitality of the First Flavian Cohort of the Britons is known far and wide and that they must be ready to receive their imperator with open arms."

On the battlements above the gates, I noticed auxiliaries standing at attention in shining armour. It was evident that they had spent many watches polishing their gear in anticipation of my arrival. I tried as best I could to conceal my exhaustion and forced a smile. "The reputation of the First Flavian Cohort has indeed spread throughout the Empire", I said, loud enough for all to hear. "Even though I am in a race against time, I refuse to miss out on the opportunity to spend a night amongst heroes of Rome."

A great cheer erupted from the battlements.

Sucessus nearly burst with pride and his chest swelled a few inches. "Come, lord", he said, and signalled for us to follow him. "My wife has been toiling in the kitchen nonstop since I told her the emperor himself will be visiting our humble fort."

After I inspected the troops in the fading light, the tribune insisted that we accompany him to his quarters. He dismissed the burly Briton guarding the door and ushered us into the *atrium*. "Hello Love, I'm home", he called out.

A lithe, blonde woman, at least ten years Sucessus's junior, appeared from the adjacent room. She froze when she noticed that her husband was not alone, then her gaze settled on the purple cloak wrapped around my shoulders and she dropped to her knees. "Lord Emperor, is it really you?"

"*Salve matrona*", I said, and waved her to her feet. "Tribune Sucessus tells me that you are an excellent cook. We have come to find out whether he speaks the truth."

While the tribune poured wine into cups, his wife and a servant appeared with a large serving bowl filled with steaming meat pottage and a tray stacked with fresh baked loaves, cheese, olives and an amphora of honey.

"I met Ursina in Virinum when I travelled through the passes along the Iron Road to collect a consignment of *gladii*", he said. "Her father's people have worked iron since the time the barbarians ruled Noricum. Celts may be savages, but they sure know how to fashion blades and stew boar."

Sucessus's jest was rewarded with a glare from his wife. I had no doubts that it would not go well with him after our departure.

"Well, er", he stammered. "I, er…"

Ursina placed a firm hand on Sucessus's arm to silence him. "Husband, the emperor and his men are exhausted from many days in the saddle. They surely wish to take repast and retire to their beds."

Our host nodded. He waited until all around the table had received a bowl brimming with hot stew before inclining his head to ask for the blessing of their favoured god. "May Moccus make you strong in war, fortunate on the hunt, and wise in counsel", he said, and shovelled a heaped spoon of pottage into his mouth.

Not only was the pork good, it was tastier than anything that my cooks managed to produce in the imperial kitchens. "I have never had better", I said, noticing that Gordas was cleaning the sauce from his bowl with a chunk of bread. "Where did you learn this craft?"

Ursina blushed and issued a warm smile as she ladled another helping into our bowls. "When I was a girl, lord, many times did I travel with my father through the hidden passes in the Iron Mountains. Even during winter he managed to get his blades to market. In the deep vales he would hunt boar, and when evening came I cooked the meat with honeyed figs and sweet raisin wine. There is nothing better to put back strength in a man's sinews than the sacred meat of boar."

* * *

Early the following morning, once we were clear of the wall and the massive gates creaked shut, Cai turned in the saddle to face me.

"You do well, Lucius of Da Qin", he said. "Many say you harsh and merciless, but people of fort will tell tale of humble emperor who has time for subjects. Story spread like fire in dry field."

"Pity", Gordas said from my left. "Their words will reach the ears of your enemies, Eochar, and they will be emboldened by your weakness."

* * *

The sun had barely peeked over the horizon when we cantered past Lauriacum. There, we turned away from the Mother River, heading west and south towards Iuvavum.

By midday, after we passed by the walls of Ovilava, a stiff northerly breeze picked up. Overhead, clouds raced south only to find their way blocked by the towering mountains. Soon the distant peaks were obscured by a veil of dark grey that slowly spilled down from the cliffs into the foothills.

We continued thundering west until we arrived at Tergolape, a small settlement on the western bank of the Ager. It was a market day and a handful of peasants were bartering their produce and wares.

I reined in at the edge of the marketplace, close to where an old woman was selling seared meatballs and small loaves. She eyed my gold-embroidered purple cloak with suspicion as she exchanged her wares for silver. "You must have a care, lord", she said. "Only the emperor is allowed to wear a purple cloak."

"I know that", I said, and pointed at the ominous clouds gathering in the south. "Will it rain?"

She must have noticed my seal ring, which made her eyes go wide before she dropped to her knees. "Forgive me, Lord Emperor", she croaked.

"Well, will it rain?" I asked again, and swallowed down the food with a gulp from my wineskin.

"It is the *Nordstau*, lord", she said. "Before the sun rises tomorrow, the wind will be ripping trees from the earth. In the passes the snow will rise up to the waist."

I flicked her an *aureus* and nudged my mare to a canter.

Chapter 12 – Nordstau

Iuvavum, arguably the most important trade centre in the whole of Noricum, possessed no defensive wall. Being far removed from the Danubian border there was no imminent threat and thus no garrison. I realised all too well that to enter the Alpine passes, the Semnones cavalry who had crossed the river somewhere to the east near Castra Regina, would have had to pass by the defenceless town, and dreaded what we would find when we arrived at the settlement.

On the western bank of the Salzach, little remained of what once was the old town centre of Iuvavum. Judging by the churned-up soil, a large hostile force of horsemen had inflicted the damage. We made our way along the main thoroughfare which was flanked by smoking ruins of *insulae* and *tabernae* where until recently people had lived or eked out a living by vending meat, bread, fish oil or wine. Apart from the occasional barbarian corpse, almost certainly due to disagreements over the division of spoils, the ravaged streets were devoid of Roman dead.

We continued down the road towards the stone bridge that spanned the swift-flowing river and were surprised to find that the larger part of the city, situated on the far side of the river, appeared to be unscathed. As we walked our horses along the stone paving above the water, we noticed major cracks in the blackened masonry while wood ash still swirled in the breeze around our mounts' hooves.

"The townspeople built a pyre on the bridge to keep the enemy from crossing", Gordas said. "Look, all the boats are drawn up on the eastern bank."

Gordas cleared his throat and pointed at a group of men approaching, led by a man dressed in the robes of a quaestor. The delegation halted a few paces from us and bowed low out of respect for their emperor.

"Quaestor Publius Carbo at your service, Lord Emperor", the oldster said. "For many days, we have made sacrifices at the temple of Jupiter so that we may be delivered from the depredation of the savages. Thank the gods that you and your legions have finally arrived."

He stole a glance past my shoulder, a frown of concern furrowing his brow.

* * *

We spent the evening at the residence of the quaestor, a man who was more familiar with trade than war. While the freezing wind tore at the shutters and ripped tiles from the roof, we reclined on couches in a chamber heated by a hypocaust.

"It has been eight days since Legate Marcellinus and Tribune Proculus honoured me with their presence", the functionary said while he sipped from a silver goblet. "They were pursuing the tribesmen who had ascended the passes a few days before."

"When the first wave of savages arrived, we evacuated the old town on the western bank and stacked the bridge with seasoned logs and olive oil", he explained. "We hardly had time to thank the gods for sending the legions to our rescue when a second force of Germani horsemen unexpectedly fell upon us from the west. Fortuna favoured us because we still had enough wood and oil stored near the bridge to fire it at short notice. Many of the citizens feared that the Semnones would simply bide their time and wait until the embers had cooled, but the raiders seemed to be in a hurry and lingered for hardly half a watch before they disappeared into the foothills to the south."

"Will the passes be traversable within the week?" I asked.

"Lord", he replied, "I have been quaestor of this city for almost thirty years. When the *Nordstau* comes, the trade with Italia comes to a grinding halt for at least two weeks."

Our host took another sip of wine.

"I am sure the eastern routes across the Alps are useable", he said. "But that means you will first have to travel to Pannonia before crossing to Aquileia, which will take the best part of two weeks."

"We do not have the luxury of time", I replied.

Later, alone in our chambers, I sought the counsel of my barbarian friend.

"You have seen the storm", I said to the Hun. "Will we be able to take the Illyrians across the mountains?"

Gordas walked to the window and opened the shutters. The strong gust nearly ripped the wood from his grip and a spray of white powder landed on the heated floor. For twenty heartbeats he studied the icy gale, then closed the shutters and turned to face me. "Five thousand Huns mounted on steppe ponies would struggle to cross the passes", he said. "Eochar, if you are foolish enough to take the Romans into the highlands, hundreds of their mounts will succumb while trying to wade through the snow. The ones that survive will be too weak to ride into battle."

I realised that my friend was right, but I could not be idle while knowing that on the other side of the mountain, Vibius and Hostilius were about to be destroyed by an overwhelming force of Germani.

Then Arash came to me and I recalled the words of Ursina, the Celtic wife of the fort commander at Arelape. "*. . . many times did I travel with my father through the hidden passes in the Iron Mountains.*"

* * *

Rather than abate, the storm picked up in intensity during the hours of darkness.

The following morning we dismissed the objections of the quaestor, donned our sealskins, and departed as soon as it was light enough to travel. In the vicinity of Iuvavum, near the mountains, the road was buried under almost two feet of snow which slowed our pace to that of a marching legion. We pulled our cloaks tighter, lowered our heads and struggled on into the teeth of the wind.

Less than half a watch later, the blizzard let up, so much so that we flipped back our fur-lined hoods. Once we had left the high ground in our wake, the skies cleared, but the frigid northerly blow fuelling the *Nordstau* remained.

Iuvavum was a prosperous city, which must have been the reason why the horses the quaestor had requisitioned were by far better than the ones we had taken from the forts along the *limes*. The cold weather also meant that our mounts could canter for longer without rest.

With a third of a watch of daylight remaining, we passed by Lauriacum for the second time in two days. Not long after sunset we arrived at Arelape, home to the Britons of the First Flavian Cohort. I was not fool enough to canter up to the gates, but called out a warning when we were a hundred paces away. "Stand down soldiers of Rome, your emperor has returned."

As soon as the torches flanking the gates illuminated our little group, the watchers on the wall raised their *pila* in salute. "Imperator!" they boomed, as the iron and oak gates swung open.

* * *

"Your visit is all that my men have been talking about over the last two days, lord", Sucessus said. "And now you have graced us with your presence twice within the week."

"Have you had word of my cavalry?" I asked.

"Less than a watch ago, I received a missive from Aelius Flavius, the magistrate of Cetium", he said. "He expected the Illyrian cavalry to arrive before dark. They are there to replenish their supplies."

"How far east is Cetium?" I asked.

"Twenty-two miles, lord", the tribune replied. "Do you wish for my men to escort you to Cetium?"

"No, but I want a message delivered to the Illyrian commander tonight. Tomorrow when the sun rises, I need you to be ready to ride. It is a mission that may well decide the future of the Empire."

"Will we ride against the enemy, lord?" he asked, his jaw set in grim determination.

"No", I replied. "We go south, into the mountains, and it will not be me, but your wife who will lead the way."

Chapter 13 – Perchta

The Illyrians arrived before the end of the first watch of the morning. It was an impressive spectacle as every rider led a packhorse that carried their armour as well as the scale and chain that are strapped to the warhorses before riding into battle. At the rear of the cavalry formation I noticed a long line of mules, each animal encumbered by bundles of rations for the soldiers, as well as feed for their mounts.

I was as pleased to be reunited with Kasirga as Gordas was to ride his favourite mare again. The absence of a scowl on the Hun's face indicated to me that he was satisfied with the condition of his mount, which prompted me to compliment the tribune of my guard whom I had left to command the black riders during my absence.

"You have acquitted yourself well, tribune", I said. "And it seems that you have procured sufficient supplies for crossing the mountains."

"I made sure that the horses were put to pasture every day", he replied proudly. "Whenever possible they received rations of oats and lucerne to increase their stamina in preparation for crossing the Alps south of Iuvavum. The quartermaster at Cetium was at first reluctant to part with the supplies earmarked for the northern forts, but I told him that if he does not comply he would soon get the chance to speak with you in person."

"We are not going to Iuvavum", I replied. "A spring blizzard has closed the passes."

"But lord, if we use the eastern routes, it will take us all the way back to Emona in Pannonia", the tribune protested. "The detour will add many days to our journey. What is more, we will run out of rations for the men and feed for the horses."

"That is why we are going south, into the Iron Mountains", I said.

"You know the ancient paths of the Taurisci?" the tribune asked, respect thick in his voice.

"No", I sighed. "But I brought someone who does."

* * *

Later that day, Cai and I trailed behind Gordas. The Hun had fallen in beside Ursina and Sucessus, his interest piqued by her skills.

"Your wife is no stranger to the saddle", the Hun said to Sucessus, who rode beside him.

"Epona was her father's favoured god", the Briton replied, referring to the horse deity of the Celts. "He made sure that they were taught to ride from an early age."

In contrast, Sucessus sat in the saddle in a manner that convinced me that he would tumble from the back of his mount at any moment. He must have noticed my concern.

"My father, like his father before him, revered Niskus, the river god", he offered. "I swim better than I ride, lord."

* * *

We continued our journey south, Ursina leading us through the mountains along a web of cart paths. At times we struggled up or descended along impossibly steep scree slopes devoid of any life, while at other times we trotted through vales where the canopy was so thick I doubted whether the sun had pierced it in a thousand years.

Where the track ran across outcrops of rock, the grooves that iron-rimmed wheels had cut into the stone hinted at centuries of use. "Before Rome developed its insatiable appetite for power, my people traded with Italia", Ursina said when she noticed my eyes straying to the ancient markings. "Before your people became our masters, they were our friends."

Sometimes I rode with Gordas and Cai and on other occasions Secundus and Ganna kept me company, but the conversation was thin as my mind was focused on the fate of Hostilius, Vibius and the men they commanded. I wondered whether my friends were still in the passes or whether they had already descended into the valley of the Po. Were they still pursuing the Semnones? Had they become aware of the second barbarian force pursuing them? Or mayhap the treacherous snake, Belimar, had already led them into a trap and the carrion eaters were fighting over their bloated corpses.

I tried to banish the dark thoughts and focused on covering as much ground as possible, until, sometime after the sun had set, Gordas and Cai offered their counsel on the foolishness of travelling the passes at night.

* * *

Early afternoon, five days after departing from Arelape, Gordas, Cai and I rode ahead with Ursina along a track meandering through an ancient forest of oak and hornbeam. We descended into a wispy mist that seemed to get thicker the farther we progressed. A mile down the path Gordas tilted back his head and sniffed the breeze. I, too, noticed a peculiar smell carried on the wind.

"We are approaching the great swamps", Ursina said. "My people call it the Place of Water. There are tales of dragons and spirits that dwell in the mist, but other than flying vermin, I have never laid eyes on these evils."

I had hardly ever passed through a town without a myth or legend of some sort or other, so I took little notice of the Celt woman's words and rather focused on swatting away the buzzing critters that wished to feast on our blood.

Soon after, we arrived on the banks of the narrow but swift flow that fed the marshes. A dilapidated structure that I would not afford the honour of referring to as a bridge, spanned the river the locals called the Glan. After inspecting the rotten wood, I instructed the Illyrians to cross in pairs. When a beam cracked under the strain, I had no choice but to allow only one horse and rider at a time, which meant that traversing the river became a whole day's affair.

Later that evening, Cai, Gordas and I sat beside a fire on the western bank, the fog thick around us. We were low on rations and rather than watch while my men suffered, we partook of a simple meal of wheat porridge and milk.

"If the Celt woman can be believed, we are half a day's ride east of the road that leads from Iuvavum across the mountains to Italia", I said. "I expect that by now the Roman army as well as the Semnones will be clear of the passes, assuming that the barbarians have not attacked our friends somewhere on the mountain tracks."

Gordas, who preferred meat and cheese to porridge, set aside his half-full bowl of slop. "The Germani have close on forty thousand horsemen", he said, and took a swig from his cup. "What use are horses in the confines of a mountain pass? The Semnones war leaders will wish to appease their nobles. They will not order the attack until they come across open ground fit for cavalry."

Earlier I had come to the same conclusion and the Hun's words served to set my mind at ease.

"Germani lure tiger down from mountain. But tiger still has fangs and claws", Cai said. "Belimar wear dagger in smile. Enemy will use Quadi king to trap tiger."

Cai was right. Unknowingly Vibius and Hostilius harboured a viper - a snake that was sure to sink its fangs into their flesh when they least expected it.

"Our friends are in grave danger", I said, and stood from the furs. "Let us retire so that we may depart early on the morrow."

I was exhausted from the day's journey and fell asleep almost as soon as I lay down. For the mosquitoes, flies and midges that find sustenance from sucking our lifeblood, the toil was about to begin.

It must have been sometime during the second watch of the night that I woke up, my face and neck on fire from countless stings of the flying vermin who ruled the wetlands. I swatted away another buzzing bloodsucker, rolled from the furs, strapped on my blade, and went outside to lay down beside the smouldering embers in the hope that the smoke would drive away the little critters.

I ducked from the tent and frowned as I noticed that all four praetorians who were on guard duty lay on their backs, snoring softly. Just then the moon appeared from behind clouds and I saw a dark, human-like shape bent over the half-eaten bowl of gruel that Gordas had earlier abandoned beside the cooking fire. I froze in my tracks and my hand dropped to the hilt of my sword.

The humpbacked creature sensed the weight of my gaze and slowly raised its head until its eyes met mine. The coals reflected red from dark holes set deep within its skull while the congealed slop dripped from its maw. From behind the apparition, in the dark wood, I heard sounds and scuffling that sounded much like children in distress.

The creature must have heard it too, and as it turned its head towards the sound I saw the white flash of teeth as it issued a grimace, or mayhap a leer. With a swiftness that belied its deformity, the thing gained its feet, twirled around, and limped into the undergrowth.

Again, cries of anguish reached my ears. I steeled myself, drew my blade from the scabbard, and darted into the dark wood in pursuit. I followed the footfalls and rustle of leaves, occasionally catching sight of the hunched shape where moonlight penetrated the canopy.

Four hundred paces into the forest the apparition slowed its pace, coming to a halt in a small, leaf-strewn clearing bathed in the silver rays of Mani. Its features were hidden beneath the hood of a black cloak, but as it turned to face me I caught a glimpse of lank silver hair and a beak-like nose. It extended a bony hand wrapped in thin skin with a corpse-pale pallor.

It was impossible to tell whether it was a man, woman or mayhap neither.

"What business have you with me, favourite of Arash?" the creature croaked.

"Where are the children?" I asked.

"They are mine", it snarled, spittle flying from its purple lips. "And I will keep them for all eternity."

I took a step forward, and from underneath its cloak appeared the blade of a dagger, the curved iron resembling that of a sickle.

"No magic can stand against my blade. I will slit your belly and fill it with straw", it shrieked to distract me from its sudden lunge.

My sword flashed from low to high and the gnarled hand that clutched the blade twirled into the undergrowth. I stepped to the right, transferred my weight to my left foot, and swung the blade horizontally, aiming at the base of the neck of the screeching creature.

I stood unmoving for at least a hundred heartbeats until the moon vanished and a thick fog started to spill from between the trunks. The sobbing I had heard before morphed into giggles before they vanished into the night.

Back at my tent I found the guards still slumbering, but an all-consuming weariness washed over me and I ducked through the door and collapsed onto the furs.

* * *

Cai listened to my words with a face of stone.

"Some dreams seem like it real, Lucius of Da Qin", he said when I was through. "It happen when body tired and mind beset with concern."

"It was a creature from beyond the Black Gates. That is why your guards failed to find a body", Gordas concluded. "Only because the lord of the field of blood had blessed your blade were you able to defeat the apparition."

Ursina, who rode a few paces behind, nudged her mount to fall in beside us. "My father often spoke of a creature that roams these ancient woods", she said, and indicated the forest with a sweeping gesture. "My people call her the *pergan*, the *hidden one*. The old hag with a goose foot hides her features underneath a hooded cloak and limps around the forests at night. When young children pass before being under the protection of a god, the *pergan* collects their shades."

"You have done well, lord", she concluded. "My father said that the creature can only be defeated by a blade blessed by Dagda, the god who wields the mace of wrath. You have freed the shades of the children."

I nodded to show that I heard her words. What I failed to reveal was that I, too, believed that my encounter was not a dream because when I woke that morning, I found a curved dagger strapped to my belt.

Chapter 14 – Scout

At noon we arrived outside Sanctium, the *mansio* that had been built to harness the hot springs. The healing water still bubbled up from the depths, but the way station and the baths that once were sanctuaries for weary travellers had been reduced to a heap of stone and charred timber.

We skirted the ruins and bade farewell to Sucessus and his woman on the banks of the Dravus before crossing the bridge to join the road that connected Iuvavum with Italia.

When we reached the other side of the river, Gordas dismounted and crouched beside his mare, his eyes locked on the surface of the track. After a span of heartbeats, he reached out and gently ran his fingers across the imprints left by a heavy wagon. "Thousands of Germani riders passed along this track, six, maybe seven days ago", he said, and swung back onto his horse. "The legions are four days ahead of them."

"The Semnones horsemen are holding back, concealing their presence", I said. "They will only show themselves when they arrive on ground of their choosing."

"The legions believe that they are hunting the barbarians", Gordas replied. "They, in turn, are being stalked by the Germani horsemen."

"To save our friends from the evil that Braduhenna and Belimar have hatched, we will need to engage the Semnones' main cavalry force", I said. "We number but five thousand riders while we will be facing forty thousand horsemen."

"When ride tiger, best not dismount, Lucius of Da Qin", Cai said, hinting that the die had been cast. "Day is ending and road narrows. Soon we know will of gods."

I nodded, because as always, Cai was right.

* * *

Three days later we emerged from the passes into the valley of the Po. Although we had travelled as swiftly as possible, we were yet to lay eyes on the massive barbarian army.

"The Germani are like wolves that have tasted blood", Gordas said after he had inspected the passage of the horde. "When the pack moves in for the kill, their blood runs hot and their sinews do not tire. Only after they have gnawed the last bloody morsels from the carcass do they lie down to rest."

In a surprising development, the Semnones had not advanced towards the south, but had turned west onto the Via Postumia, heading for the fertile lands bordering the Po in the heart of Italia.

"The barbarian infantry that our friends are pursuing are leading the legions to Mediolanum", I ventured. "There, on the flatlands, the horsemen of the Semnones will be most effective."

Gordas grunted, which I took as affirmation. "Although the Germani run like a wolfpack, we have narrowed their lead to four days", he said. "Within the week we will catch them."

I had been praying to Arash to deliver the enemy into our hands, but I was yet to conjure up a viable strategy to deal with the overwhelming force if, or when, the god answered my pleas. I could not help but feel like a little mongrel dog chasing down a great, lumbering bear.

* * *

Late afternoon seven days hence, we arrived outside the crumbled walls of Cremona. Two hundred years before, during the rule of Emperor Vespasian, the city had been destroyed in a civil war and never recovered to more than a small settlement hugging the northern bank of the Po.

The barbarians had not wasted their time by besieging the larger, well-fortified cities like Verona and Mantua, but had washed over the smaller settlements and farms along the Via Postumia in a wave of destruction. A veil of acrid smoke still hung above Cremona. Even from half a mile away the reek of death was nauseating.

Gordas, whose people were no strangers to ravaging cities, took in the scene with a raised eyebrow. "The Germani were here yesterday" he said while regarding a raven perched on the headless corpse of an unfortunate peasant who failed to reach the hills in time.

I was acutely aware of the fact that the probability of encountering the Semnones army was steadily increasing with every passing day. For that reason, I employed a proportionately larger number of scouts to ensure that we would not be overwhelmed in an ambush. My tent had hardly been erected when one of the outriders and his officer, a *veteranus* of the Illyrians whom I recognised, were escorted into my presence.

Both men saluted in the required manner.

"Report, Decurion Aurelius Cornelius", I ordered.

"Lord Emperor", the officer replied, pleased that the ruler of the world knew him by name. "Antestinus here has discovered the whereabouts of the foe. I know you like to hear it directly from the horse's mouth, lord, so that's why I brought him along."

I nodded to show that I agreed with him, which pleased him even more. "Tell me everything, Antestinus", I commanded.

The scout nervously cleared his throat. "We swam our horses across the river this morning while it was still dark, lord", he said. "Them savages are always watching the bridges so it pays to be careful."

"Once on the southern bank, I rode west along the hidden game paths in the thicket", he continued. "Fortuna favoured me because I was watering my horse when I heard riders babble in the native tongue of the Germani. Three mounted scouts passed less than twenty paces from me and I decided to follow 'em."

"What did they talk about?" I asked.

"I speak only a few words in their tongue, lord, but the sods led me straight to their camp near Placentia", he grinned, but the smile vanished almost as quickly as it appeared. "By the gods, lord, there are many of 'em. At least forty thousand riders. And they're well equipped, lord, although they're a mismatched lot."

"Apart from spearheads, the Semnones do not smithy their own war gear, neither do they acquire it with coin or through barter", I said. "Their armour and blades are the trophies gathered from countless wars. It is their way to boast about whom they have vanquished so that they may strike fear into the hearts of their enemies."

The scout nodded to show that he understood.

"Where exactly is their camp located?" I asked.

"Placentia lies between two rivers, lord", the scout replied. "The Trebia on the far side and the Nura on this side." A frown creased his brow and I knew that he lacked the words to explain it to me.

"Draw it in the sand", I said, and gestured for a guard to hand the man a dagger.

The scout accepted the knife, bent down, and drew a straight line running from west to east. "This is the Po, lord", he said, and marked a spot at the centre of the line, south of the river. "And this is where Placentia lies."

I motioned for him to continue.

He drew two more lines in the sand, perpendicular to the first, one on each side of the town. "The Trebia and the Nura both spill into the Po", he continued, and pointed at the area between the two tributaries. "South of Placentia, between the rivers, there is only flatland where none can hide."

"And to the south?" I asked.

The scout used the blade to scrape deep indentations into the soil. "Ten miles to the south, the hill country rises from the plain and the farmland gives way to forests and deep ravines."

He drew a cross beside the Nura, at the southeastern edge of the sketch and I could see that he was pleased with his handiwork. "This is where the enemy horsemen have their camp", he said. "It is in a dense ravine of maple and ash, about ten miles south of Placentia. Truth be told, lord, I don't think I would have found 'em if it weren't for those outriders I stumbled upon. I looked for their tracks, but they did well to disguise them."

"Did they have fires?" I asked.

"No, lord, I saw no smoke rising."

"Do you know where the legions and the other Germani force, the infantry, are encamped?" I asked.

"If I had left the cover of the trees, the enemy would have seen me, lord", the scout replied sheepishly, "but from what I could make out from their babbling is that the Romans are camped west of the Nura, five miles south of the Po."

I passed him a purse of gold coins and handed one to his decurion as well. "Rome honours those who serve her well", I said, and dismissed them.

Cai and Gordas followed behind as I ducked into my tent. "The Semnones must be about to execute whatever evil they've been planning", I said. "We must act with haste. Tomorrow at dawn, we will strike camp and ride west to Placentia."

"To attack the Semnones?" Gordas asked while Cai poured wine.

"No", I replied, and accepted a cup. "We will skirt the position occupied by the barbarians and join forces with our friends. I will warn them of Belimar's treachery. First we will deal with the traitor and then we will crush the invaders."

* * *

Nik, Bradakos and I sat around a hearth inside our tent. My father leaned forward and used an old rag to lift a small copper pot off the glowing embers. He placed it on a warm, flat stone between the furs and the fire and stirred in a handful of coarse salt before decanting the creamy contents into three cups.

Both Bradakos and I accepted the hot salted milk with a nod.

"Who, do you think, has been Rome's greatest adversary, Lucius?" my father asked.

"Armenius", I said, and took a deep swallow of the hot liquid.

Nik raised an eyebrow. "Why?"

"Because he destroyed three legions in the forests of Germania", I replied with confidence.

"What about Hannibal?" Nik asked.

"Hannibal?" I asked.

Nik gestured to a thick scroll lying on my sleeping furs. "Did you not read that this afternoon while I was out riding with the king?" he asked.

I lowered my head in shame. "No, father, I disobeyed you. I rode with Bradakos and practised shooting pheasants from the saddle", I said, and gestured at the four fat plucked fowl that were ready to roast above the fire.

"Hannibal destroyed more than one hundred and twenty thousand soldiers of Rome. He fought the legions three times within the span of two years, emerging victorious every time", Nik revealed. "And, unlike Armenius, Hannibal did not ambush the Romans, but met them in open battle inside the borders of Italia."

"But… but that is more than twenty legions' worth of soldiers", I said. "No one can defeat twenty legions."

"Hannibal did", Nik replied.

"Tell me how he did it", I demanded with the arrogance of youth.

"Hannibal's story is contained in that scroll", Nik replied, indicating the document. "And why listen to my telling of it if you can hear it in person from the men who fought Hannibal?"

I eyed the scroll, suddenly eager to learn the tale. "May I read it now?" I asked, and rose from beside the fire.

Nik stopped me with a raised palm. "Sit down, Lucius", he said. "You will cook the fowl that you have taken down with your arrows. The birds have given their lives so that we can fill our stomachs. You will respect them as is required of the hunter."

That night, when all were abed, I lit a small oil lamp and unrolled the scroll.

Somewhere around the last watch of the night, I woke with a start.

The dream had been so real that I felt a pang of sadness, not only for the loss of my father, Nik, and Bradakos, my mentor, but also for the life on the plains that I had left behind to fight the enemies of Rome.

I smiled when I thought of what I had read that night, nearly forty years earlier.

My grin vanished and the cold fist of fate gripped my heart when it suddenly dawned on me. It was the same scroll that I had seen in the hall of Belimar, the traitor.

* * *

Two-thirds of a watch before dawn, while Cai and Gordas were assisting me to don my armour, the officer commanding the Illyrians was ushered into my tent. "Lord", he said, and saluted in the required manner.

"Rouse the men", I said. "Make sure that they and their warhorses are armoured and prepared to ride into battle. We leave at dawn", I added, and dismissed him with a gesture.

"I understand, lord, and I will obey", he replied, and turned on his heel.

"Wait", I said when the officer was about to duck from the tent.

He paused at the doorway.

"Make sure that your men break their fast", I said.

A slight frown flashed across the officer's face, but he kept his counsel. "It will be as you command, Lord Emperor", he said, and hurried to do my bidding.

* * *

At sunrise I led the Illyrians over the bridge that spanned the Po.

"Five hundred years ago, Hannibal destroyed a Roman army on the banks of the Trebia", I said to Gordas, who rode abreast of me.

The Hun barely raised an eyebrow.

"When the legions were about to crush the Carthaginian infantry they were ambushed from the rear", I added, which earned me a shrug.

"Ambushed by a large force of cavalry concealed in the foothills to the south", I revealed, which this time around served to pique Gordas's interest.

"Not unlike the Semnones horsemen who we know are hidden in the ravines", he said. "But how would the wild men know about the exploits of a foreign general who lived half a thousand years ago?"

"In the hall of Belimar, I saw a scroll detailing the campaigns of Hannibal", I said, "but thought nothing of it at the time. Last night I had a dream …"

"It was the god of war warning you, Eochar", Gordas concluded. Then a frown wrinkled his brow and he asked, "Why do you not send a messenger to warn the legions?"

"Vibius and Hostilius are not aware of the Semnones cavalry that followed them from the passes and through the valley of the Po", I said. "They have been chasing the Germani for weeks and I have no doubt that they will try to engage the invaders at the first opportunity."

"Which means that the Romans will attack the Semnones at dawn today", the Hun said, arriving at the same conclusion that I had.

The Hun had hardly spoken the words when the faint din of a far-off battle arrived on the back of a westerly breeze.

I met Gordas's gaze. "The time for messages and deliberations have passed, my friend. We ride to war, to a battle that may very well decide the fate of the Empire."

Chapter 15 – Trebia (April 271 AD)

Meanwhile, earlier the previous evening in the Roman legionary camp on the western bank of the Nura…

Vibius leaned forward, his bodyweight supported by his palms that were pressed flat against the wood of a hip-high table.

Hostilius also studied the vellum map that depicted the plain bordered by rivers to the north, west and east, and hill country to the south. The Primus Pilus used his dagger to cut a piece of dried meat from a larger chunk and positioned it on the map, inside the open-sided square created by the rivers, near the eastern bank of the Trebia. "According to the scouts, this is where the Germani are camped."

Vibius issued a nod to show that he agreed with the grey-haired tribune.

"We've been chasing the savages for weeks", Hostilius said. "Until now they've shown us nothing but a clean pair of heels. Our boys are tired, but the gods know, they're keen to get stuck in."

"Is it possible that the enemy is setting a trap?" Vibius asked.

"One thing I've learned from Domitius is never to underestimate the cunning of savages", Hostilius confirmed. "Just because they're dirty, have no honour and reek of unwashed swine doesn't mean that they're stupid."

Vibius grinned in response to the Primus Pilus's outburst.

"But", Hostilius continued, "I can't figure out how in hades they will be able to trap us. Besides, we will be fighting on the flatlands where one can see for bloody miles and miles."

"Based on the reports of the outriders, the barbarians' numbers correspond to the numbers who broke out of the fortifications on the Danube", Vibius said. "So it appears that we have the whole lot of them cornered."

A junior tribune appeared at the door of the tent. "Legate", he said, addressing Vibius, "the commander of the *foederati* wishes a word with you."

Vibius issued a nod and Belimar was ushered into the *praetorium*. "Have you come to a decision?" the Quadi king asked.

"Tomorrow morning at dawn we will attack the Semnones", Vibius said. "Unlike the previous time when we met on the field of battle, no quarter will be given."

A leer settled on Belimar's bearded face. "I agree, legate", he growled. "No quarter must be given or expected."

* * *

On the morrow, by the time that the eastern horizon was aflame with gold and purple, the legions marched from the Porta Praetoria, the main gate that always faced the enemy camp.

While the infantry advanced in double column across the plain, the Illyrians left the marching camp by means of the rear gate close to the river so that they could water their horses from the Nuro before riding into battle. The eight thousand *foederati* under the command of Belimar poured from the side gate facing the north. They waited until the tenth cohort had exited before falling in at the rear of the column.

It took the best part of two-thirds of a watch to cross the flatland to where the invaders were encamped on the eastern bank of the Trebia, a few hundred paces north of the edge of the forested ravines.

Hostilius, who rode beside Vibius, pointed at the sprawling sea of tents where the Semnones were feverishly scurrying about. More than forty thousand warriors were drawing up for battle, their left flank anchored against the river and their right protected by the treed defiles to the south. Their two-mile-wide frontage extended at an angle to the river and faced the northeast, with their camp located behind them on the triangular piece of ground bordered by the river and the forest.

When a mile and a half separated the Romans from the enemy, the last of the tribesmen found their place in the line. The ramshorn blared, and as one the Semnones began beating their spear hafts against the flats of their painted shields while rhythmically chanting in their savage tongue to invoke Wodanaz, the dark one.

"Either they knew we were coming", the Primus Pilus said, "or the Semnones are more organised than run-of-the-mill savages."

"Are you having second thoughts?" Vibius asked.

"Too late for that now", Hostilius said, and raised his right arm as a signal for the *buccinator*. In response, a series of shrill notes echoed over the plain and the column came to an abrupt halt. With an efficiency that told of countless hours of training, twenty Roman cohorts fanned out across the flatland to take up their positions.

The two legions deployed on the right and left flank respectively, with Belimar's Quadi occupying the centre. Compared to the Semnones, who stood twelve ranks deep, the combined Roman and *foederati* force had barely enough men to fill six ranks.

The commanders of the Roman army sat on horseback, ten paces behind the rear ranks of the Quadi, at the centre of the line. Amongst the men of their retinue were the two *aquilifers*, the chosen men who held aloft the gold eagle standards of the legions, each gilded haft decorated with silver *phalerae* to commemorate their victories.

"I hope your plan works", Hostilius grunted, and took a quick look over his shoulder at the black-clad Illyrians waiting fifty paces to the rear.

"It will work if the legions do what they're supposed to do", Vibius replied, his eyes never leaving the thousands of chanting Germani, five hundred paces distant.

"Don't you worry about the legions", Hostilius replied. "Let's hope that Belimar doesn't get carried away when his blood is up. That's what tends to happen with savages."

"Even if he wants to, I doubt whether the Quadi will fare well against the Semnones whose ranks stand more than twice as deep", Vibius said.

"Only one way to find out", the Primus Pilus growled, and nodded to the signifer.

As one, the second and third Italian legions started across the open ground. Although separated by almost a mile, the white stork banner of the *Legio II Italica* bobbed in unison with the standard of the third legion which depicted a she-wolf suckling the founding fathers of Rome.

Ten heartbeats later, Belimar's horn bearer relayed the signal and the *foederati* surged forward to catch up with the Romans who were already thirty paces ahead, the warped line of the Quadi appearing almost comical compared to the disciplined advance of the legions.

* * *

When forty paces separated the two-mile-wide fronts, a dark shower of spears and javelins rose from the Semnones' ranks. Almost simultaneously, one hundred and twenty centurions boomed, "*Testudo!*" The command had hardly been spoken when the bottom edges of two and a half thousand shields slammed onto the dirt. The men in the second rank lifted their *scuta* above their heads and slid the iron-bound edges over the top rims of the front rankers' shields. Before the first spears rained down, the legions were sheltered by a near-impenetrable wall of laminated willow.

Again, the Germani surged forward and cast their missiles, but the shields of the legionaries bore the brunt of the onslaught.

When the enemy was thirty paces out, the Romans abandoned the *testudo* and skipped forward, hefting their wood-hafted *pila* fitted with metal shanks ending in small pyramidal heads of hardened iron. On the command, thousands of heavy javelins streaked through the cold morning air. The armour-piercing tips effortlessly punched through the painted wood, allowing the thin, two-foot-long shanks to pass without resistance and pierce torsos and limbs, effectively pinning hundreds of foes to their shields.

The Semnones' advance faltered. Then the second wave of Roman spears struck, and hundreds, if not thousands, were taken out of the fight as the barbarians reeled under the onslaught of the legions. But even if every *pilum* had maimed or killed, the remaining warriors would still have outnumbered the Romans. It took only a span of twenty heartbeats for the Germani to gather their courage and with a roar they surged forward, trampling the corpses of their fallen.

The men in the front rank of the Roman line drew their shortswords and waited in silence, their brows furrowed in concentration. When the onrushing foes were ten paces away, the veterans charged forward in unison, their shields presenting an unbroken wall of wood. At the moment of impact, the front rankers braced their shoulders against the arcs of their *scuta* while the fists of their comrades behind them tightened around their leather harnesses.

The two armies came together in a deafening clash, the deep ranks of the barbarians barely being halted by the thin line of the legions. Thousands of baying tribesmen, eager to come to grips with the foe, shoved their brethren against the shields of the legion. Although the press was tight, the Semnones stabbed with their unwieldy spears and chopped down with their axes in an attempt to break the cohesion of the legionaries.

The barbarian blades were deflected by curved scuta and well-forged armour and the line held, but still it bent under the immense pressure. On the command, the front rankers lunged back with their right feet and dropped down onto their left knees while tilting the bottom edges of their shields forward and up.

With their kin pushing from behind, the men in the front rank of the Semnones were caught off-balance and the leading warriors took a stumbling step forward.

At that very moment, assisted by the rear ranks, the Roman veterans powered forward from the crouch and slammed their oval *scuta* up into the shields of the unbalanced barbarians - a move that they had perfected through endless hours of mock battle. Coming from below, the legionaries' heavy *scuta* struck the bottom lips of the Semnones' round shields, momentarily tilting them inwards.

The Germani were no fools, especially the experienced warriors in the front ranks. Realising the danger, they slammed their shields down to protect their lower bodies. If they had been battling other clansmen, it would have been sufficient, but against the Romans it was too little, too late. Thousands of honed *gladii* flashed low, wielded by sinews forged of iron. The thin tapered points pierced armour while the double-edged blades smoothly slipped into groins, stomachs and legs. Accompanied by what seemed to be a singular, feral roar, the veterans used their immense strength to twist the iron as they ripped it from the bodies of the foes.

The roar of the legions were followed by moans and cries from hundreds of mortally wounded tribesmen.

Hostilius's gaze remained fixed on the legions while a proud grin settled on his lips. "Told you my boys know their business", he said, and wet his parched throat with a swig from his wineskin.

Vibius failed to reply as his eyes were fixed on the *foederati* at the centre of the battlefield where the Quadi and the Semnones had not engaged, but were staring at one another over the rims of their shields.

Just then, a ramshorn wailed and the *foederati* turned their backs to the Semnones. Eight thousand Quadi hefted their spears, bellowed a war cry, and surged towards the command group.

"By Mars, the bastards betrayed us", the Primus Pilus growled as his hand dropped to the hilt of his blade. Then he issued a primal roar, dug his spurs into his gelding's flanks, and led the small group of mounted men in a death-defying charge.

* * *

The battle plan that Vibius and Hostilius had decided upon was nothing new. It was a proven strategy that had been employed with great success on the field of battle. While the legions were required to hold their ground, the Quadi at the centre were supposed to give way under the onslaught of the Semnones. As the *foederati* ranks in the centre were pushed back, the first line cohorts on the far right and left flanks would advance, enveloping the Semnones in the process. When the foe had committed all their men, the Illyrian cavalry, which were held in reserve, would flank them and attack them from the rear.

Late the night before, after the council of war had been concluded, Belimar had sent a warrior, one of his closest ringmen, to the war-witch inside the Semnones camp. In the dead of night, the man had returned to his master and recited the instructions of Braduhenna, who had devised a plan of her own.

* * *

There was not a man amongst the Illyrians who would have hesitated to follow Hostilius through the Black Gates of Hades.

Confronted with the death-defying charge, the Illyrians followed their commanders into the fray without the need for a command. As one, the black riders kicked their armoured warhorses to a gallop, each plucking a lead-weighted war dart from the inside of his shield.

Before the handful of Roman horsemen were swallowed by the horde, a shadow passed over them from behind as thousands of *plumbatae* darkened the morning sky. The barbed missiles rained down on the Germani, their charge faltering as they were forced to lift their shields above their heads. The second wave of war darts struck three heartbeats before Hostilius rammed his spear into the torso of a Quadi who happened to be in his way. His horse crushed the next warrior in line and the third's head was lopped off by a single backhanded slash from the Primus Pilus's *spatha*. But a dozen men cannot defeat a mob of eight thousand, and the charge was halted by the tight press of shield-bearing warriors who were salivating at the prospect of claiming the heads, blades and armour of the Roman commanders.

A Germani rammed his spear into the side of the guardsman beside Hostilius, and with a roar of victory the unfortunate was pulled from his saddle to be hacked to pieces.

Another barbarian, a red-bearded brute, buried his axe in the skull of Vibius's horse. The animal collapsed, and Vibius went to ground three paces to the left of Hostilius. The first man brave enough to try and kill the legate paid for it with a skull crushed by the Primus Pilus's warhorse's hooves. While the second man who had tried to claim Vibius's head reached for his opened throat, a Quadi got his hands on Hostilius's leg, but lost his appendage to a slash from the Primus Pilus's blade. Hostilius parried another man's spear, but a longsword flashed from behind, parted the links of his armour, and cut into the sinews of his back. His horse swung around and he managed to flip his sword to his left fist. Before the attacker could push his advantage, Hostilius buried his blade in the man's neck. The Quadi staggered backwards, ripping the hilt from the Primus Pilus's grasp as the corpse went to ground.

Unconcerned for his own safety, Hostilius kicked a warrior in the face who kneeled over an unconscious Vibius while trying to ram his dagger through the Roman commander's mail. The man dropped his blade and fell sprawling into the press of savages.

The Primus Pilus jerked the head of his horse around to confront another attack from the right, just in time to see a giant, ruddy-bearded warrior bring a massive bearded axe to bear. But Hostilius had nothing to parry the strike with and helplessly he watched as a sneer of triumph split the brute's bearded face as the honed blade came around for the kill.

Defiantly the Primus Pilus met his killer's gaze. "Mars forgive me. I failed you, Domitius, and I failed Rome", he muttered as he waited for the inevitable.

There was a blur of gleaming lances and dark armour as a wall of iron-encased horseflesh slammed into the ranks of the Quadi. The wave of death struck the barbarian infantry at a gallop, impaling, crushing or maiming nearly all in the first three ranks.

Hostilius swung down from the saddle. With his good hand the Primus Pilus grabbed Vibius by his armour and heaved his bleeding friend onto the neck of his horse before mounting behind.

"Tribune!" he heard the shout of a standard-bearer rise above the chaos. "We must get you and the legate to safety. The savages outnumber us five to one, we will not hold them for long."

The Primus Pilus looked to where the Roman cavalry were fighting for their lives, trying to hold back the overwhelming numbers. Then he noticed that the officer was still staring at him expectantly, and he realised with a shock that the man was waiting for a command.

"Sound the retreat", he said through gritted teeth. "We will withdraw from the field to the safety of the camp."

While the morbid command of the *buccina* echoed over the field of blood, Hostilius jerked the head of his horse around to lead his men to safety.

For a span of ten heartbeats, he stared at the scene unfolding before him. Then he turned to face the signifer. "Cancel that", he growled. "Signal for the legions to converge on this position. Here, on the soil of Italia, we will make our last stand."

Chapter 16 – Turn of the Tide

We reined in on a low rise overlooking the flat ground where the two legions and half the Illyrian cavalry were facing off against the Semnones. To the left of the battlefield lay forested ravines and to the right an open plain bordered by the Trebia on the far side.

War had been my trade for most of my life so it took only a moment to decipher what was unfolding. "Vibius and Hostilius deployed their Quadi allies in the centre to draw in the enemy and to envelop them with the legions on the wings", I said to Gordas.

"The traitor has already shown his hand", I added, pointing at the centre. "The Quadi have switched their allegiance, but the Illyrians have driven them back so that they are unable to attack the legions in the flanks."

"Come", I said. "We will turn the tide."

But Gordas grabbed my reins. He pointed left, to the edge of the forest where thousands upon thousands of horsemen were spilling onto the plain. "Look, the war-witch and her allies are springing their trap", he growled.

I realised that my actions in the next few moments would not only determine the fate of my friends, but also that of the Empire. I commanded only five thousand riders and knew that to commit the Illyrians to the field would not change the ultimate outcome, but at best delay the annihilation of the Roman army.

I closed my eyes and begged the god of war and fire to come to my aid.

Arash was never far from the field of blood. In my hour of need, the lord of war answered my pleas. In my mind, I heard the words of Cai, "Sometimes stomping grass will scare viper, Lucius of Da Qin."

I turned to the commander of the Illyrians. "Take four thousand men", I said, and pointed at the ridgeline of elevated ground running from west to east along the plain. "Canter towards the Trebia, but be sure to stay on the far side of the ridge, away from the enemy's gaze."

The prefect nodded.

"When you are half a mile from the banks of the river, deploy in a single line facing south", I continued, "but remain hidden from the eyes of the foe. Every fifth man is to tie his spare cloak to a lance which he will hold aloft like a standard. When you hear the notes of the *buccina*, advance at a gallop but halt six hundred paces from the enemy."

"I understand and I will obey, Lord Emperor", he said, and led his men west.

My eyes remained fixed on the battlefield where the legions were reorganising into a defensible formation while the Illyrians tried to keep the treacherous Quadi from breaking through the Roman line.

At the same time, the Semnones cavalry were thundering closer, keen to wipe the Romans from the field. It became a race against time, one I feared my friends would lose. But two thousand of Vibius's Illyrians broke away from where they were holding the Quadi at bay, spread out into a single line, and spurred their tired horses to charge the horde of barbarian riders bearing down on them from the woods.

"The black riders are brave, like the wolf", Gordas grunted from beside me.

Faced with the heavily armoured riders, the Semnones cavalry slowed to dress their line as best they could. When the Illyrians were seventy paces away, the tribesmen kicked their horses to a gallop to meet the Romans' charge. Volley after volley of war darts rained down on the Germani before the lines came together in a clap of thunder. Many hundreds of the foe must have perished in that moment, but so many thousands remained that the Illyrians were overrun in sixty heartbeats.

The brief delay had bought enough time for the two legions to join.

My Hun friend, who had been regarding the spectacle with a face of stone, nodded his elongated head to show that he approved of the Illyrians' actions. "They sacrificed themselves for their brothers", he said. "The god of war and fire has accepted their offering. Tonight, they will feast in the hall of Arash."

The legions, who were now surrounded on four sides, formed a great hollow square. The remaining Illyrians who had battled the Quadi, mayhap a thousand or two, retreated into the relative safety in the centre of the formation.

I breathed a sigh of relief.

But it was to be only a temporary respite, as the army of the Semnones and Quadi immediately went over to the offensive. Like an island in the centre of a raging torrent of spears, the thin ranks of the Romans bent under the enormous pressure exerted by almost a hundred thousand foes.

"The legions will not hold longer than a sixth of a watch", Gordas said. "They are trapped like a marmot in the den of a wolf."

At that moment the sun peeked from behind the clouds and the rays reflected off the gold and silver of the eagle standards of the legions. I took it as a sign.

I turned around to face the thousand remaining Illyrians arrayed behind me. Like statues hewn from the black stone itself, they sat unmoving on their great warhorses.

I drew my famed sword and pointed to where the battle raged. "Our brothers are being slaughtered by the spears of invaders and traitors", I said. "With our lances and blades we will cut a path through the ranks of the enemy - a path that the legions may use to retreat. Mayhap it is too late to save our own lives and those of our comrades, but it is never too late to salvage our honour."

"Hear my words - before the gods of Rome, I free you of your sacred oath to your emperor", I boomed. "Join me if you wish, otherwise ride away to your families."

I turned Kasirga's head towards the field of blood, patted his great muscular neck, and dug my heels into his flanks. Within seven strides my stallion was at the gallop. Halfway down the hill I looked over my shoulder and noticed that not a single rider had chosen to remain behind.

I nodded to the signifer. On my instruction he tilted the wolf head standard and a shrill wail emanated from its iron maw. Without breaking stride, the Illyrian formation transformed into a giant wedge with Gordas and me at its tip. I stole a glance at the Hun and noticed that a wide grin was plastered on his scarred visage. "If I go to the gods", he said, "make sure my family knows how I perished. My death will be a thing of legend."

I nodded, stowed my lance, and clipped my shield onto the saddle. Then I retrieved my strung bow from its holder, dropped my horse's reins, and took four of my best arrows in my draw hand.

The Semnones, who were still a hundred paces distant, had been alerted to our presence. Some hardly bothered to glance over their shoulders, while others in the rear ranks closest to us reluctantly turned to face the threat. Overall, the horde paid us the same heed as a horse would a midge.

There was no need for words. Both Gordas and I knew what needed to be done. We fitted arrows, drew the sinew strings to our ears, and released.

Our shafts struck the necks of two horses in the Germani line. The mortally injured animals bolted to the side, opening a gap of sorts in the ranks of the foe. Two more three-bladed arrows struck horseflesh and the gap widened. We each released six more arrows in half the number of heartbeats, stowed our bows, and retrieved our shields and lances.

Seamlessly, the wedge of Illyrians slipped into the hole that we had carved into the horde. I lowered my lance and the armour-piercing tip effortlessly passed through the torso of a Semnones rider who still faced away from us. The deadly honed iron stuck to its path and skewered a second warrior, forcing me to relinquish the spear. Slowly, the pinned-together corpses tumbled from the saddles, but I slapped them aside as Kasirga crushed the next horse barring his way. Another warrior paid the ultimate price before my stallion's charge faltered, its momentum spent.

A young, inexperienced fighter came at me from the right, but an Illyrian lance snaked out from behind and skewered the fool's neck. A bold warrior tried to get at me from the left but Kasirga was ever alert, twisted and kicked out at the rider, his enormous hooves pulverising the shoulder of the warrior's unfortunate mount that collapsed, pinning its rider underneath.

A large, grey-haired champion with a magnificent pleated beard and many arm rings slashed at me one-handed with a short-hafted war axe, but I caught the head on the lip of my shield and my thrust passed over the rim of his own shield and pierced his eye.

And then the dark one, Wodanaz, the lord of the raging horde, played his hand.

As the corpse of the greybeard tumbled to the side, I spun around to face the next threat. Somehow the body of my victim obscured the tip of a spear aimed at my leg. When my eye caught the gleam it was already too late, and I knew that the lance would pass through my leg and pin me to the saddle.

But Kasirga was more alert than me and he managed to twist his great neck, taking the spear on my behalf. My horse groaned in pain, reared onto his hind legs and crushed the man's skull with a single slash from a hoof. I forced myself to look down and noticed that the Germani's spear was a one-in-a-thousand strike. The honed tip had passed through the leather armour where a previous strike must have removed a metal scale.

Kasirga regained his footing and swayed to the side. Then the prince of horses issued a small whinny and collapsed. I had grown up with my mother's people and vaulted from the back of my falling mount, rolling as I struck the ground. In that moment I caught a glimpse of the front ranks of the legions, fewer than ten paces away.

But it may just as well have been on the other side of the Black Gates.

I righted myself and, unconcerned for my own life, kneeled beside my dying horse. I ignored the warrior bearing down on me and heard only a faint grunt in the background as Gordas's lasso must have plucked him from the saddle.

"There is no greater honour than to sacrifice oneself for another", I whispered as I stroked my horse's neck. "Soon, I will join you on the fields of Elysium, my friend."

Kasirga's eyes glazed over and I knew that his shade had passed to the other side.

Mayhap it was the warrior-spirit of my horse or maybe the lord of war and fire came to me. I felt the terrible grief morph into a red-hot anger that threatened to consume all. All around, the foes were converging, keen to claim the head of the man who wore the fur-lined purple cloak.

My right fist tightened around the hilt of my blade and my left around the haft of my battle-axe. I ducked to avoid a spear that would have crushed my skull, skipped from the path of the horse, and severed the warrior's arm at the elbow. The next man was too slow and my blade cut deep into his knee before I plucked him from the saddle and vaulted onto his mount. I spurred the borrowed horse into another rider, my blade opening his throat before he could even lift his shield. A stocky blonde-bearded man with a fine longsword and good armour cut at me backhanded. I deflected his blow with the flat of my blade and in reply the metal spike of my axe split the riveted plate of his helmet and pierced his skull.

Suddenly the Germani were not so keen to claim my head, and many retreated in the wake of the blood-smeared apparition who killed all who dared to face him. But there will always be fools who overestimate their own prowess, and half a dozen more warriors succumbed to my iron before I had cut a bloody swathe through the foe to reach the Roman ranks.

Where the legionaries were waiting.

Like water released from behind a sluice, the Roman infantry spilled into the path that the last of the surviving Illyrians were battling to keep open. The legionaries took advantage of the enemy's confusion and formed ranks on both sides of the escape route, allowing the legion to retreat through the corridor.

With the tired sinews of the legionaries invigorated by hope, the barbarians failed to break their line.

Just then the standard-bearers of the legions passed me by. They escorted two men bearing a makeshift stretcher trailed by a horse carrying a rider who was barely keeping the saddle. He was hugging the neck of his mount while bleeding from a deep wound in his back.

"Wait", I commanded.

The men carrying the stretcher halted. I approached and looked down on the bloodied, bruised face of Vibius who lay unmoving on the canvas. "Does he live?" I asked.

"The legate is somewhere between this world and the next, lord", the closest Roman replied. "But he still draws breath."

Prompted by my voice, the injured rider raised his head. "Domitius", Hostilius croaked. "I knew you would come and …", but he got no further. His head slumped and he slid from the saddle, succumbing to the loss of blood.

I sprinted closer, steadied the Primus Pilus before he fell, and gained the saddle behind him.

From the elevated position I noticed that the Germani were recovering from the surprise of our charge. Thousands of barbarians had disengaged from the press and were streaming around the formation in an attempt to envelop the Romans once again and cut off our retreat.

It was time to roll the last dice.

"Order the Illyrian cavalry to attack", I commanded the signifer, who immediately pressed the *buccina* to his lips.

A dust cloud rose from the far side of the ridge and moments later the northern horizon came to life with a line of black-clad riders stretching as far as the eye could see. Although dust obscured the rear ranks of the Roman cavalry, hundreds of standards proudly rose above the haze, hinting at the size of the massive force.

A collective moan emanated from the barbarian ranks as they laid eyes on their approaching doom. For a span of thirty heartbeats the war leaders remained mum, but then a ramshorn echoed across the field of blood and the tribesmen flowed away from the battle like rain from a newly oiled *sagum*.

Chapter 17 – Pyre

"Farewell, my friend", I said, and thrust a flaming brand into the oil-soaked wood.

"It is right that you honour him, Eochar", Gordas grunted from beside me. "It is the old way."

I watched as the flames embraced my trusted companion of so many years. After the fire had freed Kasirga's shade from the bonds of the flesh, the smoke guided it into the heavens, across the bridge of stars to the great beyond.

Gordas raised an eyebrow. "When you, too, cross the river, will you take Kasirga as your horse to ride across the fields of Elysium?"

"Of course", I replied, still reeling from the loss.

"Then I will lay claim to Simsek", the Hun stated in his matter-of-fact way.

"I will take them both", I countered.

"Not if I get there first", he replied.

I slapped his scaled shoulder. "Come", I said. "Let us go and see if the Easterner's ministrations are working."

* * *

Although Cai had managed to revive Vibius and stem the flow of blood from Hostilius's gaping wound, the atmosphere in the command quarters was darker than the halls of the lord of the dead's abode.

I noticed a stack of wax tablets on a desk in the corner of the tent, all tied together with twine, and immediately recognised it for what it was - a casualty report.

Hostilius failed to meet my gaze. "Almost two and a half thousand Illyrians lost their lives", he whispered. "The bodies of the fallen legionaries are still being gathered and loaded onto carts. I estimate four thousand, maybe more."

The Primus Pilus lowered his head in shame. "Nearly six thousand sons of Rome are dead because of my incompetence."

"And mine", Vibius added, his voice sounding like a hoarse croak.

"How many survived?" I asked.

When no reply was forthcoming, I said, "Let me tell you. Eleven thousand of the Empire's soldiers survived because of you. I was the one who invited the wolf into the fold. I was the one who trusted the traitor, not you."

"You saved us and our men from certain death, Lucius", Vibius said.

Thankfully Gordas intervened to stop the conversation that was leading nowhere.

"Once the bleeding has stopped, the body heals itself from the wounds suffered in battle", the Hun growled. "But the lesions of the shade can only be cured by the blood of the enemy."

None argued with his sage counsel.

Just then the duty tribune entered with a scout in tow. "Lord Emperor", he said. "Our outriders have found the enemy."

I gestured for the man to give his report.

"Lord Emperor", the scout said, "the Germani are heading east."

"Are they retreating to the passes?" I asked.

When the man averted his eyes, I knew the answer and I felt my throat constrict.

"No, lord", he said. "They have skirted our camp. Their outriders are already reconnoitring the Aemilian Way."

"Jupiter Best and Greatest!" Hostilius exclaimed as soon as the scout was out of earshot. "The savages are on their way to Rome."

"How do we stop a hundred thousand with only seven thousand Illyrians and fewer than eight thousand legionaries?" Vibius sighed. "Have the gods destined us to oversee the fall of the Empire?"

I felt the darkness of despair trickle into my mind and spread its black tentacles inside my skull. "The Empire has already been broken into three parts", I said, and slumped down onto a couch. "Mayhap the gods have doomed Rome and we are fighting a battle that cannot be won."

"Best go sleep, Lucius of Da Qin", Cai suggested. "Rest first, then seek will of gods."

* * *

"Are you sure?" I asked the scout while I wiped my face with a damp cloth in an effort to wake up.

"Yes, lord", he replied, his eyes wide. "I saw them with my own eyes."

"How many?" I asked, and stretched to dispel the stiffness from my sinews.

"Maybe five thousand riders, lord", he said. "And the same number of footmen."

"To which tribe do they belong?" I asked. "The Semnones?"

"The footmen are clad in furs, just like the Germani", he confirmed, and a frown appeared on his brow. "The riders wear robes and the flanks of their mounts are painted for war. To me, lord, they look like…"

"Like Scythians?" I asked.

"Yes, lord", he replied.

I felt the breath of the god of war and fire drive away the darkness of despair and rekindle the flame of hope that had once burned within my chest.

"How far away are their outriders?" I asked.

"Less than a watch, lord", he said.

I dismissed the man with a gesture. "Wait for me outside. Once I have donned my armour, you will take me to them."

* * *

"Greetings, Lord Emperor", my daughter said, and inclined her head in the way of the Scythians.

"You are welcome in my lands, Queen Aritê", I replied, and pressed my palm to my chest. "Is your husband not accompanying you?"

"Naulobates has been delayed", she replied. "He is leading a hunting party."

"Boar or deer?" I asked.

"Germani", she replied, and issued a grin that chilled my blood.

Her gaze settled on my horse, a fine gelding from a pure Spanish bloodline. "Where is the son of Simsek?" she asked.

"He gave his life to save mine", I said, and felt my throat constrict. "I have sent his shade ahead in the way of our people."

It was clear that my words pleased her, but still a frown appeared on her brow, her gaze fixed on my mount. "It is not fit for a prince of the Roxolani to be seen on the back of a mule", she said.

Gordas, who sat abreast of me, suppressed a grin, clearly enjoying the exchange.

The queen of the Roxolani barked a command to a hulking oathsworn riding in her wake. "Bring him to me."

"Lady", her ringman replied, and galloped towards the rear of the massive Scythian column.

A hundred heartbeats later Burdukhan returned, leading a magnificent horse by a halter. I felt a pang of sadness because the stallion's features reminded me much of Kasirga, bar the fact that the young horse was a gray with a black mane and matching tail.

"He is the son of Kasirga", she said with pride. "In his veins flows the blood of Simsek and the great warhorses of the Sasanians."

I dismounted and approached the horse, coming to a halt five paces from him.

He issued a nervous nicker and strained at the halter.

I spoke softly in the language of the Sea of Grass and kept my distance. It took a hundred heartbeats for his curiosity to get the better of his fear and he cautiously inched closer. As soon as he relaxed, I slowly raised my hand and rubbed his muscular neck. But he shook his head, whinnied and retreated, disapproving of my familiarity.

"If he does not take to your father, I will gladly look after him, Queen Aritê ", Gordas said. He glided off the back of his mare and spoke in the language of the Huns, which all horses seemed to understand. The animal did not shy away and allowed the Hun to run a palm across his muscular back. "You see, Eochar, he likes me."

"He likes you because you reek of mare's milk", I said - a terrible insult in the land of the Huns. Then I smiled and added, "He thinks that you are his mother."

Gordas removed his fist from his dagger before he doubled over with laughter. When he had righted himself, he tapped his armoured chest with a fist. "In here, you are a Hun, Eochar. Give the sewers that you call Rome to the dirt eaters. Join me, and let us ride east to the endless plains of the Sea of Grass."

I placed a hand on his shoulder. "It is a tempting offer, my friend", I said, and turned to face Aritê who wore an amused expression.

"Has he been named?" I asked.

"Yes, father", she replied. "He has been trained for war but I have not allowed any rider to bond with him. That honour is yours."

I nodded in approval. "What is his name?" I asked.

"Intikam", she replied. "He is named *Wrath* because he will be the one who brings death and retribution to your enemies."

Chapter 18 – Onion

Ducking into the command tent, it was not Hostilius nor Vibius who greeted me, but a grinning Diocles.

"Lord Emperor", he said, and inclined his head.

I realised then how much I had missed the company and advice of my aide. Ignoring his extended arm, I embraced him like one would a brother. "It is good to see you", I said.

"What tidings do you bring from Rome?" I asked.

"I have conceded to Zenobia's request", he said bluntly. "The mint in Antioch will produce coins that bear not only your image, Lord Emperor, but also that of her son Vaballathus."

It was a bitter potion to swallow, but Diocles had acted on my instructions, doing that what needed to be done.

"In return for the concession, the grain shipments from Aegypt are continuing uninterrupted", he said.

A great weight lifted off my shoulders. "You have done well", I said. "It must have been difficult to convince the Senate."

Judging by the pained expression on Diocles's face, I imagined it was an understatement. I decided to rather speak of his ordeal when we were both rested.

"How did you manage to avoid the invaders?"

"Eight days ago, I took ship from Rome", he explained. "When I landed at Genua, there were rumours of Germani warbands ravaging the Po valley. The following morning, I rode north crossing paths with many fleeing to the coast. Yesterday afternoon, I arrived at Camillomagus where the townsfolk spoke of a great battle on the banks of the Trebia."

I wanted to ask Diocles whether he knew the outcome of the battle, but he was one step ahead.

"I have been informed of the setback", my aide replied diplomatically.

"You're not in Rome anymore, Greek", Hostilius growled from across the room. "No need to dip your words in honey."

"The Semnones are heading to Rome", I said. "And last night we did not have a force large enough to stop them."

"So how in hades did you manage to lay your hands on reinforcements while you were sleeping?" Hostilius asked. "Did you summon wraiths from the underworld?"

"Something like that", I replied, which deepened the Primus Pilus's frown.

At that moment the morning sun projected a large, ominous shadow onto the canvas of the tent. Moments later, a heavily muscled arm pulled aside the flap and a hulking barbarian clad in a loose robe and wolfskin cloak stepped inside. A feral grin split his bearded, tattooed face to reveal a mouthful of savage, filed-down teeth.

"Father", he said in broken Latin, and pressed his right palm against his chest as a sign of respect. "The wolves of the Heruli are at your service."

"Greetings Naulobates", I replied in the language of the Sea of Grass. "You are welcome at my hearth."

We were interrupted by the prefect of the Illyrians. "Lord", he said. "We are about to send the shades of the fallen riders on their way. My men will view it as a great honour if you presided over the sacrifices."

I turned to face my friends. "While I tend to the fallen, make arrangements so that the army may be resupplied and ready to march. Tonight, when the dead are at peace, I will convene a council of war."

* * *

Once the sun had dipped below the western horizon, we all congregated inside the command tent.

"The wolf is weak when it is separated from the pack", Aritê said, and accepted a cup from Diocles. "We will ambush the warbands of the enemy and overwhelm them one at a time."

"As far as we know, the invaders are not aware of our reinforcements", Diocles pointed out. "Maybe we should conceal the presence of the Scythians until we are able to surprise the enemy."

"I refuse to hide in the shadows while the dirt eaters ravage the lands of my father's people", Aritê said. "We must destroy the vermin as quickly and ruthlessly as possible."

"I agree with the queen", Hostilius said, no doubt just as eager to salvage his honour as my daughter was to spill the blood of the invaders.

"When strong, appear weak", Cai advised. "When near, appear far away."

"My daughter is right", I said. "It is not the way of the Scythians to conceal themselves. Queen Aritê and her mounted archers will harass the enemy and pick off the undisciplined warbands that get separated from the main host."

I made no mention of the wolves of the Heruli. Although my son-in-law had the appearance of an uncouth savage, his mind was as keen as the blade he carried at his side. "Unlike the brave riders of the Roxolani, the Heruli have no qualms to remain in the shadows", he said. "As long as the queen is willing to share the spoils of war."

Aritê smiled sweetly and placed a hand on her man's scaled shoulder. "What is mine, is yours", she said. "You need not ask."

"Likewise, my love", the big man replied.

Vibius rolled his eyes. "When do we attack?" he asked, also keen to restore his reputation.

Diocles had always been the voice of reason, and it was no different then. "We have eight thousand legionaries at our disposal and seven thousand black riders", he said. "The Roxolani and Heruli have contributed another ten thousand to our force, which makes twenty-five thousand in total. Between the Semnones, Quadi and Alemanni, they can field a hundred thousand warriors of which almost forty thousand are mounted on good horses."

"Strength of enemy, also weakness", Cai pointed out.

"Diocles is right", I said. "Our forces are outnumbered four to one. Many still bear wounds and the morale of our army is in tatters. If we act too soon, we will be crushed by the invaders, Rome will go up in flames and the Empire will cease to exist."

I gave the harsh consequences of rash action a few heartbeats to sink in.

"It is early spring", I continued. "There are yet no crops that can be looted from the fields nor are there pastures to be found that are able to sustain thousands of horses. The foraging parties of the Semnones will have to travel far to feed the warriors and their animals. Their progress south will be slow."

"Even if we get to fight on the ground of our choosing, we will not prevail without the help of the gods", my son-in-law said.

His pious words earned him a loving look from my daughter, whose rule was guided by the gods of the Sea of Grass.

"Naulobates is right, the existence of the Empire hangs in the balance", I said. "I will send orders to Rome. The custodians of the sacred texts must enter the vault of the Temple of Apollo to observe the rites as described by the oracles of old. It is the only way to ensure the good graces of the gods of Italia."

Hostilius issued a gasp. "My *ava* told me that the Sibylline Books were last consulted in the aftermath of the great fire during the time of Nero."

"For two hundred and seven years the holy books have gathered dust", Diocles confirmed. "It is an auspicious time to curry the favour of the gods." But my aide's expression did not match his words.

"You have reservations?" I asked.

"For many years the power of the Senate has remained unchecked", Diocles said. "The emperors were either weak or occupied with usurpers or civil war. And then Gallienus started to meddle with the age-old privileges of the ruling class…"

"It's those same bastards who had Marcus poisoned", Hostilius sneered.

Diocles nodded in agreement. "They had Emperor Claudius Gothicus murdered because they feared him. They were fearful of what he might do to them if he uncovered their treachery and scheming."

"If they knew the current emperor like we do, they would have tried their best to keep Marcus in good health", the Primus Pilus said. "The previous emperor was a proper soldier, strict and disciplined, but forgiving by nature. Domitius can't even spell mercy, never mind dish it out."

Hostilius looked at me as if he only then realised I was present. "Don't take offence, Domitius, I say it like it is, whether you're in the room or not", he said, and chugged the remaining wine in his cup.

"None taken", I said.

Diocles cleared his throat to bring the discussion back to point. "Yes, the Senate fears you, Lord Emperor", he said. "And I have no doubt that they will try their utmost to discredit you and to make sure you fail. I would not be surprised if they fail to consult the Sibylline Books and sacrifice Rome itself just so that they can blame you for the calamity. The mint master's corruption is but the outer layer of the onion."

"Draft the missive nonetheless and request of them to observe the rites", I said. "When the time is right, I will take my blade and peel off the layers of deception one at a time, until we get to the root of the evil."

Chapter 19 – Attrition

"Do not look to the left, Father", Aritê cautioned. "We are being watched from the high ground over yonder."

Although I studied the forested hill from the corner of my eye, I made sure not to turn my head. "Where are Naulobates and his wolves?" I asked.

"As we speak, his warriors are moving in the shadows, encircling the scouts", she grinned.

Moments later, a scream of anguish emanated from the wooded hill before it was cut short, no doubt by a Heruli blade. It prompted my daughter's smile to morph into a leer. "It is time to go hunting", she said, and reached down to retrieve her strung bow from its case.

* * *

Hostilius, Gordas, Diocles and I sat in the saddle beside my daughter. Vibius, who still felt the effects of his head injury, had remained with Cai in the camp. The Primus Pilus, also not fully recovered from his wound, had joined us after all attempts at persuading him to stay behind had failed.

We waited at the edge of a woodland on a low hill overlooking a thriving farm. On the flatland below, beyond the gentle southerly slope clad with olive groves and vineyards, lay the outbuildings of the large agricultural estate - all except the grand villa and bath house that had been built far from the slave quarters. This practice ensured that when the wealthy owner visited from the city, he would not be forced to endure the sight and smell of the men and women who toiled from first light to last.

Some labourers were tending to the vineyards and olive trees while others were toiling in the fields with hoes and spades. Goats, cattle and a handful of horses grazed peacefully in paddocks bordering pressing rooms. Inside the large warehouses, amphorae of wine and olive oil would be stacked on the ground floor while grain and fodder would be stored on the well-ventilated level above.

"I can't help but think we're protecting the estate of some stinking rich senator who probably had a hand in Marcus's murder", Hostilius sighed.

"Then it's a good thing we did not warn the overseer, eh?" I said. "Else they would have been busy carting whatever is left in the stores into the hills."

The Primus Pilus grunted his agreement.

"The Germani are no fools", I said. "They will suspect a trap if the slaves are looking over their shoulders."

"Are you even sure we're staking out the right place?" Hostilius asked, and rubbed the small of his back. "We've been sitting for the best part of a third of a watch."

"Have no fear, centurion", Aritê replied. "Before long, your iron will taste the blood of the Semnones, although…" My daughter paused mid-sentence, distracted by movement on a pasture below. Moments later, a goat scampered across the open ground.

"Although what?" the Primus Pilus asked.

"… Although your spear does not have the range of our bows", my daughter said, indicating Hostilius's favourite weapon for hunting. "You might end up being no more than a spectator."

"Spectator my arse", the Primus Pilus growled, hefting the weapon with his left hand. "What it lacks in range, it makes up for in penetrating ability", he countered, and mimicked a thrust. "Besides, I prefer close-quarters work."

Hostilius gestured to Diocles on his far side. "I'll deal with the well-armoured ones", he said. "The Greek can use his swords to put the wounded out of their misery."

"They come", Gordas growled, which prevented my aide from issuing a retort.

Below us, a mounted foraging party numbering almost five hundred barbarian riders crested the rise on the far side of the estate. Simultaneously, a party of slaves noticed the arrival of the raiders. As one they yelled an alarm, discarded their implements, and started fleeing up the hill to the safety of the woods.

I deferred to Aritê, who patiently allowed the foe to approach. Satisfied that they were close enough, she raised her bow above her head, screeched a chilling war cry, and kicked her mare to a gallop. The unfortunate bondsmen and women who were running up the hill froze in their tracks when they laid eyes on a thousand mounted Scythians thundering down upon them from the forest.

"Seek shelter amongst the olive trees", I boomed as we approached. Slaves, like legionaries, were trained to follow orders without question. Hearing my words, they scampered from our path into the groves.

Faced with the charging Scythians, the Semnones halted in their tracks. It took only three heartbeats for the leader of the Germani to realise the futility of engaging with the horse archers who not only outnumbered them, but whose arrows could kill from a distance. He boomed a command and the raiders wheeled around, intent on returning the way they had come.

But my daughter had hunted on the steppes more times than she cared to remember and knew all the ways to herd and trap fleeing prey. Confronted with the backs of the raiders, she plucked two arrows from her quiver, issued the command, and released. Hundreds of missiles whooshed from the strings, arced high and slammed down into the backs of the fleeing Semnones, the first volley emptying more than half the saddles of the invaders.

Aritê raised a hand and the Scythians lowered their bows and reined in amongst the bodies writhing on the ground, all riddled with shafts. The remaining raiders thundered away, keen to escape the blades of the Roxolani.

My daughter vaulted from the saddle and claimed the scalp of a moaning Semnones. She took the trophy and smiled in satisfaction as the second force of Scythians crested the hill, blocking the route of escape. "I promised Burdukhan I would leave enough scalps for him and his men", she said as the first volley of her ringman's band slammed into the trapped foe. "Contented warriors are loyal warriors, you know."

While the Scythians took trophies, looted the bodies and hacked the useable arrows from the flesh of the Germani, Hostilius walked amongst the fallen, every so often spearing a warrior who still drew breath. "Not really something I would boast about around the cooking fire", he scowled. "But I guess making a contribution is better than sitting in the tent with one's feet up, eh?"

* * *

For the best part of three weeks, we pursued the invaders who continued their advance along the Aemilian Way.

The Germani were traversing some of the richest farmland in the whole of Italia. Although we trapped and killed thousands of enemy foragers, the main force remained too numerous to hem in. For every farm we managed to save, ten were put to the torch. For every invader we killed, ten survived.

But like Cai had predicted, the success of the Semnones was also their weakness. They accumulated hundreds, if not thousands of wagons filled with the riches of the land, slowing down their advance to less than seven miles a day.

With every passing day we whittled down their numbers, but like a plague of locusts crawling across the land, the invaders' march south were slow, yet inexorable. One afternoon, just east of Forum Cornelii, Hostilius, Gordas, Diocles and I scouted out the camp of the enemy from high ground, remaining mounted although we were on the crest of a hill. The enemy was aware of the Roman army pursuing them so there was no need for stealth.

Hostilius whistled through his teeth. "How many of the bloody savages have we put out of their misery?" he asked.

"Reports estimate that we have killed somewhere between eight and ten thousand foragers", Diocles replied.

"Doesn't look like it", Hostilius said. "Even if we kill another ten thousand of them before they get to Rome, it still won't be enough."

We rode back to camp in relative silence, all preoccupied with their own gloomy thoughts. The only remaining option was to meet the enemy on the field of battle. I realised that with the

Romans outnumbered four to one, even the advantage provided by favourable ground and sound strategy may not be enough to tilt the scale in our favour. If we were to suffer another defeat, not only Rome, but the whole of Italia would burn.

Back at camp, Vibius was waiting for us to return. In his hand he held a scroll bearing the seal of the Senate. "This arrived a third of a watch ago", he said. "It is addressed to you, Lucius."

"I'm sure those old farts have opened the Sibylline Books", Hostilius said. "You'll see, Domitius, things will take a turn for the better once the gods have been placated. With so many people turning from the old ways, it's about time that the gods rattle their cages."

I had no doubt that the scroll would be long-winded so I passed it to Diocles to give us the gist. While he read the words, his grin slowly faded and was replaced by a look of concern.

"Out with it, Greek", Hostilius barked.

"The Senate has rejected your request to consult the sacred texts, Lord Emperor", my aide said.

"For what reason?" I asked.

Diocles flopped down on a divan. "This scroll contains many words, but says very little", he replied. "They cite monetary constraints as an excuse, but I can give you the real reason, if you wish to hear it."

We all knew that few men in the Empire understood the machinations of the Senate better than Diocles, so I filled our cups with wine and indicated for my friends to be seated on the couches.

"I never confronted Felicissimus, the master of the mint, with his corruption", Diocles said.

"It is as we agreed", I confirmed. "When I am in Rome I will personally expose his corruption and my justice will be swift."

"During my weeks in Rome, I took it upon myself to gather as much information about the mint master and his dealings", Diocles revealed. "I believe that he is in the pay of a small group of powerful senators."

"The men who call themselves the Harbinger, the one with many heads", I said. "We know all this."

Diocles nodded. "For that reason, I reached out to Senator Pumilio to, er…, assist me in expanding my understanding of the Harbinger's activities."

My aide's revelations were getting interesting.

"Pumilio's network of spies is still gathering information which they will share with you on your arrival in Rome, Lord Emperor", he continued, "but there are some preliminary findings, that, although premature, might shed light on the decision by the conscript fathers."

"Stop talking like a bloody lawyer, Greek", Hostilius growled. "Just tell us the long and the short of it."

"The Harbinger has been sending consignments of gold north to the areas devastated by the invasions. Indications are that at least some of the gold has gone across the Danube", he revealed, and took a swig from his cup. "In addition, the Harbinger's agents have been purchasing ravaged farmland at a fraction of the market price to create great agricultural estates."

"Are you saying that those bastards are paying the barbarians to ravage Italia?" Hostilius asked.

"I am saying that it is one of the scenarios", my aide replied. "And if it is true, it explains why they have been lobbying the Senate not to open the Sibylline Books. Just imagine the wealth they will gather by purchasing all those ravaged farms around Rome."

"And the power they will wield once they own the land", I added.

"The Romans are playing with fire", Gordas said. "Unlike the harsh and savage home of the Semnones, Italia has been tamed. The Germani will covet these fertile lands with a moderate clime, and they will claim it for their themselves. Then the farms that the Romans have purchased will be nothing more than worthless scraps of paper."

"Write to them again. Offer to pay all the expenses from the treasury", I commanded my aide. "But this time I want you to be clear. If they decide not to consult the immortal gods, I insist to have the list of names of the senators who failed to vote in accordance with my wishes."

Chapter 20 – Rites (May 271 AD)

Mid-afternoon five days later, we arrived on the western bank of the Rubicon. The river, made famous by the Divine Julius Caesar, was just twelve miles north of Ariminum and twenty-five miles south of Ravenna. It was not lost on me that we had come full circle in the last seven months. It was then, while meeting with a delegation of the Senate in Ravenna, that we first received word of the Semnones invasion.

"The scouts report that the savages have reached the coast", Hostilius said as he stomped into the *praetorium* after inspecting the defences of the marching camp. He poured himself a cup of falernian and chugged it. "It seems that the Germani have skirted Ariminum", he added with a shrug. "Besides, why would they lay siege to walled cities when they can march into Rome without even having to climb a fence?"

We were interrupted by Diocles, who clasped a scroll in his hand. "A missive arrived bearing the seal of the Senate", my aide announced. "The Sibylline Books will be consulted, and the vote was unanimous."

"What happens now?" Hostilius asked.

Diocles not only followed the old ways but, like with most subjects, he was well read in the old religious texts. "The *Arval* priests will circumambulate the old city while the Vestal Virgins chant the hymns in accordance with the sacred verses", my aide replied. "Afterwards, the bull, ram and boar that had accompanied them will be sacrificed, and the *Ambervalia* proclaimed."

"Do they really believe that Ceres and Bacchus will protect them in their hour of need?" Hostilius asked.

"I believe that in this case the sacrifices will be dedicated to Mars the Avenger", Diocles said. "The god of war will be invoked and the festivities will be in his honour."

We heard the clopping of hooves outside and moments later Gordas entered through the door. He, too, poured himself a cup and gulped it down. "The Germani have made their camp on the banks of the river you call the Metaurus", he said. "Just off the Roman road near the great sea."

"Have you reconnoitred the hinterland?" I asked.

Gordas issued a grin which indicated that he had not only done as I had asked, but that he discovered something of interest. "A few miles inland, where the farms of the dirt eaters give way to wooded high ground, there is a great loop in the river. The ground is flat and suitable to horsemen."

"Can the river be crossed on horseback?" I asked.

"It is deep and the current is strong", Gordas replied. "But a good Scythian horse will gain the far bank in a hundred heartbeats."

"By now, in Rome, the sacrifices would have been made to Mars the Avenger", I said. "Tomorrow at dawn we will roll the dice and establish not only our fate, but also that of the Empire."

"Good", Hostilius replied, and downed another cup. "It's about bloody time."

* * *

Before the start of the second watch of the morning, our scouts confirmed that the Germani were still looting the surrounding countryside and making no effort to break camp, which prompted me to set the wheels in motion and call my friends to the *praetorium* for a council of war.

When I had outlined my plan, I was met by frowns all around, except from Cai. "It good strategy to remove ladder once enemy is on roof", he said.

Hostilius harboured doubts. "I know that Naulobates and his men are like wraiths in the night", he said. "But how are you going to know the layout of the Semnones' camp?"

In response to the Primus Pilus's question, I indicated for the duty tribune to allow my visitors to join us. Moments later, Secundus and Ganna entered the tent. Ganna was a purebred Semnones woman and Secundus had lived with the clan long enough to have adopted their ways. They were both dressed in tribal garb and would not look out of place amongst their kinsmen.

"How will you get into their camp?" Hostilius asked.

"We will have amphorae of wine in the back of our cart", Ganna replied in the language of the Germani. "Anyone with eyes in their head can see that we are not Romans, and besides, most of my kinsmen will sell their own mothers to get their hands on an amphora of falernian."

The Semnones girl had a point.

Hostilius shrugged. "Suppose so", he admitted. "But what will be your excuse for leaving again?"

"The guards will be told that we will return with more wine", Secundus grinned.

"When the moon shows itself in the sky this night, I will be waiting for you at the side of the road, one mile north of the Germani camp", Naulobates said.

"We will be there", Secundus replied, inclined his head, and led his wife from the tent.

I followed them into the daylight. Before they departed I called Secundus aside. "Do what you can", I said, and handed him a pouch bulging with gold.

He accepted the coin, but appeared markedly uncomfortable, as if he wished to ask for a reward. "There is something I would like if I succeed, lord", he said.

"Name your price", I sighed, and motioned for him to continue.

Upon hearing his terms, I could not help but grin. "Done", I said, and clasped forearms to seal the deal.

Not long after, Aritê led five thousand Roxolani horse archers south towards the great loop in the Metaurus River.

At dusk, I watched as Vibius and Diocles rode out the gate in the vanguard of the remaining Illyrian cavalry, followed by

Hostilius and the *aquilifers* who proudly held aloft the golden eagles of the two understrength legions.

As was their way, the Heruli waited until dark before they stirred. Before the end of the first watch of the night, the wolf warriors jogged from camp, heading towards the woodlands bordering the river.

Cai was assisting me to don my armour when Naulobates came for me. "It is time, lord", he said, and inclined his head to the Easterner. "Mani will show himself soon."

"I will join you in a moment", I replied, upon which he nodded and left the tent.

Once Cai had checked the buckles of my armour he draped a purple cloak over my shoulders and then a wolfskin cloak. When he was done, he placed a hand on my shoulder and nodded. "I know. I will be careful", I said, turned around, and ducked into the night.

Even though the area outside the *praetorium* was well lit, I failed to locate the Heruli. "There they are, lord", one of the guards flanking the entrance said, indicating a shadowy area to the right. A few flashes of white appeared, no doubt Naulobates and his men grinning at my discomfort.

"Come", I said, and gestured to where Gordas was waiting with the horses.

* * *

We waited a hundred paces from the edge of the cobbles while Naulobates fetched Secundus and his woman. Sixty heartbeats later, he returned with Ganna, but there was no sign of her husband.

"Where is Secundus?" I asked.

"He is negotiating a purchase", she said. "He will either be successful or I will bury him in the morning."

Her words shocked me into silence, but she added, "We owe you everything, lord. My husband is well aware of the risks."

In detail, she briefed us on the layout of the Semnones camp. When she was done, Ganna glimpsed at the handful of wolf warriors. "Beware the white tent of the protectors, lord", she said as she turned to leave. "It is pitched beside the one you seek."

*　*　*

Guided by the thin silvery light of a waxing moon, Gordas and I walked our horses closer to the sprawling barbarian camp. I still grieved over Kasirga and missed my companion terribly. Each day for the past weeks, I had made time to ride and bond with Intikam, but the powerful young stallion was not yet ready to ride to war so my daughter had given me a horse from her private herd, a large gelding as black as night.

A hundred paces from where the first tents were pitched, two torch-bearing sentries stepped into our path, their spears levelled. I noticed more watchmen, mayhap a dozen, congregated around a fire, twenty paces from the path.

"Where do you go at this early hour of the morning, friend?" one of the warriors growled.

"I am the Scythian guard of the ruler of these lands", Gordas replied in the tongue of the Germani, and casually started picking at his teeth with his thumbnail.

The warrior's gaze shifted to me and he issued an amused chuckle. "Then you must be the emperor of Rome." Despite the Semnones's sense of humour, he was no fool, and threateningly trained his weapon on my stomach while raising his torch to have a closer look.

I did not offer a reply, but flipped back the edge of the wolfskin to reveal a purple cloak and a black muscled cuirass inlaid with gold and silver. The cloak, dyed with Tyrian purple, was worth more than a warrior would earn in a lifetime. A man who possessed such a garment, never mind the cuirass, would be the envy of his clan.

It took but a moment for the guard's grin to morph into a sneer and he drew back his spear to bury the blade deep in my groin.

But the darkness itself seemed to take on physical shape as Naulobates gained his feet two paces behind the guard. The hulking Heruli clasped a calloused hand over the sentry's mouth and I saw a brief, dull flash as he rammed the iron of his blackened dagger deep into the base of the warrior's skull, just below the ear. Adroitly, he wrenched the torch from the dying man's clenched fist as he collapsed onto the dirt.

Before my son-in-law's ringman lowered the second guard's corpse gently onto the ground, there was a slight commotion at the fireside and the sentries' chatter died away.

I nodded and Gordas nudged his horse to a walk. We continued along the meandering path leading deeper into the camp, passing through a sea of shelters of all shapes and sizes. They were not laid out like a Roman marching camp, but according to clan and tribal affiliations. Every so often we passed by a group of warriors still consuming the previous day's liquid spoils beside a smouldering cooking fire. Apart from raising hands in mutual greeting we paid each other little heed. From time to time, I noticed shifting shadows at the edge of my vision. I knew not if they were friend or foe, but I was certain that Naulobates's men kept pace with us.

After what seemed like an eternity, but could not have been more than a few hundred heartbeats, we passed through a twenty-foot-wide clearing that reminded me of a firebreak. On the far side of the open ground was a collection of a dozen spacious pavilions.

To our right, I noticed a white canvas tent. The design was distinctly Roman, yet unfamiliar, and I could not help but wonder if it was a relic from the time of Varus and the Battle of the Dark Woods. Beyond the white tent was a richly embroidered hide enclosure with two torch-bearing guards flanking the closed leather flap. Both spear-wielding warriors were tall and well armoured with scabbarded longswords strapped to their belts.

I swung down from the saddle and strode towards them, open palms at my side. When I was ten paces away, the guard on the left issued a command in his native tongue, clearly annoyed, yet unwilling to disturb the slumber of the important occupants inside the embroidered tent. "Halt", he hissed from between clenched teeth.

"I come at the behest of the war matron", I whispered, just loud enough to make the words difficult to discern.

The guard nearest to me, a brute with a dark, plaited beard and a boar-crested helmet, slid his longsword from its sheath and approached until only two paces separated us. "Who are you?" he growled softly and leaned in to hear my answer.

I undid the clasp of the wolfskin and allowed it to tumble to the grass, revealing my magnificent gilded armour and fur-lined purple cloak. "Tell Braduhenna that the emperor of Rome is here for her", I whispered.

I wish to believe that the gasp he issued was not one of surprise because my blade left the scabbard in a blur, flashed like lightning, and opened his throat to the bone. The remaining guard drew a deep breath to issue a primal roar of rage, but the air never reached his lips as the razor edge of Gordas's battle-axe split the plate of his helmet and embedded deep in his skull.

Two of Naulobates's ringmen picked up the fallen torches. One led his lord through the embroidered flap of the large pavilion while another slit open the canvas of the white tent, allowing a handful of wolf warriors to enter before he ducked in as well.

After twenty heartbeats had passed and a few muffled cries had reached our ears, Naulobates appeared from the tent, a writhing human shape draped across his shoulder. The big man nonchalantly hefted Braduhenna onto the back of our spare mount. The ease with which Gordas lashed her in place betrayed that he was no stranger to kidnapping.

"How long do you need?" I asked Naulobates.

"If you can, give us a hundred heartbeats, lord", he said, and he and his men disappeared amongst the tents.

I counted to one hundred and twenty in my mind, noticing that the eastern horizon was already grey with the first light of the approaching day. I cleared my throat and shouted. "Hear me, men of the Semnones!"

I waited ten heartbeats and repeated my words.

All around, bearded faces wearing confused expressions were appearing in the doors of tents.

"Warriors of the Semnones!" I boomed in the tongue of the Germani. "You have come to my lands, trusting in Wodanaz, the lord of the raging horde. But your god is a feeble god of forests and marshes. He has no power in the lands of Rome. See how easy it is for me to take your witch. Her gods are powerless to protect her against the wrath of the gods of Rome!"

The first call to arms echoed through the unending rows of tents. For effect, I made my horse rear up.

"Tell me again", I asked Gordas. "How do you get a wolf pack to give chase?"

"You run", he growled.

Chapter 21 – Metaurus

"Then it is time to run", I said, pulled at the reins and dug my heels into the horse's sides. Within ten heartbeats the enormous stallion was at a gallop. We weaved through the mass of tents at breakneck speed, our powerful mounts crushing the odd warrior unfortunate enough to stumble onto our path.

By the time that we were halfway through the camp, the first of the tribesmen had gained their saddles. Forty heartbeats later, when we cleared the last of the tents, at least five hundred horsemen had taken up pursuit. Some were desperate to save the war matron while others were salivating at the prospect of taking the emperor.

I had long before realised that two riders would not be sufficient to lure the bulk of the Germani into a pursuit. A pack of wolves would never chase down mice, no matter how alluring the little creatures are. I looked over my shoulder at the very moment Aritê chose to lead her horsemen into the fray.

More than two thousand Scythian horse archers thundered down at the Germani flank, releasing two volleys of arrows in quick succession. For the sake of being able to give chase, most of the pursuers had disdained to don their armour and almost half of the foes fell to the wayside, barbed shafts piercing their or their mounts' unprotected flesh.

A feral roar of rage rose from the Semnones camp as they witnessed their brethren fall victim to the shafts of the hated people of the plains. War horns wailed and thousands upon thousands of riders galloped from amongst the tents.

My daughter steered her horse abreast of mine. "The dirt eaters despise Scythians", she said. "They will come because they count our horses, not our arrows."

I studied the horde baying for our blood. "Are you sure you have enough shafts?" I asked.

Aritê answered my question with a grin. Then she gestured towards the witch. "May I have her when you are done?" she asked.

"No", I replied, causing my daughter to frown.

"Why not?" she asked.

"I have entered into a trade", I revealed. "But you may be able to purchase her from Secundus's woman if you offer enough coin."

* * *

The Germani had hardly settled into the chase when they reeled from another attack in the flank - this time it was Burdukhan who led the other half of the Scythian riders from the opposite direction. Many fell, but it prompted the war leaders to commit the remainder of the Semnones horsemen.

Suddenly the Germani wolves were chasing bigger prey - they realised that the honour of rescuing their war matron and claiming the emperor would be reserved for a handful of riders, leaving little to the others. Five thousand Scythians would provide enough loot and sport for all. The Semnones, whose best warriors fought from the saddle, knew the value of Scythian mounts. Animals bred on the plains were extremely difficult to come by, as the people of the horse would never willingly sell their prized mounts to dirt eaters.

But first they had to catch us.

Aritê had given her warriors strict orders. Every few hundred paces, the Roxolani riders released shafts at the horde, which resulted in a steady stream of arrows. The barrage proved sufficient to empty the odd saddle, but not enough to discourage the pursuers from continuing the chase.

"It is time for our paths to separate", I said, unclipped the brooch holding my cloak in place, and passed the purple garment to Burdukhan, who was also mounted on a black gelding.

My daughter's ringman accepted the cloak and draped it around his shoulders with a flourish.

"It suits you", I said, and the hulking oathsworn grinned in reply.

"May Argimpasa smile upon you", I said to my daughter, and indicated for Gordas to pass her the reins of the horse carrying Braduhenna.

"And may Arash the Destroyer guide your blade", she blessed me in turn.

Thousands of hooves pounding the dirt had raised a veil of dust. Gordas and I veered away to the right while my daughter and her horsemen led the Germani to the loop in the Metaurus.

* * *

The Hun and I reined in at the head of the black riders on the far side of the low hill where Diocles was waiting with the Illyrians.

"I trust that all is going according to plan, lord?" my aide asked.

"So far, so good", I replied, relinquished my horse to be armoured, and indicated for Diocles and Gordas to join me at the crest of the rise.

While Gordas assisted me to don my Illyrian armour, we studied the scene playing out on the flatland below where the mounted Semnones spearmen had seemingly herded the Scythians onto the U-shaped ground created by the loop in the Metaurus. At the open end of the U, squadrons of horse archers were taking turns to hold the Germani at bay. They released their arrows at close range before wheeling about, only to return when their brethren withdrew. Soon the Germani halted, amassing their forces across the mile-wide gap, blocking the route of escape. Unbeknown to them, large numbers of Scythians were swimming their horses across the river at the belly of the U, three hundred paces distant.

When the war horn of the Semnones wailed, the mounted lancers raised their shields and levelled their spears. The remaining Scythian horse archers who were harassing them manoeuvred their mounts around and withdrew at a gallop with the horde in close pursuit.

The fleeing Scythians were forced to slow down as they approached the riverbank that had been stirred into a muddy mire by the horsemen who had already crossed.

The Semnones must have relished the inevitable slaughter and spurred their horses to a gallop. But somehow the thrill of the chase caused them to disregard the bowmen already amassed on the far bank, only forty paces distant.

Four thousand shafts rose into the morning sky and descended on the Semnones who were already drawing back their spears to skewer the horsemen crossing the river. Before the Germani could recover, another two volleys of poison-smeared, barbed arrows slammed into their ranks, allowing almost all the fleeing Scythians the time to urge their horses from the water and up to the safety of the southern bank.

Meanwhile most of the Semnones, in their eagerness to get to grips with the hated mounted archers, had allowed themselves to be drawn into the trap that we had set for them.

The river was too wide for spears to breach, so they amassed on the northern bank of the Metaurus and settled on hurling insults at their arch enemies. The Scythians watched from the other side of the forty-pace-wide water, silently daring their pursuers to enter the river and fall prey to their arrows. At their centre, a purple-cloaked warrior sat on a black horse, beside him a bound and gagged woman draped over a saddle.

"Here they come", Diocles said, pointing to where Hostilius and Vibius were leading the two under-strength legions towards the loop in the river. The legionaries were marching at double pace to reach the open side of the U before the Semnones woke up to the danger.

We watched in silence as the drama played out less than five hundred paces distant, willing the legions across the open ground. They were halfway across the gap when there was a stir in the ranks of the Semnones facing off with the Scythians. Hundreds of Germani spearmen in the rear ranks started milling about, nervously glancing over their shoulders. I knew it would be only heartbeats before the ramshorn blared.

"The black riders are needed", I said, jogged towards my horse, and swung up into the saddle.

The signifer fell in behind Diocles, Gordas and me, and raised the iron wolf head standard. The breeze passed through its metal maw and a wail echoed across the plain. In response the column of black riders surged forward, first at a trot and then at a canter.

The standard-bearer relayed my orders and as we cantered down the easy slope, more than seven thousand Roman horsemen deployed in attack formation, their ranks nearly fifteen riders deep.

To our right the legions were racing over the open ground to close the trap. At their head, I noticed Hostilius raise a hand in salute. I reciprocated, and on my orders, the signifer tilted the ash haft to alter the pitch of the iron standard. The Illyrians levelled their lances, dressed the line, and kicked their armoured horses to a gallop.

The Germani must have realised the danger. They spurred and whipped their horses to reach the gap that Hostilius and his legions were attempting to close. I steadied my armour-piercing lance, pulled my black oval shield tight against my torso, and selected a target.

The warrior thundering down on me shifted his round shield, revealing a savage snarl. The braids of his greying beard and the plait of thick blonde hair protruding from underneath his Greek-style helmet moved in rhythm with the gait of his mount. With his right hand he wielded a stabbing spear fitted with a leaf-shaped iron blade. A longsword hung from his side.

But I had moulded the Illyrian cavalry on the heavy horsemen of the Roxolani and the near impervious cataphracts of the Sasanians. Before the barbarian could bring his stabbing spear to bear, the thin iron tip of my lance passed through the layers of laminated willow of his painted shield and pierced his chest, lifting the corpse from the saddle. Half a heartbeat later, my heavily armoured warhorse slammed into the side of the riderless mount, throwing the smaller animal onto the warriors behind. I relinquished my lance, plucked the iron-flanged mace from my saddle, and crushed the skull of the helmetless rider who was preoccupied with staying on his horse. Because of the weakness of the thrust, the spear blade of the next man to face me was turned aside by my scale armour and he paid the ultimate price for the error.

"Now!" I boomed to the signifer, and the shrill note of a *buccina* signalled the withdrawal.

Before the reeling Germani could reorganise, the black riders retreated and the legions closed the door of the trap.

"Advance!" Hostilius boomed.

Centurions echoed his orders, the legionaries hefted their scuta, and eight thousand Romans, six ranks deep, pushed forward.

Some of the tribesmen charged the wall of laminated wood and spears, but all they gained was death. Unwilling to run into a solid wall, the horses balked and dug in their hooves, throwing their riders onto the blades of the Romans.

But the Semnones soon realised the futility of trying to breach the legions' ranks. The foe's ramshorn blared and at least a third of the riders dismounted and charged the advancing legionaries.

The Roman ranks bent under the sheer weight and relentless pressure of the onslaught, but Hostilius and his centurions rallied their men, desperately keeping the foe from breaching their line.

I watched the battle unfold and I knew that the badly outnumbered legionaries would not hold for long.

"Do it", I said.

Gordas strung his horn bow and retrieved a pitch-smeared shaft from a pouch. He dismounted, unbuckled a small clay flask from his hip and kneeled on the downwind side of his mare. Shielding his toil from the breeze with an open palm, he carefully decanted the smouldering embers onto the pitch, fitted the fire arrow to the string, and released it high into the sky.

In reply, the southern sky darkened and five thousand Scythian arrows slammed into the Semnones.

Two heartbeats later, five thousand more arrows left the strings of the horn and sinew bows. The barrage of missiles did little damage to the shield-bearing warriors on horseback, but for the ones who had dismounted and were fighting on foot, it was a whole different story. They were facing the legions with their backs turned towards the hail of arrows. Hundreds fell in the first volley and even more in the second. I saw the legion's ranks level out and soon the centurions were bellowing orders for the centuries to advance.

Slowly the jaws of the wolf were closing around the prey.

But Cai, who had intimate knowledge of the writings of the ancient masters of the East, had counselled against cutting off the enemy's path of escape. "Remember, Lucius of Da Qin", he had cautioned. "To capture, one must set free." Cai's counsel was one of the reasons I had chosen the ground. On the western edge of the battlefield, the riverbank was bordered by a hundred-pace-wide strip of oak and hornbeam forest. Further to the west, the ground gradually rose, flowing into hill-country and the densely treed foothills of the Apennines.

To the eyes of the Germani, the woods would be a sanctuary.

The legions relentlessly pressed forward. Every few heartbeats the skies darkened with Roxolani arrows. And more and more Germani heads turned towards the west - towards the woods where they could escape the blades and arrows.

I noticed two mounted fighters canter towards the forests. Twenty more followed. Then half a thousand. Within a hundred heartbeats, the horde was streaming into the greenwood to escape their fast-approaching doom.

Hostilius gave the signal for his men not to pursue the fleeing Germani as the last of the tribesmen galloped into the shadows.

Gordas and I walked our horses over to where the Primus Pilus was leaning on his bloody blade. Judging by the blood and gore spattered on his face and armour, it was evident that he had gotten his hands dirty.

He pursed his lips and regarded the Hun. "You were right", he said. "Nothing like the blood of the enemy to wash away a stain of dishonour."

Gordas issued a grunt which hinted that he had prior experience of the issue, and unclipped a wineskin from his saddle.

The Primus Pilus leaned closer and accepted the proffered skin with a nod. He drank deeply and regarded the woodlands for long. "Pity so many of the bastards got away, though", he said. "It leaves a bitter taste in the mouth."

My own gaze was also fixed on the hills when a far-off wolflike howl rose from the greenwood. I stole a quick glance up at the sky. "They should have known better than to ride into the woods when the sun is low in the sky", I said. "I've heard that the hills around these parts are infested with wolves."

A chorus of screams rolled down the forested slopes to reach our ears.

"The two-legged kind?" Hostilius asked.

"That's what I am told", I replied.

Chapter 22 – Trade

Hundreds of Semnones lost their lives when the advancing legions mercilessly forced them into the swirling waters of the Metaurus. Many more died with a spear in the fist, either skewered by Roman blades or pierced by Roxolani arrows. But the worst of the slaughter did not take place on the field of blood. Until well after dark, blood-curdling howls rose from the surrounding woods where the wolves of the Heruli were going about their grim toil with relish.

Despite destroying the cavalry of the Germani, we were acutely aware of the fact that almost fifty thousand enemy infantry remained but a few miles away. For that reason, I ordered the construction of a marching camp so that we could sleep without fear of having our throats opened by Semnones blades in the middle hours of the night.

Come the end of the first watch of the evening, an eerie silence descended over not only the camp but also the surrounding hills. Hostilius looked over his shoulder at the dark woods silhouetted against the sea of stars. "Sounds as if Naulobates's men are finally done", he said, and took a swig from his cup.

He had hardly uttered the words when more high-pitched screams emanated from the hillside. Unlike before, the wailing continued for what seemed like a hundred heartbeats.

"Maybe I spoke too soon", the Primus Pilus said, and cut a chunk of mutton from the carcass grilling above the flames.

"You are not wrong. The wolf warriors have vanquished the enemy", Gordas confirmed while he tore out the lower jaw from the sheep's head. "They are respecting the brave ones amongst the Germani", he added, cut out the tongue with a flick of his dagger, and sank his teeth into the succulent flesh.

"To me it sounds like men being tortured", Vibius said, and popped an olive into his mouth.

Few understood the ways of the clans of the Sea of Grass better than Gordas. "No", he said. "The Heruli are performing the blood rites", he confirmed, and wiped the greasy juices from his lips with the back of his hand. "The shades of the brave are prepared so that they may be welcomed on the other side."

Diocles visibly winced at the thought and changed the subject. "Whatever are you going to do with Braduhenna, Lord Emperor?" he asked.

"Never mind the witch", Hostilius growled. "The Germani footmen still need to be dealt with before they continue their advance on Rome. And, may I remind you that Maximian and Nidada are most probably still amongst the slaves taken by the savages."

The realisation that the Primus Pilus's sons remained captive caused the elation to be banished from around the fire. The arrival of an unexpected drizzle added to the sombre mood and prompted us to continue our conversation inside the command tent.

Hostilius's gaze was still fixed on the wine that he swirled in his cup when, a third of a watch later, the officer of the guard ducked into the *praetorium*. "They have arrived, lord", he announced.

I sighed and gained my feet. "There is an unfortunate disciplinary issue I have to deal with", I explained, and started towards the door, pausing just as I was about to exit the tent. "Tribune", I said, looking straight at Hostilius. "Mayhap you will assist me?"

"You've never needed my help to kick arse, but if you insist", he scowled, chugged the wine remaining in his cup, and ducked through the flap which I held open.

A few paces from the door of the tent Ganna and Secundus stood side by side, surrounded by six praetorian guards. Beside them two emaciated men shivered in tattered legionary tunics, their hair lank and their beards matted and lice-ridden. Even from ten paces away the stench was almost overwhelming. But yet… both wore wide grins.

"Leave us", I instructed the praetorians, who saluted and stomped away into the night.

"What in hades have we here… ?" Hostilius growled. Then he grew silent and his jaw dropped.

"By the gods!" the Primus Pilus shouted, sprinted forward, wrapped his arms around them, and simultaneously lifted his two boys up in a bear hug.

I cleared my throat. "What do you believe the charge should be, Tribune Proculus?" I jested. "Desertion, or failing to abide by the legions' hygiene standards?"

Hostilius wiped his cheeks with his sleeve and retreated a few steps until he drew level with me. "I wouldn't bother about the wording of the charge, Lord Emperor - that's for the Greek to decide", he said. "I think I would like to recommend a punishment."

His hands went to his hips and he regarded the two pitiful creatures. "Seeing that we're never going to get that reek scrubbed off them, we might as well put them on latrine duty for the rest of their careers."

"I can't say that I have heard of permanent latrine duty before", I said. "But I will sign the decree if you can get Diocles to write the orders. But…", I added, addressing Maximian and Nidada, "if you can manage to get rid of the stench within a third of a watch, you may join us for dinner."

Once the two had been escorted to the river, Hostilius turned to face me.

"Thank you, Domitius", he whispered. "I will never forget this." But then he paused and issued a sigh. "But please don't tell me that you had to trade them for the witch."

I nodded solemnly. "I'm afraid I have to admit that I did just that", I replied.

The Primus Pilus pursed his lips. "You know how I feel about my boys", he said. "And I'll gladly give my life in exchange for theirs, but returning Braduhenna to her kin wasn't a good idea. That woman will cause the death of many Romans."

"Who said I traded her back to the Germani?" I replied. "I released the war matron into the hands of Ganna. In return, she and Secundus bribed the slave herders to sell the boys to them. It could not be done earlier because Braduhenna would never have permitted it."

"And what, if I may ask, will you do with the witch?" Hostilius asked Ganna in the tongue of the Germani.

The Semnones woman issued a feral grin that reminded me that she was a pureblood savage. "No, you may not ask, Roman", she hissed. "But I assure you that she will never bother you again. Not in this life, or the next."

Hostilius raised an eyebrow and shrugged noncommittally. "Now that you've explained it to me, it sounds like a fair trade", he said.

"Where will you go?" I asked Secundus.

"We cannot go back to Germani lands", he said. "And my family has denounced me. I will pray to the gods to show me the way."

I called out to Diocles. "Tribune", I said once my aide had joined us. "I recall you mentioned that you have become aware of a problem with traders avoiding taxes by smuggling goods through the Alpine passes."

Diocles nodded, his expression serious. "You recall correctly, Lord Emperor", he replied.

"What remedy do you suggest?" I asked.

"We should select a *quaestor* and dispatch him to Pons Drusi", he said. "But there are few men who have, er…, sufficient experience and local knowledge to combat the activities of smugglers."

We both stared at Secundus, who regarded us with suspicion.

"Citizen Secundus Reguntus", I said. "As reward for services rendered to the Empire, you are hereby appointed as special *quaestor* reporting to the emperor. You will reside in Pons Drusi where you will ensure that smuggling is eradicated. My aide will draft the orders."

* * *

It was already the middle of the first watch of the morning when the scouts returned from reconnoitring the camp of the invaders.

"Did your horses go lame, or did you get lost?" Hostilius scowled when they eventually returned.

"Tribune", the decurion replied. "The barbarians have struck camp so it took some time to locate them."

"Bollocks", the Primus Pilus said. "It's not been light for long. How far could they have gone in so little time?"

"They must have departed yesterday evening, tribune", the scout replied. "Their vanguard is already near Ariminum."

"They must have marched straight through the night", I mused.

The decurion confirmed with a nod. "We found many abandoned wagons stacked with loot - the draught animals still harnessed to the yokes."

"The savages don't easily abandon plunder", Hostilius said.

"If you don't mind me saying so, Lord Emperor, I think you've put the fear of the gods into the hearts of the savages", the decurion said. "The straggler or two we managed to catch confirmed that only a handful of their cavalry made it back to camp after the battle at the river. The survivors told horror stories. They swore that you are a priest of the lord of blood, and that you summoned an army of spectres from beyond the Black Gates to fight by your side."

I dismissed the decurion with a gesture.

"Looks like Naulobates did a proper job", Hostilius grinned.

Chapter 23 – Deception

"We could permit the Semnones to escape unmolested", Vibius suggested. "That will save many Roman lives and allow us to travel to the capital, like we wanted to do in the first place."

"We have injured the wolf", Gordas said, and paused to empty his cup with one gulp. "It will not do to allow it to return to its lair where it will recover its strength. When spring arrives, it will hunger for the flesh of the flock. No, I say we pursue the beast and kill it."

"I stand with the Hun", Hostilius growled.

Diocles tended to see things from a different perspective. "The barbarians have taken a massive amount of loot", he said. "I have no qualms allowing them to return to their homeland, but the treasury is in dire need of the funds. Reclaiming the plunder will boost the morale of the army and allow us to finance upcoming campaigns."

"Heaven not gained in single stride", Cai counselled, earning him frowns from all around.

"Best pursue Germani", he said when it was clear that none could decipher his words.

"We will pursue the invaders", I said, and decided not to hide the real reason from my friends. "Belimar of the Quadi is amongst them. He has feigned friendship and thrust his blade into our backs when we least expected it. Thousands of Romans lost their lives because of his betrayal. The shades of the fallen will not rest until they are avenged."

Hostilius slapped his knees with his open palms and gained his feet. "Then we had better get going before the savages get too far ahead, eh?" he said, and started for the door.

* * *

Like Gordas rightly observed, the enemy had been wounded, but never mind how much I longed for vengeance, the Germani wolf was still a powerful adversary - one I did not wish to face without the aid of the Roxolani and the Heruli.

I found Aritê near the battlefield bordering the Metaurus where her men were rounding up the last of the horses of the slain. According to our standing arrangement, the Roxolani claimed the captured animals as their part of the loot.

"Pathetic creatures, aren't they?" she said as she regarded the Germani mounts that, truth be told, were easier on the eye than Scythian horses.

"Their horses are weak because they select breeding stock based on appearance", she scoffed. "Scythian stallions first have to survive the rigours of the steppes, then they fight to win the right to sire offspring."

She regarded the captured herd for long.

"How feeble they look compared to my stallion", she said.

My daughter's mount possessed the traits valued on the Sea of Grass. A large muzzle, wide nostrils and prominent, hairy ears. Its neck and chest were both short, but well muscled like a wrestler's. The large ribcage and deep girth hinted that it possessed enormous lungs and a large, strong heart. Its hindquarters were well shaped but sinewy, and its legs short and thick. There was no doubt in my mind that, if put to the test, Aritê's horse would still be able to run at a gallop long after the best of the Germani horses had collapsed and died from fatigue.

"I do not want these horses in my lands", she said. "Their blood will weaken our herds."

"Rome could buy them from you", I suggested. "But, like you have said, they are pathetic creatures, so they will no doubt come cheap."

She twisted in the saddle to look me in the eye. "Roman horses are already weak", she said. "Maybe these will strengthen the blood of your herds."

Although Aritê's words were not far from the truth, I issued a noncommittal shrug. "One gold coin for every twenty horses", I offered.

"It is better to steal from the enemy than to rob one's allies", she replied, and sounded much like Cai. "One *aureus* for fifteen."

"That equates to nearly three thousand coins", I said, and faked thinking on her offer. Then I sighed, as if defeated. "I will pay what you ask if you help me to collect the funds from my agents."

"Of course", she said. Then she narrowed her eyes and asked, "Collect it from whom?"

"The coin is still with the Semnones", I said. "But with a little help from you and your husband I am sure we will be able to relieve them of it before they reach the passes."

"Only if you pay me one coin for ten horses", she replied.

I accepted with a smile.

* * *

We left the battered infantry at Ariminum. I harboured a growing suspicion that, like the Divine Julius Caesar had done so many years before, I would have to take the legions across the Rubicon soon. I knew that in the streets of the Eternal City, cavalry would be of little use, therefore I needed the legions to regain their strength for what I feared was a confrontation that had been years in the making.

Two days after the battle, seven thousand Illyrians and their spare horses rode from camp. Unlike my predecessors, I did not mind for the Scythian mounted archers to ride in the vanguard with Naulobates's wolves following at a jog. All in all, I commanded a force of almost twelve thousand horsemen and five thousand footmen.

Hostilius, Gordas, Vibius, Diocles and I rode abreast of Aritê, Naulobates and their oathsworn. Cai, who cared little for war, had opted to ride with the slaves and the pack horses trailing the Illyrians.

We had not been long on the road when a handful of Scythian riders came galloping our way. They reined in at a respectful distance and approached at a walk. "Lady Aritê", the leader of the group said, inclining his head in respect.

"Speak", my daughter commanded.

"The Germani have passed the town the Romans call Faventia", he reported. "They are travelling at speed and leave behind many stragglers", he added, and gestured to three severed forearms with hands still attached dangling from a cord tied to his saddle.

"They will make fine covers for your quivers", Aritê replied, the warrior beaming with pride at the words of his queen.

She turned to Burdukhan. "Take five hundred men and harass their rearguard from a distance", she said. "If Lord Naulobates is agreeable, we will send two hundred wolf warriors to make sure that the enemy gets no rest during the hours of darkness."

"As you command, lady", he said, inclining his head.

Burdukhan detached from the column, called out the names of the clans whom he wished to accompany him, and led them in pursuit of the scout. In much the same way Naulobates dispatched two hundred warriors who followed the riders at a jog.

"We could catch up with the Germani tomorrow", my daughter said, clearly impatient to lay claim to their portion of the loot.

Naulobates raised an eyebrow. "You have shown me how the horse lords of the steppes ride down prey", he said to his wife. "At the start of the hunt, they allow their quarry to outpace them so that the poor creatures believe that they have evaded their pursuers. But the Scythians keep up a slow and relentless pursuit until the body and the spirit of their prey are crushed."

He gently placed a hand on my daughter's armoured shoulder. "Give heed to the way of your people, my love", he said. "Let us chase down the Germani and break their bodies and their spirits. When they have lost all hope will we attack and kill them all."

*　*　*

For two weeks we harried the retreating horde. The Illyrians ambushed their foraging parties while the Scythians disrupted their column with hit-and-run tactics. When evening came, Naulobates unleashed his wolves. In their wake the Semnones left a grim guard of honour - the rotting corpses that lined both sides of the Aemilian Way.

By the time we arrived at Placentia on the banks of the Po, we must have whittled down their numbers by five, maybe six thousand. Although forty thousand warriors remained, they were exhausted and hungry. Judging by the small bands of deserters that Aritê's riders regularly stumbled upon, the morale of the Germani was at a low point.

Hostilius leaned over the table and pressed a meaty finger onto the *itinerarium*, indicating a spot not far from where we had made camp. "Three days ago, the Germani crossed the Po and made their camp on the northern bank, less than a mile west of the crossing. The savages' camp is surrounded by a ring of ox wagons lashed together to protect them from cavalry attacks. We can't safely use the bridge before they've gone, but the good news is that they're packing up", he said. The Primus Pilus traced his finger upstream, to where the turbulent waters of the Ticinus surged into the Po. "If I were in their boots I would follow the Ticinus River into the passes of the Alps."

"I agree with Tribune Proculus", Diocles said, and used his gold and ivory stylus to indicate the town of Ticinum, forty miles west, close to where the two rivers met. "West of the town, fields and pastures gradually give way to woodlands. The hill country is less than ideal for the deployment of cavalry and more suited to the tactics of the enemy."

"Then it is time", I said, drawing grins from both Hostilius and my daughter. "Tomorrow, once the enemy has departed, we will cross the river and destroy the invaders before they reach the safety of the woods."

When all stood to retire to their furs, Cai remained seated.

"What most important thing in war, Lucius of Da Qin?" he asked.

Cai had been my mentor for most of my adult life and I knew from experience that it was worth heeding his words.

"Deception" I replied. "All strategy in war should be based on deception."

"Good", he said, and patiently sipped from his cup, waiting for me to draw my own conclusions.

"Our plan to whittle down the enemy numbers has been effective", I replied, not willing to admit that I had erred.

"You think Germani stupid?" he asked after a hundred heartbeats.

"No", I conceded.

"Germani have eyes", he said, and tapped a finger against his temple to insinuate that they would have no difficulty seeing through my plans. "They see horses and expect you attack where ground is flat."

"What should I do?" I asked, suddenly feeling like a child being scolded by a tutor.

"It simple", the Easterner replied. "Do unexpected or opponent will."

* * *

Our strategy to weaken the enemy had been sound. But, like Cai had pointed out, it had been glaringly transparent.

When Hostilius stormed into my tent shortly after sunrise, I expected the news to be bad.

"The scouts report that the enemy's camp is deserted", he said.

"Were you not expecting them to strike camp?" I asked.

"I was", Hostilius admitted. "Early this morning the scouts noticed that no smoke rose from behind the *wagenburg*", he said. "They found that although the wagons and oxen remained, the camp was deserted. What's even more surprising is that there was still much loot inside most of the wagons."

"What kind of loot?" I asked.

"Mostly bulky stuff like bags of grain and large amphorae of oil", the Primus Pilus said. "No sign of any weapons, armour or coin."

Gordas was no stranger to taking loot. "An ox can travel no more than twelve miles from sunrise to sunset", the Hun growled. "The dirt eaters fooled us. They loaded all the valuable loot onto mules, packhorses, and the backs of their warriors."

"By now they could be many miles ahead of us", my daughter said. "We must fall upon their column before they reach the woodlands", she added, and stood to leave.

I waved her back to her seat. "The Germani expect us to pursue them", I said.

"Then what will you have us do, father?" she asked.

"The unexpected", I replied, and noticed a ghost of a smile playing around the corners of Cai's lips.

Chapter 24 – Ticinum

"I have decided to dispatch the Illyrian cavalry in pursuit of the barbarians", I said.

Hostilius frowned. "Why not the Scythians? Aritê's horsemen will most definitely catch the Semnones before they reach hill country. Even though they'll be riding their spare mounts, I doubt whether the Illyrians will be able to overhaul the Germani."

My daughter made no comment, but looked at me in a way that suggested that I had taken leave of my senses.

"I do not want the Illyrians to catch them", I said, which deepened Hostilius's frown. "Although I want the barbarians to know that they are being pursued."

Diocles spread out a map of the area surrounding the Po and weighed it down with empty cups. Starting at our camp near Placentia, I traced a finger west along the southern bank and pressed down on a spot forty miles upriver. "Within the hour, I will lead the Roxolani and Heruli to the ford near Camillomagus. There, we will cross to the northern bank. The invaders will not know of our approach because we will be screened from the eyes of the horde by the fast-flowing Ticinus."

"The gaze of the foe will be on the Illyrians pursuing them", I continued. "They will not expect to be ambushed from the west."

"Your plan might prove exceedingly difficult to execute, Lord Emperor", Diocles remarked. "The area around the city of Ticinum is flat, open country."

"That is why the Scythians and the Heruli will conceal themselves inside the walls of the city", I replied.

"How in hades are you going to get ten thousand warriors and five thousand horses inside the walls?" Hostilius asked.

* * *

It was close to the start of the second watch of the night when the city gates on the far side of the bridge spanning the Ticinus creaked open. A heartbeat later, four torch-bearing militia appeared, escorting two grey-haired functionaries garbed in the robes of senior magistrates.

"Lord Emperor", the man in the lead said as he approached.

I extended my right hand.

"How may we be of assistance?" he asked once he had pressed his lips to the imperial seal ring.

"Within a third of a watch, ten thousand *foederati* and half that number of horses will enter the city", I said. "They will remain within the walls until the first watch of the morning."

The mouth of the magistrate opened but no sound escaped.

Once he had managed to gather his wits, he replied, "What you ask is impossible, Lord Emperor."

"Lord Magistrate, I trust that you realise that legally, through the application of the tribunician powers, the person of the emperor is sacrosanct", Diocles said, his tone haughty and cold. "Which, by extension, makes it a capital offence to obstruct his will."

The magistrate frowned.

"Allow me to explain it to you", Hostilius growled. "If you fail to make room for us I will lop your head off."

The functionary raised both his open palms in a placating gesture. "Mayhap I failed to express myself correctly, tribune", he croaked. "What I meant to say is that although the task is impossible, I will do it nonetheless."

Come midnight, the streets of Ticinum resembled a stable of gigantic proportions while the forum, baths and theatre threatened to burst at the seams with fur-clad warriors.

* * *

Mayhap owing to Diocles's warning, the magistrate offered us his magnificent villa. I declined, preferring to spend the night in one of the towers along the eastern wall.

Just after sunrise, Hostilius kicked my foot. "I think they're coming", he said, and led me to the window where Gordas was watching the approach from the east.

I squinted into the rising sun and managed to make out the vanguard of the Germani column appear around a bend a few miles down the road.

"It is unusual for Germani to be sober at this hour", Gordas growled. "The dirt eaters are running. They know the black riders are coming for them."

Just then I noticed a dozen or so barbarian horsemen galloping towards the walls. The Semnones scouts reined in four hundred paces from the ditch, no doubt familiar with Roman ballistae. For a span of a hundred heartbeats, they studied the handful of spear-wielding militiamen patrolling the rampart. When they were satisfied that the city posed no threat, they turned their mounts around and cantered back to the approaching column.

I turned to face Naulobates and Aritê. "Ready your men", I said.

"What would you have us do?" my daughter asked.

"I will cut off the head of the serpent and squash it with a hammer blow", I said. "Daughter, you will be my blade, and you, Naulobates, will be my hammer."

Upon hearing my words, the big man grinned, beaming with pride. "It will be as you say, lord", he replied, and turned on his heel to do my bidding.

While we strapped on our armour I watched the Semnones column approach. Although the horde was mostly infantry, the nobles and their ringmen were mounted. At the front of the group of five hundred riders, a strapping champion held aloft a grisly standard. The bleached skull of what was once an enormous brown bear was perched upon a spear, with a thick chain of bronze twisted around the haft.

"Wodanaz, the dark one, watches over them", Gordas said.

"There!" Hostilius exclaimed, and pointed at a boar banner fifty paces farther back along the column. "It is the standard of the Quadi."

"Come", I said. "With the help of Arash the Destroyer, we will claim both."

* * *

As soon as the nobles riding in the vanguard had passed by the walls of Ticinum, the gates facing north, east and south creaked open.

Aritê led a thousand riders from the northern gate, while Burdukhan thundered across the bridge spanning the ditch on the opposite side of the city at the head of four thousand mounted archers. Naulobates and I followed in my daughter's wake with three hundred chosen men, the best of the wolf warriors of the Heruli.

Before the Semnones had time to react, wave after wave of deadly missiles left the horn and sinew bows of Aritê's archers and slammed into the reeling Germani. Like a serrated blade drawn across a serpent's neck, the deluge of shafts cut a swathe through the barbarian column, separating the nobles and their oathsworn from the rest of the horde.

To discourage the infantry from rallying in support of their chieftains, Burdukhan's archers enveloped the body of the snake. The Germani had no choice but to cower behind their shields, it being their only refuge against the Scythian onslaught. A few warriors, champions no doubt, braved the storm of arrows in an effort to reach their sworn lords. Soon their arrow-riddled corpses lay crushed beneath the hooves of the Scythians swarming into the gap between the severed head of the column and the leaderless body.

The arrows of the Scythians decimated the ranks of the Germani horsemen. Within fifty heartbeats the Semnones nobles had lost all cohesion - the fear and confusion imparted by the surprise attack proving stronger than the bonds that bound together the clans. Their formations fractured into small groups where sworn men clustered about their lords.

While Naulobates led his spear, axe and sword wielding wolves into the fray, I frantically tried to locate Belimar's standard. "There goes the traitor", Gordas growled, indicating a hulking rider holding aloft the banner of the Quadi.

I caught a glimpse of the banner, but the group of riders vanished amidst the confusion of battle. Ten paces away, a stocky Semnones warrior mounted on a large gelding mistook the Hun's gesture as a challenge. He boomed his defiance, lowered his thick hunting spear, and using his heels, urged his horse towards us.

Gordas's battle-axe was still in his fist when, from the left, the blunt end of Naulobates's bearded axe scythed the Germani from the saddle. The warrior had hardly hit the ground when the Heruli's weapon came around again, the honed blade cutting deep into the stunned man's neck.

A kinsman or brother of the slain man roared and spurred his horse forward to exact revenge. But Naulobates was ready. Adroitly he flipped his weapon to his left hand, and in a move that requires immense strength, the big man swung his axe backhanded. The heavy head of the bearded weapon overcame the weak parry of the foe and crashed into the man's torso, his splintered ribs piercing his lungs as easily as they did his heart.

Before others detached from the group, my son-in-law's warriors swarmed over the remaining clansmen. Naulobates's mind was as sharp as his axe, and he pointed to where Belimar and his ringmen were fighting their way to freedom, their standard moving ever farther away. "Leave these men to me and do what you must, lord", he said, and stepped aside.

The Quadi signifer was first to notice our approach. He shouted a warning, drew his long blade from the saddle and adjusted his grip on the haft of the standard, a clear indication that he wished to use it as a club. But his effort came to nothing as the heavy, armour-piercing arrow that fishtailed from Gordas's string at point-blank range split the plate of the man's helmet and lodged deep in his skull.

Behind the fallen standard-bearer I noticed the Quadi king. His body was clad in armour fit for an emperor while his head was encased in a full-face gilded helmet. A Heruli was trying to pull him from the saddle, but Belimar had learned the blood trade on the sands of the arena. His blade lashed out like a striking adder and cut deep into the wolf warrior's shoulder. The attacker dropped his blade and Belimar pushed home his advantage with a thrust that split the rings of the Heruli's armour and pierced his chest.

"Traitor!" I boomed loud enough to be heard over the din of battle.

The Quadi king's head jerked around and his eyes searched the battlefield. When he picked me out in the melee, a sneer split his bearded lips. He called out to rally his oathsworn and dug his heels into the sides of his stallion. Two of his ringmen answered their lord's call and the trio powered towards us, their blades raised.

We responded in kind.

I left the ringmen for Hostilius and Gordas and ducked underneath Belimar's vicious horizontal sweep that was meant to take my head. The blade clipped the crest of my helmet and rocked my head to the side. For a moment I feared that I would taste his iron before I could recover, but the heavy longsword had been swung with such vehemence that Belimar failed to control the blade before I steadied myself. My sword flashed like lightning and the tip split the rings of the traitor's mail, piercing his shoulder. He winced, skilfully backing his horse to avoid my follow-up thrust, and swung again, this time backhanded, but lower, so that I could not escape the path of the iron.

I met his powerful blow with the flat of my blade, close to the hilt where it is strongest. Rather than blocking the blow I gave way, allowing his blade to slide along mine, guiding it on its path. When his arm was within my reach, I grabbed his elbow in a grip of iron and jerked it towards me.

When grabbed, most men instinctively counter by pulling in the opposite direction. Belimar was no exception.

I tightened my grip on his elbow, but rather than pull, I kicked my mount towards him and pushed, adding my strength to my horse's momentum.

The Quadi king tumbled from his horse and went to ground heavily, losing his longsword and his helmet in the process. He lay still, his head turned away from me, no doubt dazed by the fall.

I vaulted from the saddle and pressed the tip of my blade against my opponent's jugular.

The prone man turned his gaze to me. I must have gasped when his eyes met mine because the man staring at me was not Belimar, the Quadi king.

"The king has fooled you, Roman", he sneered. "You will never catch my lord, by now he is halfway through the passes."

Slowly I increased the pressure of the blade, but defiantly he spat in broken Latin, "Do what you wish, Roman, but I will never reveal which route he took."

Keeping the blade in place, I stole a glance to where Gordas was kneeling beside a mortally injured oathsworn, using his dagger to skilfully remove the man's scalp.

"I am sure you won't tell me", I replied in his native tongue, using my chin to gesture to the Hun. "But I am willing to wager a goodly sum that you will soon tell my friend", I added, and slammed the hilt of my blade against the side of his head.

Chapter 25 – Passes (June 271 AD)

"He knows where Belimar is", I said while Hostilius heaved the unconscious imposter onto the neck of Gordas's mare. "But he swore an oath not to tell."

My savage friend raised an eyebrow in amusement, his hand already fingering the blade of his dagger. "I will speak with him", he said, and trotted away to find a secluded spot.

We were surrounded by fallen Semnones nobles, their bodies either riddled with Scythian arrows or pierced by the blades of Naulobates's men.

A hundred paces away, the battle still raged.

"We've squashed the head of the viper, alright", Hostilius said as we gained our saddles. "But the fight is far from over."

We watched as the Scythians swarmed around the Semnones column, their arrows picking off the weak or careless who lowered their shields. Like a mongoose chewing on an adder, Naulobates and his warriors were devouring the column from the head down.

Bot not everything was going our way.

I knew that the Scythians' quivers were almost empty and sooner or later even the iron-hard wolf warriors would tire. Then, leaderless or not, the numbers of the Semnones would tell.

I was mouthing a prayer to Arash when, two or three miles down the column, a dust cloud rose into the cloudless sky.

Hostilius noticed it too. "Vibius comes", he said.

"Let us join them", I said, and turned my mount's head towards the east.

But the Primus Pilus reached out and grabbed my horse's halter. "Don't be a fool, Domitius", he growled. "Even I can see that your gelding is spent." He gestured towards a rocky hillock half a mile away. "You have done enough. We will watch from the high ground."

My friend was right and I relented with a nod.

Upon reaching the rise, we led our horses up the slope, dismounted, and sat down on a boulder like two friends attending a play at the theatre. Half a mile to the east I spied the Illyrian column. They were not moving along the road, but parallel to it, about three hundred paces south of where the Scythians had hemmed in the Semnones. Strangely, the

Germani had not responded to the arrival of the Roman heavy cavalry.

Hostilius pointed to where the Roxolani were thundering up and down the column of the foe, their ululating war cries echoing across the flatland while they released arrows at any man fool enough to present a target. The hooves of their horses had trampled the fallow fields to powder, enveloping the barbarians in a hazy brown veil. "The savages don't react because they can't see the Illyrians", the Primus Pilus said.

Just then the cavalry column wheeled to the left so that their extended line faced the Semnones. In the centre of the Illyrian formation I noticed Vibius, mounted on his chestnut gelding.

A lone rider garbed in splendid scale armour detached from the Roxolani archers and cantered towards the Roman commander.

"Aritê", I said.

Hostilius nodded. "The Scythians will engage in close-quarters work", he said. "The enemy shield wall needs to be weakened so that the Illyrians can strike the death blow."

He had hardly finished speaking when my daughter rejoined her warriors. As Hostilius had predicted, the attacks of the mounted archers immediately intensified. Instead of releasing their shafts at a distance of fifty paces or more, they braved the spears so that their armour-piercing arrows slammed into shields from thirty or forty feet away. A fair number of Roxolani fell to the javelins of the Semnones, but many more Scythian arrows split the wood of shields to pierce flesh.

While the mounted archers decimated the ranks of the foe, the Illyrians reorganised their formation. Every hundred paces, they left a ten-pace-wide gap in their line.

Once it was done, I noticed Vibius raise his right hand.

Ten heartbeats later he lowered it and, at a trot, the Illyrians started towards the dust-engulfed enemy. Within twenty paces they were at a canter.

The Scythians broke off their relentless attack and seamlessly flowed through the gaps between the columns of charging Romans. Aritê's horsemen did not rein in but streamed around the hostile force, heading for the rear of their formation.

The dust was as thick as a morning fog on the Mother River when two volleys of barbed war darts rose from the near-straight ranks of the Illyrians. They spurred their warhorses to a gallop, lowered their lances, and thundered into the haze. Four heartbeats later, a sickening crunch emanated from the dust cloud as the wall of iron-encased horseflesh slammed into the reeling ranks of the foe.

"Those bastards are done for", Hostilius said. "No army, not even the mighty legions, can weather such an onslaught."

Slowly the dust settled.

Down below, on the field of blood, the Illyrian horsemen were lancing the wounded while the Scythians were making sport of riding down the survivors who were trying to flee to the safety of the distant hills.

I noticed a lone rider trotting towards us.

Gordas guided his mare up the rocky hillside and reined in beside the boulder. Then he took a cloak from his saddlebag, sliced a broad piece from the green woven wool, and wet it with his waterskin. The garment appeared suspiciously familiar, and I recalled that it had been draped over the shoulders of the oathsworn who had worn the Quadi king's armour.

Hostilius gestured at the cloak. "Did he tell you were Belimar went?" he asked.

Gordas disdained answering the question, instead issuing a savage grin while he meticulously wiped the congealing blood from his calloused hands and scarred forearms.

* * *

Twenty paces ahead, a summer downpour had loosened the clots of black Alpine soil from the roots of a fallen elm and deposited it on the road stones.

The Hun swung down from the saddle and released the reins of his mare to allow it to graze on the lush grass bordering the road. Then he took a swig from his wineskin while surreptitiously eyeing the hills. Once he was sure that none were watching, he crouched to examine the tracks up close.

"Six horses", he said. "Three carry warriors, the others are straining under the weight of heavy burdens."

"I suspect the packhorses carry the coin that the Harbinger has paid the Quadi king as a reward for his treachery", Diocles surmised.

"The blood gold will be their undoing", Gordas mused while running an open palm across a particularly deep imprint.

"Without the burden of the coin they would have been through the passes by now."

We had been tracking Belimar and his two companions for three days. Earlier, Gordas had persuaded the wounded oathsworn to tell his secret. He revealed that the Quadi king and two ringmen were heading north through the Septimer Pass towards Raetia.

"How far ahead are they?" Diocles asked.

"Their Germani horses are tired", Gordas replied. "We will find them on the road before the sun sets."

"We need to catch them before they leave the confines of the passes", I said. "Once they arrive in Raetia and enter the border towns, we will not be able to track them."

Hostilius had dismounted to stretch his legs. "Then we had better get going", he sighed, and heaved himself back up into the saddle.

* * *

We travelled north along the valley of the Posterior Rhine, following the paved road that hugged the heavily forested western slope. For long the Empire's treasury had been scraping the bottom of the proverbial barrel and it showed in the state of repair of the road surface. It was high summer, so although the end of the first watch of the evening was fast approaching, the sun was yet to set. We were tired from riding hard all day and disheartened that we were yet to catch a glimpse of our quarry. While Hostilius and I watered the horses from the rushing waters, Diocles studied the *itinerarium*.

"We are ten miles south of Curia Raetorum", he announced with a finger pressed onto the vellum. "From there, many roads branch out to the north."

I listened to the words of my aide, but my eyes remained trained on Gordas who was slowly clambering up a large boulder to gain a view of the road ahead. The Hun had hardly reached the top when he turned around and scampered down the rock with the agility of a mountain goat. He vaulted into the saddle and snatched his bow from its pouch. "Come", he said while he strained against the wood and sinew to slip the loop of the string into the groove of the nock.

It took another five heartbeats for me to follow suit. Hostilius hefted his heavy hunting spear and Diocles slid his *spatha* from its sheath.

Without a thought, we abandoned the spare horses at the river's edge and thundered up the incline to catch up with Gordas who was already thirty paces ahead.

As I crested the rise, I laid eyes on our prey. Three hundred paces down the road, three riders leading packhorses were making their way north. The sound of our horses' hooves slamming against the stones must have reached their ears. They twisted in their saddles, gaped for half a heartbeat, and dug their heels into the flanks of their mounts.

Unlike the Germani, who broke in their horses for the saddle, Scythian animals are encouraged to retain a feral streak. We gave our mounts free reign, allowing them to choose their own path along the broken surface. We thundered along the paved road that the legions of old had carved into the hillside, following the twists and turns of the mighty waters fifty feet below. Around a bend, the path straightened out and the road descended onto a plain of green pastureland. I reached for my quiver, took two arrows into my fist, and drew the braided sinew past my ear. At the perfect moment, when all four hooves of my stallion were in the air, I released.

The tamarisk shaft fishtailed from the string and arced high in the greying sky. Then the armour-piercing arrow disappeared against the backdrop of green before it slammed into the shoulder of one of the men. The wood, horn and sinew bow endowed the heavy shaft with enormous power and it struck the rider with the force of a war hammer, throwing him from the saddle. Unlike Scythians who are taught from boyhood to jump clear of a falling horse, the Quadi kept a hand on the reins. The head of his mount was jerked to the side and it stepped from the edge of the cobbles, stumbled and went to ground. The halter of the packhorse was tied to the rider's saddle and it, too, lost its footing. As it tumbled into the underbrush, the heavy bags of coin ripped at the seams, covering the cobbles in a layer of gold.

Two heartbeats later, my second arrow split the plate of the riveted helmet of the warrior on the right and Gordas's shaft skewered the neck of the third.

As we approached, I noticed that, by a miracle of the gods, my first victim had fallen clear of his horse. He had lost his helmet in the fall, but landed on the soft soil at the side of the paved surface. Slowly Belimar gained his feet, plucked the arrow from where it had lodged in the scales of his armour, and stumbled into the road.

"I will fight you for the right to return to my lands, Roman", he sneered, and slid his longsword from the scabbard.

But Belimar had burned his bridges. I had not pursued him to engage in a heroic fight, but rather to rid the Empire of a treacherous thorn in its side.

Gordas, who had an arrow to the string, gave me a sidelong glance. "Do you wish to hear his words, Eochar?" he asked in the tongue of the Huns.

"Yes", I replied. "But I would prefer to do it without a sword pointed at me."

The Hun's barbed arrow left the string and pierced Belimar's sword arm near the elbow. The weapon tumbled onto the cobbles and he staggered backwards. Two more shafts cleft the air in quick succession, dropping the Quadi king to his knees, both his legs skewered.

I swung down from my horse and drew my blade.

"You are already dead, Roman", Belimar snarled with impotent rage as I approached. "You will fall to a dagger in the night not knowing who your adversary is."

I ignored his ranting. "I cannot allow you to live", I said. "The shades of the thousands who died because of your treachery are demanding recompense. Once, you were my friend. If you wish, I will send your remains to the land of your ancestors so you may be buried beside your sister."

Inexplicably, at the mention of his sister, Belimar's snarls turned to sobs. He broke down, tears streaming down his bearded cheeks. "I fear that I have stained my hands with the blood of my sister", he wept. Then his tears morphed into a growl. "And it is all because of you, Roman!"

It was evident that Belimar was not only a traitor, but that the hatred that he fostered had poisoned his mind. I had heard enough and was about to whip the edge of my blade across his throat when he clasped his hands together in a pleading gesture.

"Please have mercy, Lucius", he begged. "Allow me the chance to sacrifice to my gods so that they will accept me in the warrior hall on the far side of the bridge of stars."

Forgiveness was not one of my virtues and I drew back the blade to end it. To my surprise, Gordas grabbed my sword arm to stay my hand. "When the shade of a man arrives in this world it is like a newly forged blade - brilliant, shiny and sharp as a razor", he said, and drew the curved sword which he kept at his waist.

Slowly and deliberately he turned the well-kept weapon this way and that, allowing me to appreciate the polished iron and the honed edge. "Like this blade that will one day pass to another generation, the shade also returns to its abode in the heavens."

"Some swords are oiled and sharpened each day", the Hun continued. "Other blades accumulate blood and dirt and never feel the caress of a whetstone along the edge. Soon such weapons become blunt and the iron caked with grime."

Enthralled, all listened to his words.

"Like a son who loathes to accept a crusted blade from a father, the creator will turn away the shade of a man that is blackened by evil", Gordas growled.

"Surely the blade can be restored", Belimar whined, obviously concerned about his own situation.

"Underneath the grime there is a blade that can be liberated", Gordas confirmed. "But for the sword to be restored, it must be cleansed in the forge. Likewise, only flames can burn away the blemishes of a blackened shade."

My eyes met Gordas's gaze. "He was your friend, Eochar", he said, and placed a hand on my armoured shoulder. "Allow me to perform the rites of fire so that his shade may ascend to the heavens."

I had been in no mood for mercy, but Gordas's plea was heartfelt.

I conceded with a nod.

"It will be best if you wait with the packhorses", my savage friend said, and reached for his saddlebag where he kept flint and tinder.

* * *

"It's the first time I've seen the Hun in a merciful mood", Hostilius reflected as another pitiful wail echoed along the valley. "Let's hope he gets Belimar's shade all cleaned up before we go to the furs."

I held out my empty cup and the Primus Pilus refilled it the brim.

Diocles had gathered the gold from the road and was examining a handful of coins by the light of the fire. "These are freshly minted coins that have never been in circulation. The required markings which identify the origin of the coins have been omitted, but I believe that these were minted on the Capitoline Hill in Rome."

Hostilius leaned over and took a couple of the coins from a pouch. He turned them over in his hand, squinting to make out the detail. "They look pretty much standard ", he said. "If you ask me, they could have just as easily been minted in Sirmium or even somewhere in the East for that matter."

My aide placed a coin on the furs beside the fire and picked up his ivory stylus. "The best die-cutter at the mint at the temple of Juno Moneta, Flavius Nasica, to be precise, has a habit to over-imbibe."

"Good for him", Hostilius said, and took a swig from his cup.

Diocles rolled his eyes. "One night Flavius was involved in a tavern brawl and sustained serious injuries. He managed to evade a blade that was meant for his throat, but the edge of the dagger scored his right eye. Although his work remains of the highest quality, his vision is not what it used to be, so he has developed a tendency to engrave too close to the edge along the lower left-hand side of the die", he said, pressing his stylus onto the coin.

The Primus Pilus took the coin into his palm, and like men of his age tend to do, held it at arm's length rather than close to his face. "If you say so, Greek", he said. "What does it matter anyway?"

"The Senate of Rome does not have a legal right to commission the production of gold coins", Diocles said. "Only the emperor has that authority. Whoever gave Felicissimus, the mint master, the instruction has committed a serious offence."

Hostilius shrugged and flipped the *aureus* back to Diocles.

Just then Gordas strolled into the circle of light and adroitly caught the coin. "It is done", he said, and flopped down onto the furs. He used his dagger to skewer a half-rare chunk of meat from where it was roasting above the flames and bit into the bloody mutton. Then he opened his fist and stared at the coin. "One has to know when to use gold and when to use iron", he said with an amused snicker.

"Where did you hear that?" I asked.

"It is the words that Belimar screamed before he crossed the river", Gordas replied absentmindedly, bloody juices dripping from his chin.

I shared a look with Diocles, who also recalled the veiled threat that Senator Bassus had issued months before.

Chapter 26 – Advice

Seven days later.

The camp of the Illyrians, just outside the walls of Ticinum, Northern Italia.

"Aritê sends her best wishes and so does Naulobates", Vibius said, and motioned for me to enter the *praetorium*.

"They have departed already?" I asked as I flopped down on a couch, surprised at my daughter's haste to return home.

"North of the Danube, rumours abound that the Crow has turned his gaze to the west", Vibius replied. "Your daughter has received warning from Thiaper, who now holds dominion over the land beyond the forests, that the Goth chieftains Veducus and Respa have sighted warbands near their eastern borders."

"I promised Veducus and Respa that in times of need, the legions of Rome will come to their aid", I said, and accepted a cup from a pouring slave.

"It's been nothing more than minor raids", Vibius said, dismissing my concerns.

Just then, Hostilius and Gordas strolled in.

The Primus Pilus grunted a greeting to Vibius and proceeded to pour a cup for the Hun as well as for himself. "Are the Goths causing trouble again?" he asked.

"The Crow watched from a distance while the clans of Tharuarus, Respa and Veducus fought against the Empire and its allies, and he revelled in the carnage. While his enemies bled each other dry, he grew stronger", Gordas said. "Still, many within the Empire foolishly use their coin to undermine one another, while the Crow spends his gold to gather more clans under his banner. Soon he will be strong and bold enough to cross the Mother River."

The Hun took a draught from his cup and licked the red wine from his lips. "We should attack and destroy the armies of the Crow before they are ready."

"Maybe", Hostilius said. "But a cautious general never leaves an enemy at the rear. I say we march on Rome and sort out the treacherous Senate once and for all. Then we can deal with the savages north of the Danube."

"I, too, wish to march against the Crow", I said. "But in the middle hours of the night, the shade of Marcus comes to me, longing to be avenged."

Gordas slowly nodded his head, his lips pursed. "I have felt it too, Eochar. You are right. His spirit must be put to rest."

Diocles walked in and I gestured for him to take a seat.

"Tomorrow we ride south along the Aemilian Way", I said.

"The Illyrians as well?" Hostilius asked, and popped a handful of dried dates into his mouth.

"No", I said. "We have no need of horsemen in Rome."

"Do you wish for me to remain with the Illyrians, Lord Emperor?" my aide asked.

Before I could reply, Hostilius spoke up. "Your place is at the emperor's side", the Primus Pilus reprimanded Diocles. "Being a Greek, you know better than any of us how those corrupt bastards think."

My aide knew Hostilius well enough to recognise the veiled compliment. "Thank you, tribune", he said.

"I helped you and Marcus to mould the Illyrians into what they have become", Vibius said. "I have no interest or inclination to go to Rome."

I nodded to show that I appreciated Vibius's words. "Once we have departed, take the black riders to Mediolanum in the north where you will bolster their decimated ranks with new recruits", I said. "Train and re-equip them, and make sure that you have enough horses. Be ready by spring. Diocles assures me that as soon as we have vended the loot captured from the Germani, the treasury will be healthy again. Write to me, and I will grant you all the gold you need to accomplish the task."

"I understand and I will obey", Vibius replied.

"What about the legions?" Hostilius asked.

"We will meet the two Raetian legions at their camp near Ariminum", I said. "From there we will take the eagles south, to the gates of Rome."

Hostilius nodded, pleased that we were finally heading for the inevitable reckoning with the Senate. "We should send Maximian and Nidada home to our wives in Sirmium", he suggested. "They are keen to return to their legion, but need a couple of weeks of fattening up before they will be able to do a full day's march again. There is nothing like home-cooked food to get one's strength up."

"I'm afraid I've made other plans", I said.

The Primus Pilus's eyes narrowed in suspicion.

"Have they arrived?" I asked Vibius.

Vibius failed to suppress a grin and nodded to the duty tribune at the door. "Show in the subjects who wish to pay obeisance to the emperor."

Cai walked through the door followed by Segelinde and Adelgunde, with Hostilius's two boys hot on their heels.

In a jest, I stood from the couch and extended my right hand.

Segelinde approached, bowed low, and pressed her lips against the imperial seal. "Imperator Caesar Lucius Domitius Aurelianus Augustus, and now also Germanicus Maximus", she said with a wink.

I raised her up and took her into a long embrace until she pushed me away to look me in the eye. "I hope that you were not planning to go to Rome without us", she said, and her gaze drifted to Hostilius, who was starting to wither under Adelgunde's glare.

"I was just telling the emperor that it's not right to go to the Eternal City without one's wife at one's side", the Primus Pilus said. "Isn't that right, Domitius?"

"Of course", I replied, indicating that they should take seats. "We are about to enter a nest of vipers where a sharp wit is as dangerous as a honed blade. The Primus Pilus suggested that only fools would fail to take along two of the keenest minds this side of the Danube."

I noticed Adelgunde's hands going to her hips and Hostilius's expression became remarkably similar to that of a horse about to bolt. Fortunately for my friend, I had another arrow nocked to the string.

"And", I continued. "Maximian and Nidada will not return to the Raetian frontier. Starting tomorrow, they will report to Tribune Diocles."

My words immediately placated the Primus Pilus's better half, who gently laid a hand on her husband's shoulder. I noticed that the two young men appeared just as relieved as Hostilius.

"Long live the emperor", the Primus Pilus said, and raised his cup in a toast.

* * *

Segelinde rolled onto her left side. She reached out and placed a gentle hand on my arm.

I had been awake for a while with dark thoughts of what would be waiting for me in the Eternal City.

"Is it time to rise?" I asked, and raised myself onto an elbow.

She pushed me back down. "You have done well, husband", she said. "By crushing the Germani, you have strengthened your rule considerably. The booty and slaves you have gained by defeating the invaders will not only bolster the treasury, but it will endear you to the soldiers. All your warriors who have survived the battles have become rich with the gold looted from the corpses of the enemy."

"There are many legions, especially the ones stationed along the Danube, that did not participate in the fighting", I said. "They have not had the opportunity to gather loot."

Segelinde scoffed at my remark. "News travels faster than a galloping horse", she said. "The legionaries who have not yet filled their bags will know that they, too, will soon share in the plunder. When you look north or east, you see unconquered enemies threatening the borders, but all the soldiers see is the loot that they will claim when their great warrior emperor leads them to victory."

"With the help of the gods, my friends and the soldiers, I have crushed the Germani", I replied. "But to unite the Empire and secure its borders, much remains to be done."

"You have given peace to the shades of many by ridding the world of Belimar and the witch", she said.

"Still, the deaths of Marcus and Kniva has seen no requital", I said.

"Vengeance is not yours", she said. "Never forget that it is the prerogative of the lord of the field of blood. You, my love, are but the blade in the fist of Arash the Avenger."

For long I thought on her words and concluded that her advice was sage.

"What do you think will happen in Rome?" I eventually asked.

"It is no longer a newly crowned emperor that advances on Rome", she said. "The man who comes to confront the thieves and traitors is not only the conqueror of the Germani and the Vandali, but also the one who is loved by the legions."

"Does that mean that the traitors will cower and fall upon their swords?" I asked in a jest.

"No", she said. "It means that their fear will make them bold. They know that you are not a man plagued by the weakness of a forgiving nature. You must be careful. We are not entering a city, we are walking into the midst of war."

Chapter 27 – Road to Rome (July 271 AD)

The Via Flaminia, near where the Roman road crests the Mountains of Poeninos (Apennines).

Hostilius shielded his eyes from the glare of the sun, squinting at the steep track leading up the slope. "You will put a curse on yourself if you don't go and speak with the oracle", he said, and wiped the perspiration from his brow with the back of his hand. "Even if she doesn't tell you what to do, maybe she'll at least tell you what not to do."

I remembered that Marcus spoke highly of the sibyl whom he had visited on more than one occasion, and decided to heed the Primus Pilus's advice.

We walked our horses up the tortuous path, negotiating nine bends on our way to the summit. After what felt like a third of a watch, we arrived at the sanctuary of Jupiter Poeninos.

The portico of the imposing entrance featured twelve carved stone columns that supported an equally impressive entablature. Underneath the open colonnade, marble pedestals displayed the same number of bronze sculptures, each depicting a god or goddess.

The presence of the legions on the road meant that there were no other worshippers visiting the temple. Gordas, who in general disliked enclosed spaces, volunteered to remain with the horses. Hostilius, Diocles and I swung down from our saddles, passed the reins to the Hun, and entered through a stone arch into a large open courtyard. A young woman, whom I assumed to be an acolyte of the sibyl, approached us. "Welcome", she said, nodded a greeting, and directed us to a doorway located on the wall to the right. "Before you enter the sanctuary, I bid you to perform ablutions with the waters of the sacred spring."

"Good thing Gordas stayed with the horses", Hostilius muttered as we made our way to the baths where we removed our clothes and armour before immersing our tired bodies in the cool water. Afterwards we dried ourselves with linen strips, donned undyed wool tunics that were provided for the use of the faithful, and returned to the courtyard where the acolyte was waiting patiently.

"You may give patronage to the god by making offerings of incense", she said, indicated a small altar and proceeded to hand Hostilius and Diocles clay burners that contained glowing coals. "You will find resin of frankincense and myrrh in the baskets below the shrine."

Hostilius issued a shrug, took Diocles by the arm, and led him towards the altar.

"Lord", the acolyte said. "Please follow me, the mother is expecting you."

We passed through a doorway on the far side of the courtyard, entering the main room of the temple where an imposing bronze likeness of the deity adorned a marble base. Jupiter was larger than life and heavily muscled, standing nearly ten feet tall. In his right hand the bearded god clutched a thunderbolt, and in his left a sceptre of power.

"Come", the acolyte said, and made a sign that I should follow her into a dark stone corridor on the far side of the inner chamber.

"Surely that leads to the *adytum*", I said, reluctant to anger the god by setting foot inside the innermost sanctuary, the holiest of places that only the sibyl and senior priestesses were allowed to enter.

"The oracle commands it, lord", she said, turned around, and started down the passage carved into the stone.

I was glad to find that the corridor did not lead to a small, dark tomb where an oracle crouched beside a chasm in the earth, but to a spacious open courtyard enclosed by high walls of stone. A large tree grew near the centre of what resembled a manicured palace garden instead of the innermost sanctuary of a temple. Judging by the massive trunk and gnarled roots, I suspected that the oak was very old and maybe even predated the temple itself. In the shade underneath the canopy, the sibyl was seated on a stone bench. The tall, blonde woman was of an age with me and dressed in a short-sleeved, undyed cotton shift that extended to her ankles. Her appearance resembled the women of the Celts, not that of a Roman matron. The priestess offered no words of welcome, and indicated with a gesture that I should join her. Her piercing gaze never wavered, creating the impression that she was divining my thoughts.

"Long before the time of Romulus and Remus, the Twelve Clans of the Rasenna ruled these hills", she said. "When Rome was little more than a town with muddy streets, the Ancient Ones streamed through the northern passes and claimed the land as their own. In time, Rome grew in strength and subjugated the Celts with the sword. Now they believe that these mountains belong to them."

I nodded in response, a reply which seemed to please the oracle.

"After the Empire disappears in the mist of time, the Germani will lord over these lands and eventually other tribes will drive them off", she continued. "Earthly kings come and go, but the one who rules from the peaks, remains for all of eternity."

I wondered which god she was referring to.

"The Rasenna called him Tin, the Senones prostrated themselves before Poeninos, and now the Romans have sculpted his likeness in bronze and built a sanctuary to honour the one they know as Jupiter", she said, and gestured to the walls. "Their hubris made them forget that gods have no interest in gold and ivory, neither do they care for stone, mortar and bronze."

She raised an open palm to stall a response. From a copper pot she filled two small stone cups and passed one to me. "Drink up, Scythian, and be quiet so that we may hear his words", she said, just as a gentle blow moved through the branches above.

I did as I was told and closed my eyes. For long I listened to the sound of the warm breeze rustling through the leaves of the consecrated oak until I imagined that I, too, could hear the voice of a god on the wind.

"Go forth, warrior. Cleanse the ill deeds of the treacherous with the sword", a dreamlike voice whispered. "Let the Tiber

run red with blood and fill Hades with the shades of the wicked. In your hour of need, let the Earth Mother show you the way."

I opened my eyes as soon as the words faded away, but the sibyl was nowhere to be seen.

* * *

"There you have it", Hostilius said after I had told all. "It's what I've been saying all along. We need to go clean up, and we need to go in hard."

"I am no tyrant", I replied. "I do not wish to be known as the emperor who turned the streets of Rome into a battlefield."

"Why do you not go to speak with Felicissimus, Lord Emperor?" Diocles suggested. "Surely he knows the identity of the powerful men who have participated in his crimes. In exchange for his cooperation maybe you can be merciful?"

Just months before, the mint master had tried to kill Diocles and my aide's magnanimous proposal took me by surprise. "Do you suggest that I pardon him?" I asked.

"No", Diocles replied. "I believe that he will be amicable to accept a quick death rather than suffering at the hands of a torturer."

Gordas's face fell on hearing my aide's suggestion. The Hun had not forgotten that it was in effect Felicissimus's fault that the blade of his *akinakes* received a nick. I believe that he counted on being offered the opportunity to exact a measure of revenge on the mint master. "Being a tyrant is better than being seen as weak", Gordas growled.

"I believe that Diocles's suggestion is appropriate", I said. "But I do not wish to draw the attention of the senators who have conspired against us. We must speak with Felicissimus, but it must be done in secret."

"I am familiar with the mint master's routine", Diocles said. "It will not be difficult to lure him into a trap."

"Good. Tomorrow we will ride ahead to meet him", I said. "In that way we will be able to expose the conspiracy with a minimum of bloodshed."

"You're forgetting that it will take the legionaries less than a watch to figure out that their emperor has gone, Greek", Hostilius growled. "I'm sure that the Senate has spies in every town on the Via Flaminia. Soon they'll put two and two together and realise that you've gone ahead."

"Good point", I said. "It is something we will have to remedy."

* * *

My aide assisted a reluctant Hostilius to strap on my armour. "It is a bit tight around the chest", the Primus Pilus said, and pulled in his stomach in an effort to fit into my ceremonial cuirass.

I took three steps back to regard the imposter from a distance. It was immediately apparent that even a village idiot would not be fooled into believing that the Primus Pilus was the emperor.

"The tribune is just too, er…, muscular to fit into your armour, Lord Emperor", Diocles said, causing Hostilius to narrow his eyes.

"Better watch your tongue, Greek", Hostilius growled. "Or I'll have you pose as the emperor and ride in the coach with the women."

I measured Diocles with my eyes and realised that Hostilius's suggestion had merit. "Not a bad idea", I said.

"But you need me to arrange a meeting with the mint master", my aide said, no doubt concerned that he would be confined to a carriage for days.

"I'm sure we can make a plan to get by without you", Hostilius said, grinning at Diocles's discomfort. "Besides, you'll only be travelling in the coach until we reach Interamna."

My aide breathed a sigh of relief.

The Primus Pilus's grin morphed into a leer. "From there onwards, you'll be transported in a litter", he revealed.

* * *

Later that evening, having accepted his fate, Diocles stepped into the *praetorium* to join Segelinde, Adelgunde, Hostilius, Gordas, Cai and me for the evening meal.

"It's been nearly two years since Postumus's death", Diocles said. "You will recall that he was murdered by his own soldiers who instated one of their own, a certain Marius, as emperor of the breakaway Gallic Empire."

"Couldn't have happened to a nicer person", Hostilius said, and took a swallow from his cup. "Postumus was a conniving bastard and reaped what he sowed."

"Didn't Marius only last three weeks?" Segelinde asked.

"Three days, Lady Segelinde", Diocles corrected her. "One of Postumus's generals, Victorinus, had Marius killed before he took the throne for himself."

"I remember that after Postumus had been killed, the leading families of Hispania kicked the Gallic Empire under it's arse and gave their oaths to Marcus instead", Hostilius said.

"Marcus always believed that the Gallic Empire should be brought back into the fold without bloodshed", I said. "He was just about to embark on a campaign of convincing the cities in Gaul to give up their rebellious ways when the Alemanni invaded."

"A few cities in southeastern Gaul did heed his words", Diocles said. "But while you and Emperor Claudius Gothicus were fighting the Germani and the Goths, Victorinus besieged the largest town and slaughtered all the inhabitants."

"Now that's something you shouldn't forget when we get the chance to deal with him, Domitius", Hostilius said.

But Diocles was not yet done. "Then you will be glad to know that I have just received word that Victorinus has been killed by one of his generals. It was a personal issue of some kind. There are rumours that it involved a woman."

"Women", Hostilius said, shaking his head.

I noticed Adelgunde narrowing her eyes.

"Like I wanted to say", the Primus Pilus said. "Women are worth fighting for."

"In any event", Diocles continued. "Tetricus, who had been the governor of Aquitania, has been raised to the purple. Apparently he has a reputation as a fair and reasonable man."

"If he is fair and reasonable, why isn't he here to submit to the real emperor of Rome?" Hostilius asked.

"That is a good question", I said. "Maybe when this is all over we should invite him to do just that."

"Maybe", Diocles replied, and I noticed that his agile mind was already weighing up scenarios.

Chapter 28 – Posca

Three days later.

Rome, the Eternal City.

Hostilius and I timed our exit from the *House of Sallust* to perfection, joining a band of worshippers heading up the Sacred Way. To our relief, no one in the group of pilgrims paid the two sagum-clad figures any heed.

The night at the *hospitia* had not come cheap, but the location near the foot of the hill served our purpose, from my point of view at least.

"Bloody daylight robbery", the Primus Pilus growled once we had gotten on our way. "Three gold aurei for one night on a lice-ridden mattress."

"At least we had a hot meal before we retired to the furs", I countered. "And stabling for the horses."

"I've had *posca* that tasted better than the excuse for wine they served with the gruel", he growled.

We had endured immeasurable hardship over the years and I knew that my friend's issue was not so much with the quality of the amenities and the food, but instead with the exorbitant price attached to it.

A man at the rear of the band of faithful must have heard the tail-end of our conversation. He twisted his head around to get a better look at the fault-finding pair, which proved difficult as the sun was yet to rise and the oil lamp on the colonnaded sidewalk was behind us, casting our faces in shadow but illuminating his. By the way he held himself and the scowl on his face, I immediately recognised him for what he was - a retired senior centurion.

"You won't have lasted a day in my legion", he sneered. "Shut your faces or I'll do it for you, you miserable bloody naggers. Why don't you thank the gods that you had had something to eat rather than complain? Judging by your looks, I'd wager that you're not the sort that's used to dining at the emperor's table."

Hostilius was a good man, but quick to anger. Before I could stop him he growled, "I'll take you up on that wager, soldier. Why don't we make it ten gold coins."

A frown of annoyance flashed across the stranger's face and I feared that there would be violence, but then he broke into a fit of laughter and slapped Hostilius's shoulder. "I take back my words, brother. I can see that you served under the eagle. If you've made it to retirement and can still appreciate a jest, you have my respect."

The man slowed his pace, fell in beside Hostilius, and extended his right hand. "Fonteius Maximus."

Hostilius gripped his forearm in the way of the legions. "Hostilius Proculus."

Judging by the expression on his face, it was clear that the Primus Pilus's name seemed familiar to the retired officer, so I tried to distract him.

"Where did you serve, Centurion Fonteius?" I asked.

"Me and my brothers served with the *I Italica* at Oescus on the Danube", he said. "We've never been to Rome so after we were discharged with honour, we thought it best to use our gold to pay our respects to the gods who kept us alive all these years."

"Which legion were you with?" he asked in turn.

"The last time we were attached to a legion it was the Third Italian", I said. It was true, as I had recently led the legion into battle.

"I heard that the Third Italian Legion fought beside the emperor recently", he said. "Have either of you met him?"

He took our lack of response as an answer in the negative.

"I haven't either", Fonteius sighed. "But I was in the ranks that day when Claudius Gothicus defeated the Goths at Naissus. I tell you, we were done for, but Aurelian pulled our arses out of the flames. I saw how he led the charge that cut a bloody swathe through the savages. If it weren't for him, me and the boys here would all be dead."

"Did you lay eyes on him?" I asked.

"No, brother, I did not", he replied. "But I saw his sword flashing like it was being wielded by the hand of a god, claiming the head of one Goth after another. I was but ten paces away. The image of his famed blade is etched into my mind forever."

As we passed the Temple of Vesta, the group slowed down. Where the street narrowed, next to the House of the Kings, city watchmen were searching passersby for concealed weapons.

Our blades were strapped to our belts, so I signalled to Hostilius that we should sneak along the colonnade, but our new friend pushed through his men to confront the guards. "Primus Pilus Fonteius Maximus, First Italian Legion", he said, and pulled away the edge of his cloak to reveal the hilt of a gladius strapped to his belt. "Emperor Claudius Gothicus gave me this blade for gutting twenty Goths at Naissus", he growled. "I swore an oath before Juno that I would never surrender it. Do you wish to take it from me?"

The officer of the guard wisely stepped aside. "Are these your men, centurion?" he asked.

He nodded. "And I vouch for every one of them", he said, and led us into the forum.

Just before we passed the Temple of Saturn, Fonteius once again slowed his pace. "Farewell, brothers", he said. "It was good to make your acquaintance." It was much lighter by then and the first time he had a proper look at our faces.

"You look familiar", he said as we gripped forearms. "You never gave me your name."

"Lucius Domitius", I replied.

"Like Aurelian", he said, clearly amused.

"Sometimes my friends call me Caesar", I replied as if jesting.

Hostilius and I walked away, leaving a chuckling Fonteius to go about his business.

* * *

The Primus Pilus and I arrived at the summit of the Capitoline just before the first rays crested the eastern horizon. We strolled onto the consecrated ground that abutted the temple of Juno Moneta and watched the sun rise above the famed hills of the Eternal City. "By the gods, I've missed Rome", Hostilius whispered, staring at the brilliant display of colours. "For what it's worth, I think you're doing the right thing, Domitius. This city is too beautiful to be despoiled by bloodshed."

Our elevated position afforded us a view of the approach to the nearby temple, and I noticed two men briskly making their way up the stone stairway. One wore a crimson toga adorned with the stripes of the equestrian order, the other was garbed in a short-sleeved tunic to show off heavily muscled arms. "That would be the mint master and his bodyguard", I said, and strolled closer to the path.

When the pair became aware of our presence, Felicissimus slowed down and exchanged words with his companion. The guard confronted us, his hand on the hilt of his sword, while the mint master remained five paces behind.

"The summit of the Capitoline Hill is consecrated ground", Felicissimus said, his tone haughty. "It is not a sanctuary for the homeless."

I was about to reply but the guard drew his blade. "Begone!" he boomed. "Before I gut you where you stand, vagrant!" he added, and drew back his weapon as if he were about to execute a thrust.

The guard must have been a man prone to violence because he acted before I could answer. I stepped in and to the right to avoid his flashing blade, pressing my left hand against his elbow to guide the thrust away from my body. He was still moving forward when my elbow came around and slammed into his temple, causing him to collapse at the feet of the mint master.

Hostilius casually strolled forward, picked up the unconscious man's weapon and dragged him into the underbrush.

"Who… Who are you and what do you want?" Felicissimus stammered.

I flipped back the hood of my sagum. "Do you recognise me, Aurelius?" I asked.

"N…No", he stuttered.

"Give me a freshly minted coin", I said.

"You… You may take them all", he said, and held out a bulging purse. "Just… Just leave me in peace."

I accepted the bag, decanted a few coins onto a palm and selected a gold *aureus* before returning them to the purse and handing it all back to the mint master who, at that stage, was shivering with fear.

I held up the gold disc to the light so that the profile of the emperor was clearly visible. Then I turned my head to the side so that he could see the likeness.

The mint master dropped to his knees.

To remove any vestiges of doubt I extended my hand adorned with the seal of the emperor, which Felicissimus kissed between sobs of fear.

"For the sake of the gods, get up and pull yourself together before people take notice", Hostilius said, and indicated that he should continue towards the mint. "I suggest we have a little chat in private."

Felicissimus gained his feet and did as he was told.

* * *

Soon we were seated on the ivory and gold inlaid couches inside the mint master's office. Having dismissed the slave,

Hostilius poured wine, took one gold goblet for himself, and handed each of us a vessel.

"If you are willing to cooperate I will reduce your punishment to ten lashes, the forfeiture of your estates and exile from the Empire", I said, and took a sip of wine. "Should you prove stubborn, you will reveal all under torture before being nailed to a cross."

"It's a bargain", Hostilius said. "A man like you surely has a stash of coin hidden somewhere in a hole. You can use that to buy your way into the good graces of a chieftain somewhere outside the borders."

The mint master refilled his own goblet and gulped down the contents. "You are most gracious, lord", he said. "Tell me what you would have me do."

Chapter 29 – Reward

Greetings honourable Senator

Although I respect your wish to keep our relations away from the public eye, considering the events that unfolded this morning, it is imperative that we meet as a matter of urgency.

For fear of the situation getting out of hand, I cannot leave my place of work. I implore you to travel to my office with haste. I am confident that with your assistance, the issue will be contained without embarrassing repercussions.

Felicissimus rolled up the letter and sealed it with hot bitumen. He refrained to put his name to the missive and neither did he press his ring onto the molten blob. Soon after, the mint master's slave hurried from the office with the scroll clutched in his fist, headed for the Caelian Hill and the villa belonging to Senator Sempronius Bassus.

My eagerness to bring swift justice to thieves and traitors blinded me to the fact that Bassus was a wily old fox and a master at subterfuge and bluff. But, just as I was about to make a mistake by playing by his rules in the arena of intrigue, he would err by attempting to overcome me with violence.

* * *

While we waited for a reply, Felicissimus consumed at least four more cups of neat wine until little remained of his fear that had been so conspicuous earlier. "Bassus was the one who came up with the idea", the mint master revealed with a slight slur of the tongue. "As a quid pro quo, he lobbied in favour of my ascension to the senatorial class." He took another swallow from his goblet. "So, Lord Emperor. As soon as you have Bassus in hand, you will let me go free?" he asked.

"I will allow you to gather your stash of coin, but nothing more", I said. "Before nightfall you and your family will board an imperial galley. The ship will carry you south across the Middle Sea to Africa Proconsularis, where you will travel to the land of the Garamantes. If you ever set foot in the Empire again, your life will be forfeit."

Felicissimus nodded, pursed his lips and lowered his eyes in resignation.

Just then, a guard, dressed in the uniform of a city watchman, knocked on the door. "Procurator", he said, addressing

Felicissimus. "Senator Bassus is at the gate. He requests an audience."

"You may let him in", the mint master said, and dismissed the man with a flick of a wrist. He drained the wine remaining in his cup and rose to greet Bassus on the colonnaded porch outside his office.

"Where do you think you're going", Hostilius said, but I waved the Primus Pilus back to his seat. "Let him set Bassus at ease."

Rather than boasting a view across the city, the second-floor portico faced the inside of the mint, allowing the procurator to cast an eye across the workshop floor from an elevated position. Felicissimus must have used it as a speaking platform to make announcements to the substantial workforce.

He had hardly exited the door when we heard a muffled scream, followed by a dull thud.

Hostilius and I rushed to the foyer to find the guard leaning over the balustrade. "He jumped, lord", the man said. "I tried to stop him but I couldn't."

We joined the guard at the railing, just in time to see a man garbed in a senatorial toga bend over a body sprawled on the stone floor twenty-five feet below. The mint master's neck was twisted at a grotesque angle, leaving little doubt as to whether he had survived the fall.

Bassus stepped over the corpse, taking care not to soil the soles of his sandals in the fast-growing pool of blood.

Slowly he made his way up the stairs, arriving on the landing twenty heartbeats later.

"What a pleasant surprise to find you here, Lord Emperor", he said, his eyes cold and calculating. "I feared that you may not return from war, so, on behalf of the Senate, I initiated an investigation into the crimes that you brought under my attention. You were right, the mint master was bleeding the treasury dry. I was about to recommend that he be charged with treason, which is a capital offence as you know."

Bassus strolled to the stone balustrade and rested his soft, ringed fingers on the smooth marble. "Let us not remember Aurelius Felicissimus for his crimes, but rather that, in the end, he had the courage to do the right thing."

"Where is the guard that saw him fall?" Hostilius asked, suspicious at the watchman's sudden disappearance.

"What guard are you referring to, tribune?" Bassus asked.

"The watchman who passed you by on the stairway", I said.

"My humble apologies, Lord Emperor", Bassus smiled and shrugged. "In my haste I must have failed to notice the man you thought you saw."

* * *

"Tell us what is going on?" a voice shouted from amongst the five or six hundred artisans and labourers who were gathering on the workshop floor to see what the commotion was about.

Before I could offer a reply, Bassus, who was still standing at the balustrade, raised a hand to silence the *head count*. "Your superior, Aurelius Felicissimus, pilfered coin from the mint. We know that some of you were not only aware of his crimes, but assisted him and shared in the ill-gotten spoils. The emperor urges the guilty amongst you to give yourselves up so that you may have an easy death."

I had dealt with men who served under the standard most of my life. To accuse innocent men of crimes they did not commit was tantamount to throwing a burning brand on an oiled pyre of brushwood.

The Primus Pilus recognised the danger signs. "You had better do something quickly, Domitius", Hostilius said. "Before things get out of hand."

I pushed Bassus aside, took his place on the rostrum, and raised both my arms for silence. Already the murmurs of disagreement were morphing into shouts of defiance. "Hear the words of your emperor!" I boomed, but my tattered clothes did little to prove my identity.

Bassus must have used the distraction to hurry down the stairs. Down below, I noticed him walk onto the workshop floor, his guards forming a protective half-circle in front of him, roughly pushing through the press of workmen to reach the exit. Most of the mint workers were still clutching the tools of their trade in their fists - hammers, iron tongs and pry bars. I witnessed a guard smash the hilt of his sword into a man's temple. The injured man's friend, a big, burly smith with a large hammer resting upon his shoulder, took exception. He swung his hammer and the iron head smashed the helmet of the guard who had lashed out at his friend. The guard's skull was crushed by the blow, showering his fellows with a spray of blood and brains.

"By the gods", Hostilius whispered from beside me. "Bassus is fomenting a riot."

The Primus Pilus's words had hardly left his mouth when the guards, no doubt ex-gladiators, lay into the workers with their swords. They cut a bloody path to the door of the mint, slaying twenty, maybe thirty workmen. But the mint was not that different from a blacksmith shop, and the workers who toiled at the furnaces shaping hot metal with their hammers were strong of sinew and they fought back, killing at least five of the twenty fighters protecting Bassus.

"It's too late to calm them with words", Hostilius growled, pulling me towards the stairs. "We either take our chances now and live, or wait around to be hammered to a bloody pulp by a blacksmith's hammer."

Within two hundred heartbeats, the crowd had changed from an inquisitive group of artisans to a violent mob baying for blood. By the good graces of Fortuna, our arrival on the floor went largely unnoticed as the crowd were still trying to prevent Bassus and his men from reaching the door.

"Don't make the mistake of pitying these men", Hostilius said, and drew his gladius. "They'll gut us as easily as a bunch of savages will", and thrust his blade into the back of the nearest workman.

I drew my sword, took my dagger into my left fist, mouthed a prayer to Arash, and followed Hostilius into the fray.

The man nearest to me, a die-worker, raised his tongs to crush my skull. I blocked the blow with my dagger and smashed the hilt of my blade against his nose, feeling the cartilage give way under the power of the strike. A stocky hammer-wielding man with a black beard stepped into his place. He had hardly lifted his hammer when Hostilius's thrust pierced his throat. Gurgling, he fell to the wayside.

"Look out", I said as a rake-thin furnace worker struck out at Hostilius from the left. Fortunately for the Primus Pilus there was not enough room in the press of people to wield a spade with deadly force. Heeding my warning, he raised his left arm to protect his head, roaring with anger and pain as the flat of the spade slammed into the meat of his arm. "Now the gloves are coming off, bastards", he boomed, and downed the thin man and two of his companions with viper-fast thrusts.

Another came at me with an iron bar. I lunged, my blade entering his eye before he could bring the weapon to bear. More men surged towards us and I turned to face them, but I felt a hand on my cloak as Hostilius pulled me through the doorway and into the sunlight.

I took a quick look across my shoulder and noticed that two hundred paces distant, Bassus and his guards were descending the stairs to reach the bottom of the hill. All around us, groups of confused pilgrims were milling about.

Hostilius and I stood shoulder to shoulder, frantically wielding our swords to prevent the mob from spilling through the narrow doorway into the open where they would be able to surround us.

Then we heard the loud thuds of iron hammers smashing into wood. Thirty paces along the stone wall, a small iron-bound door was being smashed into kindling from the inside.

"We're going to have to make a run for it", the Primus Pilus shouted. "At my signal, we kill the two in the doorway. It will stall them for a heartbeat."

Just before Hostilius put his words into action, I spied a group of pilgrims spilling from the entrance to the Temple of Juno, a mere forty paces away. It was the men we had met earlier that morning.

"It is time to repay the debt, Fonteius!" I roared, and raised my sword in the air.

The burly centurion froze in his tracks, his eyes fixed on the gleaming blade. For a span of three heartbeats he remained that way, trying to make sense of it all.

"Come, you useless bastards", he shouted to his men. "Mars is smiling down on us. Today he is giving us the chance to honour our oath to our emperor."

Chapter 30 – Legions

Every one of Fonteius's fifteen companions carried legionary-issue *gladii* concealed beneath their cloaks. Although they were all on the wrong side of fifty, they had survived many battles against the vicious tribes that made their home north of the Mother River. They had no shields, nor armour, but it was immediately apparent that they excelled at the business of war.

On their centurion's command they drew their blades and formed a half circle around the entrance to the mint. "Go, lord", Fonteius growled without taking his eyes off the chanting men on the other side of the door. "We will hold them while you escape."

"That is not what I had in mind, centurion", I said, and backpedaled until I stood beside him. Hostilius held the doorway for another five heartbeats, feigned a thrust, and shuffled back to join me in the ranks.

Like a dam wall giving way, the enraged mint workers burst from the arched doorway, wildly wielding their weapons.

"Steady, boys", Fonteius growled.

I drew a deep breath and exhaled slowly to calm myself. My world shrunk until all that mattered was the hammer-wielding man bearing down on me. I did not wait for him to draw back his weapon, but lunged, and my blade pierced his shoulder. He dropped his hammer and clutched at the wound, bright blood oozing through the gaps between his fingers as he was dragged to the rear. I dispatched one crazed attacker after another, but every time his place was taken.

For the first time in my life I was not facing those intent on ravaging the lands of Rome. Every time my blade bit, if felt as if I were piercing my own flesh. I tried to wound and maim rather than kill. But unlike me, the mint workers had no such qualms.

All around I heard screams and a clash of weapons as the legionaries stood their ground and dealt out injuries and death. Slowly but surely the numbers of the mob began to tell. Already three or four defenders were crouching on the ground behind us, nursing injured arms or legs where the heavy iron tools the attackers wielded had shattered bone.

I slammed the hilt of my blade into another temple and heard a sigh of pain to my left. I stole a glance at Fonteius to see that he had taken a heavy hit to his right arm. He flipped his gladius to his left hand and grinned at me through bloodied teeth. "How many men get the honour to die fighting beside the greatest general who ever lived?" he growled, and fended off another man trying to bash in his head with a stave.

For all his life, Fonteius had defended the liberty and lifestyles of the men of Rome. Now they were trying to kill him. Their betrayal struck me like iron thrust deep into my gut.

Mayhap it was the words of the centurion, or maybe the killer that lived inside me could only be chained for so long. A red-hot anger rose from the pit of my stomach and spread through my limbs. I felt the terrible presence of the lord of the field of blood and my fist tightened around the hilt of my sword.

I drew my blade back, all the way past my left shoulder, and moved forward and to the right. The iron of a screaming man's axe passed an inch from my head, and in turn I rammed my dagger into his eye. My blade moved like lighting and took the head of the stave-wielding worker about to crush Fonteius's skull. I felt no remorse, only the joy of Arash as the edge of the honed tip slid across the throat of another on its way into the groin of a third. I hamstrung the man to my right, took the head of the man beside him and laid open the back of the next.

Fifty heartbeats later, when I came to my senses, Hostilius's fist was clamped around my shoulder, shaking me gently but firmly. "It's alright, Domitius", he whispered. "They've had enough", he added, and pointed his bloody blade to where the last of the mint workers were fleeing back into the safety of the workshop.

On the ground between us and the door, at least twenty corpses littered the stones.

Fonteius, who was still nursing his injured arm, stared at me with an incredulous expression. "I've heard all the stories, lord", he said while he took in the carnage.

For ten heartbeats he fell silent, then shook his head, his lips pursed. "In all my years under the standard I've seen nothing like it. They lied, lord, they did. The god doesn't come to you. You *become* him."

Hostilius let go of my arm. "Come", he said. "We must get out of the city before it's too late."

"Isn't it over?" Fonteius asked.

"No", Hostilius replied. "It's only about to start."

* * *

It came as no surprise when we found Gordas in the stables of the *House of Sallust*, our horses saddled and ready. He raised an eyebrow when he noticed the blood on our robes. "Trouble?"

"We need horses for our friends", I said, and gestured to Fonteius and his men.

"There are eight horses in the back", the Hun replied. "They will have to mount double."

We had hardly exited the stables when the proprietor of the *hospitia* burst into the courtyard, shouting to a slave to bar the door to the street. "Stop", he said. "You cannot claim the property of my patrons."

"You have no qualms robbing your customers every day, innkeeper, ", Hostilius growled. "Why the sudden concern?"

I stole a glance at the horses to judge their quality, dug a hand into my purse, and counted out eight coins. "It is more than they are worth", I said.

The proprietor must have noticed my seal ring when I handed him the *aurei*, and he dropped to his knees. "Forgive me lord, I did not now", he whimpered, averting his eyes as he did so. Then he realised that the door to the street was still barred. "Open the gate for the emperor, fool", he shouted at the slave, and scampered to get out of the way of the Primus Pilus's gelding.

We had hardly turned left onto the Via Patricius when Hostilius reined in. "There's a commotion up ahead", he said. "Looks like the soldiers of the urban cohorts."

"Damn it", I said. "It slipped my mind that Bassus is the urban prefect and the four urban cohorts are under his control. They are most probably searching for us on his orders."

Without hesitating, the Primus Pilus nudged his gelding left into a side street. "We could try and reach the praetorian camp", he said, "but we don't know how deep the rot goes. Or", he continued, "we could head through the Subura towards the Hill of Gardens and try to get onto the Via Flaminia from there."

Just then we passed the Temple of Terra Mater. A frieze above the colonnaded portico depicted the earth mother reclined in a hollow, her hand stretched out towards Jupiter, her companion.

The words of the oracle came to me, '*In your hour of need, let the earth mother show you the way*'.

"Where is she pointing?" I asked the Primus Pilus.

"Who?" he asked.

"The earth mother", I replied, and reined in.

A frown creased Hostilius's brow. "Terra Mater is pointing at Jupiter", he said, eyeing me in a way that suggested that I had lost my mind.

I scowled. "To the praetorian camp or the gardens?"

The Primus Pilus cocked his head this way and that while studying the mural. "I believe she is indicating the gardens", he said, clearly still concerned about my mental wellbeing. "Are you sure you didn't take a knock to the head earlier?"

"It is something the sibyl said", I replied to placate him, and turned my mount's head to the left into the street of the booksellers, heading towards the Forum of Nerva. As we approached the semicircular portico lined with marble columns, we spied soldiers spilling into the far side of the courtyard from the direction of the Forum of Caesar.

Hostilius knew the city well, and swerved right into the long street. We cantered up the valley between the Viminal and Quirinal hills, and I noticed that, like me, the Primus Pilus also mouthed a prayer as we passed by the shrine dedicated to Fortuna. I believe to this day that it was the goddess who whispered in his ear and made him head left, towards the Temple of Salus, the goddess of safety and well-being.

A sudden racket erupted from the alleyways behind us and I twisted in the saddle to see what it was about. From the direction of the Subura, thousands of men and women surged through the narrow streets. A few wielded spears and swords but most were armed with hammers, axes and spades. "Death to the emperor! Death to the emperor!" the rabble chanted, vandalising shopfronts and setting upon any who appeared to belong to a higher social class than their own.

Hostilius regarded the stream of humanity spilling into the long street. "Better get going. It seems that Bassus has incited the head count and it's fast becoming a full-blown riot", he said, and urged his horse into another side street.

We wound our way along the backstreets of Rome until the buildings gradually gave way to open spaces. The Hill of Gardens was a combination of expansive public parks and large private estates where the very wealthy lived in peace and seclusion, yet remained close to the vibrant social life and luxuries that only the Eternal City could provide. We trotted up the hill in the shade of the Virgin Aqueduct.

At the entrance to the Gardens of Domitius, two guards were doing duty. One of them, the officer in charge, I assumed, stepped forward and held up an open palm to stop us. "Gardens are closed 'cause of the unrest down in the city", he said dismissively.

"Step aside", I commanded.

"'Fraid I can't do that", he said, his hand going to the handle of his wooden club.

"Is that the way to speak to your emperor?" I asked.

The man issued a chuckle, but when it was not reciprocated from our side, his eyes washed over us and his confidence waned. "I've got my orders, lord", he said, suddenly much more respectful. "You can't be the emperor. Can you?"

Hostilius slipped his blade halfway from the scabbard, his corded forearms criss-crossed with scars ranging from white to red. "Are you willing to stake your life on it?"

The man's gaze settled on Gordas, which was the final straw. "Enjoy the ride, lord", he said, and stepped to the side.

We continued through the serene gardens until we arrived at a high stone wall.

"The Via Flaminia is on the other side of that", Hostilius said.

We rode north along the wall until we spied a rusty iron gate built into the wall. "I wish I had one of those proper hammers the bastards at the mint were swinging", Hostilius said as he eyed the sturdy lock.

I heard Fonteius address one of his men. "For the sake of the gods, Marcius, pass it to the tribune."

Marcius issued an embarrassed grin and produced a looted blacksmith's hammer from underneath his cloak. "My son-in-law works iron, lord", he explained. "He can't afford one like this."

Hostilius gripped the tool in his hand, and with an almighty swing shattered the lock. It took two more strikes to batter the gate from its hinges so that a horse could pass through.

There were almost no traffic on the Flaminian Way and we cantered towards the Milvian Bridge that spanned the Tiber. "Look", Hostilius said. "Bassus's minions are guarding the river crossing."

A dozen soldiers of the urban cohorts had formed a line across the road at the bridgehead. Their scuta were grounded and *pila* protruded from the gaps between the shields.

We reined in just outside of the range of their javelins. I cursed myself for not having a bow and, for fear of it being discovered, I had ordered Gordas to leave his favourite weapon in the legionary camp.

I noticed the Hun fiddling with the pouches tied to his saddle. Moments later, he produced an unstrung horn bow which he proceeded to string in the saddle. From another bag he retrieved a fistful of arrows.

"You disregarded my orders", I said, my tone hurtful.

"He usually does", Hostilius chipped in. "That's why we are still alive."

One by one Gordas picked off four of the men barring our way. But the ones who remained must have been experienced soldiers and they kept their shields up, waiting for us to approach so that they could skewer us with their spears.

"I am going to need a new horse", Gordas said as he took his five remaining arrows in his draw hand.

"You will have your pick from the emperor's stables", I replied.

The Hun nodded in reply. "I will draw their spears and break their shield wall", he said. "Follow me and bloody your swords."

Without another word Gordas spurred his mare to a canter, keeping to the left edge of the cobbles.

The men of the urban cohort were born and raised in the city and they knew not of the ways of the people of the steppes. What the Huns could accomplish with a horse, Romans could never even begin to fathom.

I, on the other hand, had grown up on the Sea of Grass and immediately divined the Hun's intentions. "Be ready to follow me", I said to Hostilius.

Just before the first *pilum* streaked through the air, Gordas turned his horse to the right and headed across the road at an angle, riding almost parallel to the men of the cohorts. Like only a Hun could, he slid from the saddle and clung to the right side of his horse, using his mount as a shield. The first two spears failed to find their target, but the third thudded into the side of the animal, missing the Hun's exposed leg by a handspan. The horse whinnied in pain, which turned to a scream as another four *pila* pierced its flesh. Gordas pulled on the reins and the mortally injured animal ploughed into the wall of laminated wood at an acute angle. The animal went to ground, crushing half of the eight remaining soldiers.

My fierce friend, however, managed to land on his feet, his battle-axe in his fist, and swung the spike of his weapon into the neck of one of the Romans who were too slow to find his wits. The remaining three soldiers hefted their *pila* to skewer the crazed barbarian from a safe distance.

Apart from killing or injuring five of the guards, Gordas had succeeded in drawing the soldiers' attention away from Hostilius and me. Just as the soldiers were about to cast their javelins, my borrowed horse crashed into the nearest one, throwing his broken body onto the stones. Before the man beside him could come to grips with the surprise attack, my blade came around, striking him at the vulnerable area at the base of the neck.

Hostilius, who rode beside me, still wielded the blacksmith's hammer. He swung the heavy weapon in a great arc towards the last remaining man's helmet. The soldier managed to jerk his head from the path of the hammer, but the heavy iron struck a glancing blow against his armoured shoulder causing him to drop his *pilum* as he was flung to the ground.

I jumped down from the back of my mount and pressed my blade against the stunned soldier's neck.

"Better be quick about it", Hostilius said, and gestured in the direction of the city. A few hundred paces distant, a group of about thirty riders were thundering our way.

"Tell your master that you carry a message from the subjugator of the Germani", I said. "Tell Bassus that he, not I, was the one who chose the path of violence. He has until sundown to give himself up or do the honourable thing and open his own veins."

"What should I tell him will happen if he doesn't, lord?" the soldier asked.

"If he chooses to disobey his emperor, he only has to wait until sunrise to find out what the consequences will be", I replied.

I mounted, extended my arm, and pulled Gordas onto my horse's back. In his right fist he clutched his horn bow and in his left five bloody arrows that he had managed to hack from the bodies of the soldiers of the urban cohort.

Apart from Hostilius and Fonteius, we were all mounted double on horses that were of dubious quality. Soon our pursuers had narrowed the gap to two hundred paces.

"Take down the lead rider", I said, and ducked to the left so that Gordas could release an arrow.

The shaft flew true and the man tumbled from the saddle, the ensuing confusion buying us a few extra heartbeats. One after the other the Hun expended his arrows until his fist was empty. "They will catch us soon", Gordas said. "But they still have to kill us." He grinned like a wolf and took his axe into his fist, relishing the prospect of a bloody skirmish.

Slowly but surely the riders gained on us. About a mile down the road, while cantering down a gentle slope, our pursuers inexplicably reined in at the top of the rise behind us. A heartbeat later, an *ala* of legionary cavalry appeared on the crest of the rise ahead.

"Looks like the legions found us before we found them", Hostilius said.

Gordas, however, wore a look of disappointment as the gods had yet again robbed him of the opportunity of a glorious death.

Chapter 31 – Honour and Virtue (August 271 AD)

"Bassus will not throw himself at your mercy, Lord Emperor", Diocles said. "Being the lead senator as well as the urban prefect, he wields much power within the city."

"I wouldn't be surprised if he is meeting with the praetorian prefect as we speak", Hostilius said. "If Bassus turns the praetorians against us, we've got a proper fight on our hands."

"I am sure that he is using his influence to mould the rumours to his purpose", Diocles added. "In the Forum, paid men will stand on the Rostra and bear witness to how you, the vicious emperor, murdered Felicissimus in cold blood and then, in a fit of rage, slaughtered the mint workers without cause. They will spread tales of your rampage through the streets of the city and demand justice for your brutal acts. The blame for the riots will be laid at your feet."

"How come you sound so confident?" the Primus Pilus asked, and took a swallow from his cup.

"Because that is what I would do if I were Bassus", my aide replied.

"Bassus must know that you are approaching the city with almost seven thousand battle-hardened warriors", Segelinde said. "Surely he does not believe that he can overcome them."

"The soldiers of the urban cohorts number close on two thousand men", I replied. "They are trained and equipped in the way of the legions. In addition, four thousand praetorians garrison their camp in Rome. If the praetorians side with Bassus, he will have an army of close to six thousand men."

"And that excludes the seven cohorts of city watchmen that add up to almost seven thousand additional men", Diocles interjected.

"The *vigiles* are little more than glorified firemen", Hostilius said, dismissing my aide's words. "I wouldn't put much value on them defeating one cohort of the legions if it comes down to a battle."

"True", I said. "But in the confines of the streets and alleyways, the numbers of the *vigiles* will tell. It only takes one well-aimed clay tile cast from atop a roof to take down a veteran soldier."

"It sounds like a stalemate", Diocles said.

"Do not forget that Bassus and his cronies have ties with the breakaway Gallic Empire", I said. "I will not be surprised if a messenger has already ridden north to ask for their help. Bassus does not have to defeat us, all he has to do is hold out for a few weeks."

Gordas had been listening to our words while drawing a whetstone along the edge of his dagger. "Then the solution to our problem is clear", he said, testing the edge on his arm. "Bassus must be killed, and it must happen soon."

* * *

Hostilius raised himself from the couch, walked to the door of the tent and peeked up at the starry sky. "It's pretty safe to say that it's past sunset", he said, and chugged the last wine in his cup.

Like Diocles had predicted, Bassus did not deliver himself into my hands, nor did we receive tiding that he had fallen on his sword.

"Are we marching at daybreak?" Hostilius asked, and flopped down onto the soft cushions.

Before I could answer, Diocles appeared at the door with three cloaked and hooded figures in tow. "They have arrived, Lord Emperor", he said.

Moments later, Ursa, Pumilio and Silentus flipped back the hoods of their garments and we embraced like the old friends we were.

"How did you get across the river?" Hostilius asked. "We're told that Bassus's soldiers have barricaded the Milvian Bridge that spans the Tiber."

"We have ways", Ursa replied.

"You've sure kicked a hornets' nest, Umbra", Pumilio said in an effort to divert the attention from his business dealings. "The rot goes deeper than you think. The traitors in the Senate are blaming you for everything that's happened. And I'm told that Heraclianus, the praetorian prefect, has been convinced by Bassus that you are intent on massacring everyone in the city. I believe he has sided with the traitors."

"It's going to be a bloody business", Hostilius said, his lips pursed.

"There might be one glimmer of hope", Pumilio said. "Over the last years, I've come to know the prefect of the *vigiles*, Julius Placidianus. I would even go so far as to say that he is an acquaintance of mine - one I would like you to meet to, er…, discuss options."

Hostilius narrowed his eyes. "If he's a business acquaintance, we'd rather not", the Primus Pilus growled. "Besides, the *vigiles* are little more than a motley crew of firemen. What good would they be to us?"

"It's not what you think, centurion. Placidianus is an honest man", Ursa said. "The only times we get to see him is when we plead with him to give one of our men lashes or sticks instead of handing him over to the urban prefect for a worse punishment."

Silentus nodded his support for Ursa.

"Where and when can we meet this Placidianus?" I asked.

"Good, good", Pumilio replied, choosing to take my words as confirmation of his request. "Show him in."

Moments later, Diocles escorted a man into the *praetorium*. Unlike most who belonged to the equestrian class, Placidianus did not have an air of superiority about him, his way reminding me of that of a soldier's. "Lord Emperor", he said, and went down onto one knee.

"Join us", I said to the prefect of the city guard, indicating a couch. "Senator Pumilio tells me that you are a fair man, even though you are at odds with him most of the time."

"Although I ask the gods for guidance, lord", he replied, "I do not always receive it."

His answer showed me that he was no dullard and I noticed that, like me, Diocles suppressed a smile.

"You have seven cohorts under your command?" I asked.

"Seven thousand men, lord", he said. "And I train them like my father trained his men when he served under the eagle."

"You have barracks on the Caelian Hill?" I asked.

"The fifth cohort is stationed on the hill", he confirmed. "To guard the villas of the wealthy men of Rome."

"How come you are not siding with the traitors?" I asked.

"My men and I patrol the streets at night, lord", he said. "I have come to learn that when others are abed, wicked men go about their business. Many times, I have seen the master of the mint slip into the back entrance of the villa of Senator Bassus during the middle hours of the night. They had been planning their dark deeds for long."

"Do you know the identities of the others who are conspiring against me?" I asked. "The only way to kill the monster is to take all the heads. Years ago I cut the head from the hydra, but soon it sprouted more. I will not make the same mistake twice."

"I can give you a list of the names of the men who meet with Senator Bassus after dark", he replied. "What they discuss behind the walls of stone, I do not know, lord."

"Have you received a missive from Bassus to meet with him?" I asked.

Placidianus nodded. "I have, but that is why I came to see you first, lord."

"Where has he summoned you to?" I asked

"To his villa on the Caelian Hill", Placidianus replied.

"Go and meet with Bassus", I said. "Allow him to convince you that I am a tyrant. Tell him that your men are not trained or equipped for war. Instead, volunteer to guard the Caelian Hill with the fourth and fifth cohorts of the *vigiles* so that the urban cohorts and the praetorians are free to face the legions in battle."

"What do you plan to do, lord?" he asked.

"Tomorrow morning, at the start of the last watch of the night, meet me at the Temple of Honour and Virtue at the foot of the Caelian Hill and I will tell you", I said.

Ursa escorted Placidianus from the *praetorium*. When the prefect of the watchmen was out of earshot, Pumilio voiced his concerns. "It is obvious that you wish to go to the Caelian Hill and rid the world of Bassus and his associates", he said. "With them out of the way, the praetorians and the urban cohorts will have no choice but to pledge their loyalty to you."

"It is too obvious", Diocles interjected. "You are underestimating Bassus again, Lord Emperor. It will take him but a few heartbeats to know that Placidianus is acting on your instructions. The prefect is not adept at deceit."

"For once I agree with the Greek", Hostilius said. "That boy's too honest for his own good. Bassus will gather his cronies and wait for you to show your hand. Then he will surround the Caelian Hill with the praetorians and the urban cohorts and you will be trapped."

"That, my friends, is exactly what I am counting on", I said, and raised my cup in a toast.

Hostilius narrowed his eyes. "You'd better explain yourself, Domitius", he said.

"I will", I replied, "because there is still much work to be done before the morning."

*　*　*

Having made our way east through the countryside for the most part of a full watch, we arrived at the Via Praenestina just as the moon was about to dip behind the horizon.

Pumilio turned his horse onto the cobbles and started towards the distant lights of the city. By his sudden silence I knew that he was focused on the left edge of the road, watching for a landmark. I glanced over my shoulder at the long column of legionaries behind us. The four thousand men who had been selected from the frontline cohorts moved in near silence, apart from the occasional dull thud when a covered shield bumped against a boot.

"Ah. Here it is", Pumilio whispered, indicating the outline of a gnarled oak. Hostilius immediately raised a hand to halt the column.

We dismounted and tied our horses to the tree. Gordas lit a lantern and handed it to Pumilio, who started along what appeared to be a game path. We had hardly gone fifty paces when he stopped and kneeled in the dirt. With a few quick strokes he cleared the leaves and gravel from a wooden board and proceeded to lift it, revealing a round shaft. Handing the lantern to me, Pumilio used the footholes carved into the stone to lower himself into the blackness. A heartbeat later I heard him drop onto the floor below. "Pass the light", he said, and I complied, surprised to find that the roof of the aqueduct was a mere three feet below ground level.

"Something tells me that it is not the first time you've been here", Hostilius said.

Pumilio grinned up at the Primus Pilus. "It's been dry for almost a hundred years", he said. "And the other side is secured by a thick iron grate with a proper bolt."

"To which you hold the key, of course", the Primus Pilus said.

"Of course", Pumilio grinned as he accepted the lantern.

While one after the other legionary dropped into the stone tunnel, Hostilius, Gordas, Diocles and I rode south along the Roman road.

* * *

A third of a watch later, all of us, except Gordas, walked our horses along the Appian Way towards the Capena Gate. We reined in two hundred paces from the wall of the old kings, just outside the twin temple. Apart from two flickering oil lamps on the portico of the sanctuary, total darkness enveloped us.

"Looks pretty dilapidated", Hostilius whispered. "Honour and Virtue seems to have fallen out of favour, if you know what I mean."

Two cloaked and hooded figures appeared from the shadows. One, a bear of a man, the other of average build.

"You can leave the horses, Umbra", Ursa whispered. "Pumilio's made a proper donation for the upkeep of the temple. It's enough so that the priests will care for the animals and keep their mouths shut about it as well."

"Some may call it a bribe", Placidianus remarked.

Ursa shrugged. "As long as people can sacrifice at the altar of Honour and Virtue, who cares?"

Although it was too dark to notice, I imagined that Diocles rolled his eyes.

"Talking about bribes", Ursa said, "we had better get into the city before the watch changes. All the boys manning the gate have been bribed good and proper, but I don't know about the next shift."

We were making our way towards the distant walls when Gordas materialised from the darkness like a wraith, and fell in beside me. "Two men are following us", he said.

"Good", I replied.

Ursa whistled twice when we were close to the gate. The doors opened a crack, and as we passed through he waved at the guards, who reciprocated.

I heard Placidianus issue a sigh, no doubt dejected to see what things had come to.

Although the hour was early, we were not alone on the road. All over, small groups of whispering figures emerged from alleys and side streets. They must have been men of the *head count* intent on participating in the chaos and looting that the new day would usher in.

As we passed underneath the Appian Aqueduct, Hostilius uttered a curse as a stream of cold water spilled from a crack in the plaster above. "I thought Pumilio said that this thing is not in use anymore", he growled.

"It has been decommissioned", Diocles confirmed, baiting the Primus Pilus.

"Then why is there water in it?" Hostilius asked.

"Nowadays the lower section is used as a sewer", Diocles replied.

Hostilius scrunched his nose in disgust.

Up ahead, in the open area in front of the Temple of the Seven Suns, a crowd was gathering. We watched as a man climbed up to the first level portico so that he could incite the mob. Ursa quickened his pace to get past.

"Why are you in such a hurry, friend?" a man asked, and grabbed Ursa by the shoulder. "You're not one of the emperor's informants, now are you?"

Ursa had been working on the streets of Rome for many years. He halted and put his massive arm around the stranger's shoulders in a friendly manner. "We're on our way to the Caelian Hill", he whispered. "You're welcome to join us. Father is expecting us. You don't want to be the reason we're late, eh?"

At the mention of Pumilio's street name, the man stiffened. "No..., no... of course not, friend", he stuttered. "Just concerned about a fellow citizen's welfare, that's all."

"Only three months ago the emperor had his arse kicked by the Germani! Isn't that right, friends!" I heard the instigator shout from the makeshift podium and the man confronting us turned away to cheer on the troublemaker.

"If it weren't for the Senate's intervention with the gods, we'd all be slaves of the savages! Aurelian is punishing us because of his incompetence! He murdered the mint master on a whim!"

"I saw him murder poor Felicissimus", a voice that sounded suspiciously high-class answered from somewhere in the crowd. "The mint master had no trial."

"Death to Aurelian! Death to Aurelian! Death to Aurelian!" the troublemaker boomed. He waited until the crowd had picked up the mantra, then jumped down from his rostrum, raised a wooden club in the air, and led the chanting mob deeper into the dark city.

We had no choice but to join in and follow the crowd. Just before we passed below Nero's Aqueduct, Ursa pulled us into an arched side street that ran up the Caelian Hill.

"I must say, their instigators are doing a very good job", Diocles said when the shouts of the mob had faded away.

"All Bassus has to do now is get rid of me, and the rabble will see him as the saviour of Rome", I said.

"So let's make sure that doesn't happen", Placidianus said, and gestured to where a group of city watchmen were guarding the approach to the Caelian Hill.

Chapter 32 – Caelian Hill

The centurion of the unit blocking the road up the Caelian Hill saluted in the way of the legions when he noticed his commander approach. He paid the hooded men little heed. "Everything is quiet, prefect", he said. "All we've seen so far tonight is a few chancers skulking about, but they turned tail as soon as they noticed us."

"Inform your centuries that no one is allowed onto the hill, even if it is the emperor himself", I ordered the prefect. "If you are attacked, fall back slowly and trust in your emperor."

I could see that my words did not fully satisfy Placidianus, but he did well to curb his tongue. "I understand, lord, and I will obey."

I left the commander of the watchmen to organise his men while Ursa led us higher up the hill. A hundred heartbeats later, he turned right and immediately left again, passing the great indoor market where the wealthy spent their gold on exotic wine and delicacies. A hundred paces farther, Ursa halted in front of the gates of a villa enclosed by a high stone wall. Thrice he slammed the brass knocker against the backing plate and repeated the process following a brief pause. The heavy gate swung open to reveal a grinning Pumilio. "The watercourse is an easy, short and quiet route", he said, bade us to enter, and closed the gate behind us.

At the rear of the large villa lay an expansive garden, almost two hundred paces square. Near the stables, legionaries were scampering from a hole in the ground as if the army of Hades had been summoned from beyond the Black Gates. Already, nearly two thousand soldiers were trampling the manicured shrubs.

"I purchased this place due to its, er…, unique location", Pumilio said. "That, and the exquisite garden."

"I have heard men say that location is important when acquiring property", I replied, and removed my boot from a bed of marigolds.

I noticed a slight scowl on Pumilio's lips.

"When it is over, I will send the imperial gardeners to set it right", I said, which seemed to satisfy my friend.

We were interrupted by a knock at the gate. Moments later, Silentus arrived. "Trouble at the roadblock near the Clivus Scauri", he said. "Praetorians. About five hundred."

Placidianus had had no other choice but to divide his cohorts as all the access points to the hill required a force of watchmen. Although fewer than two hundred men guarded the Clivus Scauri, the attackers could not bring more than ten men to bear across the narrow, arched roadway.

"It's a good thing the praetorians aren't what they used to be", the Primus Pilus said. "Else it would be a slaughter."

Thirty heartbeats later, Hostilius and I led a cohort of six hundred legionaries through the gates at a jog. Diocles and Gordas remained with the rest of the force just in case more attacks occurred at other locations on the hill.

We made our way down the hill, passing underneath Claudius's waterway. As we turned left onto the slope named after the famed Scauri, the din of battle reached our ears.

"It's time to find out whether Placidianus can follow orders", Hostilius said, and raised an open palm to halt the cohort.

I indicated for the centurions of the six centuries to approach. "The first, double strength century will remain here to support the *vigiles* in their retreat", I said. Then I pointed at the two dead-end alleyways branching off either side of the street. "I want one century concealed in each of those four alleys. Stay in the shadows and wait on my signal."

Hostilius and I led the remaining century down another block before we ducked into an alleyway.

It did not take long for the clash of blades to move closer. Although it was still dark, we flattened ourselves against the stone walls to reduce the risk of discovery. Two hundred heartbeats later, we spied the first of Placidianus's soldiers backpedaling up the main street.

"Not bad for firemen", Hostilius conceded as he noticed that they had not broken ranks, but were driven back by the praetorians who possessed superior weapons and armour.

"It's now or never", I said as the last of the rear ranks of the praetorians disappeared from view.

The Primus Pilus and I led the eighty men out of the alley at a run. It took only a moment for the battle-hardened soldiers to deploy across the width of the street.

"Attack!" Hostilius boomed. In response, the four centuries of legionaries spilled from the alleys and slammed into the praetorians' flanks. At least a hundred and fifty fell to our blades within sixty heartbeats, but to his credit their commander managed to steady their ranks.

I had no desire to kill my own people and boomed, "I call on you, praetorians, to honour your oath to me, your emperor. Lay down your blades and I will pardon you."

For a moment the fighting ceased and I thought that the bloodshed would end, but the praetorian commander raised his sword in the air. "We refuse to honour a tyrant", he shouted, and his sword bit into the shoulder of a watchman who had already lowered his shield.

The praetorian centurion's words aroused the beast inside and I felt the anger surge through my body. "Kill them all", I shouted as my blade moved like lighting, scraping across the rim of a guard's shield to cut through his eye and into his brain.

Beside me I heard Hostilius roar like a feral beast as he lowered his shoulder against his shield and pummelled into the man facing him. The bottom edge of the praetorian's shield gave way under the onslaught and Hostilius rammed his blade into the top of the man's foot where the iron greave did not reach. The soldier hobbled backwards, lowering his shield for only part of a heartbeat. Utilising experience gained during a lifetime of fighting, the Primus Pilus timed his high thrust to perfection, laying open his adversary's throat.

Not long after, Hostilius, Placidianus and I walked amongst the corpses of the praetorians while the legionaries and watchmen tended to their dead and wounded. Five hundred of the imperial guard lay dead at our feet. Twenty legionaries and double the number of watchmen had perished in the skirmish. All of them lost to Rome forever.

"They will send more", Hostilius said.

"Maybe not", I said, as far to the north we heard the faint wail of a *buccina* and I knew that the remaining men in the legionary camp were launching a feigned attack on the position that Bassus and his soldiers had taken on the Milvian Bridge on the other side of the city. "They will need at least three thousand men to keep the bridge."

"Bassus is a bastard", Hostilius cautioned. "He doesn't care a rotten fig if every single soldier in this city dies. Al he wants is to drape the purple around his shoulders, no matter at what expense."

I hoped that my friend was wrong, but he had hardly uttered the words when I noticed another group of praetorians approach at the far end of the street at the bottom of the hill.

I turned to Placidianus. "Are you ready to have another go?" I asked.

"Same tactics as before?" he asked.

I nodded.

"Let's go", he said, and led the *vigiles* down the arched roadway.

* * *

By the end of the first watch of the morning, the attacks subsided. Almost a thousand of the legionaries we had led through the aqueduct had perished. Of the two thousand watchmen commanded by Placidianus, only six hundred remained alive.

The battle-hardened legionaries and the disciplined men of the *vigiles* had ambushed and killed cohort after cohort of praetorians and soldiers of the urban guard until the stacked corpses served as a grim obstacle to deter any further attacks.

"According to preliminary tallies, almost five thousand of the enemy are dead", Diocles said once we had returned to Pumilio's villa.

"They are not the enemy", I said. "They are but the blade in the fist of Bassus, who is the real traitor."

"Now that you mention Bassus", Hostilius said, and glanced at the sun, "maybe we should pay the senator a visit before he decides to cut his losses and makes a run for it."

"Since yesterday evening, my men have been watching his villa, as well as those of his six fellow conspirators", Placidianus said. "Neither he, nor his cronies, are going anywhere soon."

Hostilius strolled to the nearest ornate fountain and splashed his face to get rid of the grime and dried blood. "Better get it done, then", he said. "I say we start with his associates and leave the best for last."

* * *

Placidianus and a dozen of his men emerged from the sixth villa they had thoroughly searched. "The owner is not at home", he said, shaking his head. "I have questioned the staff and I believe that they are speaking the truth. The senator has not been in residence for nearly three days."

Over the course of nearly a watch, Hostilius's expression had slowly shifted from one of initial disappointment to a scowl of outright anger. "Bollocks with that. I'll have a word with the slaves myself", he said, and gestured for Gordas to join him.

Diocles raised an eyebrow but made no attempt to follow the Primus Pilus and the Hun into the house.

A sixth of a watch passed before the two reappeared, both wearing defeated expressions. "I think you are right", Hostilius admitted grudgingly to the prefect of the watchmen. "Even Gordas couldn't scare them into admitting that their master is hiding somewhere in a hole."

We followed Placidianus and his men up the hill to the palatial property belonging to Senator Bassus. While the prefect systematically searched the villa, Hostilius and Gordas strolled around the garden. I followed Diocles into the kitchen which was situated about twenty paces away from the main building. Many wealthy Romans preferred to not have the smoke associated with a wood fire and the odours of meat, chicken and fish pollute the incense-filled rooms of the house. Apart from the smell, fires tended to originate from a *culina*, making it even less desirable to have it near the villa. Most Romans who belonged to the senatorial class would sooner starve than set foot in the small, stuffy room where kitchen slaves toiled away most of their lives.

Compared to other *culinae* I had seen, the villa's kitchen was large. One wall of the room housed four large fireplaces, no doubt to enable slaves to prepare the substantial number of exotic dishes required for entertaining the senator's many clients. Three large brick ovens were built into the opposite wall where a low doorway provided access to a dark room which I assumed was a store of some kind.

Diocles removed an oil lamp from a shelf and ducked through the doorway, the dim light revealing a long, narrow chamber. Bags of flour, amphorae filled with garum, oil and spices and smoked joints of meat were stacked on the myriad of shelves. Against the wall to the right, a pile of firewood extended to the vaulted ceiling.

Absentmindedly my aide picked up a length of wood which caused a frown to crease his brow. "One would think that a rich man like Bassus would be able to lay his hands on dry firewood", he said.

I was about to jest that the senator had fallen on hard times, but I knew that Bassus would never be content with the smoke associated with green wood, even if the *culina* stood apart from the villa. "Something is not right", I said, and freed three large pieces from the bottom of the neatly stacked pile, indicating for Diocles to bring the lamp closer.

"It is pine", Diocles exclaimed with a gasp. "No wealthy man would stoop to burning the resinous wood used by the men of the Subura."

I retrieved a poker from the main kitchen, ducked back into the store, and gestured for Diocles to step aside. I forced the rod into the gap between the stack of thick logs and the wall. Using the iron as a lever, I toppled the wood and jumped clear just as the stack was about to fall over.

With a loud crash the logs tumbled onto the floor, dislodging a few of the dolia and amphorae stacked on the shelves.

Diocles carefully picked his way across the heap of logs towards the wall. First he bent over at the waist, then went down on his haunches and started to clear away the wood from the floor. "Lord Emperor", he said. "You would wish to see this."

I was halfway across the pile when Hostilius and Gordas burst into the *culina*, their blades bared. "What in hades was that ruckus?" the Primus Pilus said, trying to catch his breath. "We heard it from the far side of the garden."

"We accidentally toppled the wood", Diocles said. "And discovered something interesting in the process."

Soon we all crowded around the large wooden trapdoor that had been concealed underneath the stack of wood. Hostilius shrugged, used his dagger to lift a corner of the wood and heaved open the covering to reveal a flight of stone steps descending into what appeared to be an underground chamber of substantial proportions.

"Here goes", the Primus Pilus said, but I stopped him with a raised palm.

"Allow me", I said, drew my blade, and stepped onto the stones that were illuminated by the orange glow of oil lamps.

Specially made shelves had been attached to the wall on the left side of the corridor, allowing for hundreds of high-quality amphorae to be stored in an optimal position. I harboured no doubt that the wine collection was worth more than the villa itself.

I rounded the corner at the bottom of the corridor and paused inside the arched doorway that opened into a larger area. The dimly lit chamber was expansive - almost thirty paces square with a high vaulted ceiling and a marble floor inlaid with intricate mosaics. Woollen rugs sourced from the East were arranged across the tiles and endowed the room with a feeling of opulence.

On the far side, nearly twenty paces distant, seven couches were set out in a semi-circle. Seven grey-haired, toga-wearing men reclined on the divans, sipping wine from jewel-encrusted gold goblets while engaged in muted conversation. They must have heard the commotion at the trapdoor, but they continued their discourse unperturbed, a testament to the complete trust they placed in their power borne of wealth and class. On low tables surrounding them, silver serving trays boasted a selection of dates, figs, cheese, oil, loaves and cured meat. The men all wore Tyrian-striped garments which identified them as belonging to the senatorial class.

In the shadows behind the senator who was seated on the centre couch, I spied two human shapes and assumed that they were guards.

So enthralled was I by the scene that my eye almost failed to catch the sudden movement from above, but somehow I managed to jump clear of the solid portcullis that slammed down to seal the doorway behind me. From the other side of the thick wood and iron I heard muffled cries and shouts as Hostilius and Gordas struggled in vain to open the door.

To my right I noticed another guard, a strapping Germani, standing with his back facing the stone wall. Judging by the workmanlike longsword strapped to his belt and the way he held himself I was convinced that he knew his business.

"Ah, that's better", a familiar voice said from the other side of the room. "I prefer a touch of privacy when discussing matters of a… delicate nature, don't you, Lord Emperor?"

"Greetings, Senator Bassus", I replied. "What matters are you referring to?"

I was acutely aware of the fact that there was a man behind me. When I noticed the nearest smirking senator's gaze shift, I steeled myself. A slight intake of breath betrayed the guard's intention, and I imagined him drawing back his sword across his shoulder to strike the killing blow.

Although I tried my best not to show it, every fibre in my body was as ready as a wound-up skein of a ballista.

I heard the hiss of a blade cleaving air, or mayhap it was a whisper of warning from Arash. Dropping to a crouch, I drew back my sword across my left hip, my torso coiled as tight as a bow under draw. I was already uncoiling from the hip up as the shining steel of the Germani's sword passed harmlessly above my head. As my body unwound I powered upward with my legs, endowing my blade with even more velocity. The honed edge effortlessly sliced through the thick muscles of the guard's neck and cleaved his spine, the severed head thudding onto the floor next to where delicate mosaics depicted Neptune driving his chariot. A heartbeat later the headless corpse collapsed to the ground, silencing the conversation.

Bassus seemed unconcerned and waved away the incident as if it were trivial. "You have done me a favour. I have been considering getting rid of Adalbehrt for some time now", he said. "He was obedient, but tended to get ahead of himself on occasion."

I strolled closer, the bloody sword still in my fist.

The nearest senator stood from his couch. "Why do you come to us with a blade in your hand, Lucius Domitius?" he asked, and gestured to his companions. "We are but friends who sought shelter from the ravaging mob - from the riots that you caused by your propensity for violence."

"I have come for justice", I replied. "You murdered my friend Marcus, stole the Empire's gold and used the coin to persuade the Germani to ravage Italia. Your hands are stained by the blood of thousands."

A wicked grimace split the man's lips, indicating that rather than having remorse, he revelled in the accomplishment of it all. "There is no court in the city, not even in the entire Empire, that will find us guilty of a crime", the senator spat.

"I have stood in the ranks of the legions and faced the horde with only a shield and a sword", I replied. "The screaming men who came at me with iron in their fists and specks of spittle lodged in their beards were never brought to trial. Nevertheless, it was easy to know who needed killing. The barbarians, at least, have honour, but you are traitors to Rome who plunge daggers into the backs of innocent men."

"You have no right to…" But he got not further because the tip of my sword had cut deep into his throat. I twisted the weapon, jerked the blade from the bone of his spine, and the corpse collapsed onto the ornate divan.

Confronted with the bloodshed, one of the conspirators lost his nerve and gained his feet. His eyes darted this way and that like a trapped animal's, and he started for a doorway located in the far wall, no doubt a passage leading to safety.

"Sit, coward", Bassus snapped. "You have taken the oath. Choose now - you are either with us or against us."

Meekly the man retook his seat.

Bassus whispered a command, and in response one of the dark shapes concealed in the shadows behind him moved into the light and placed himself in between his master and me. In his right fist he clutched a long-bladed stabbing spear with a foot-long haft.

The man's short-sleeved scaled vest, that extended to his knees, failed to conceal a frame heavy with muscle. He was not built like the big-boned Germani champions north of the Danube, but resembled the well-proportioned athletes whose exploits I had witnessed in the Flavian Amphitheatre. His skin was dark like that of a Nubian's, but unlike the people of the Nile, the man's entire face was decorated by a pattern of two dozen vertical lines that must have been gouged with a blade. It was not only his warrior markings that reminded me of my Hun friend, but also the way he carried himself, and for a brief moment I pitied the man for being enthralled to such a wicked master.

Bassus must have noticed my interest. "You are not the only man who owns a tame savage with a scarred face, Lord Emperor", he said.

"The Hun is my friend, not my slave", I replied.

"Call it what you wish", he shrugged. "Like Obba does my bidding, your friend does yours."

"Those in the know consider the Nokarians the best warriors in the known world", Bassus continued, indicating the olive-skinned man. "The reason why they are almost never seen in the lands of Rome is because they are notoriously difficult to come by. Few slave traders are willing to brave the hinterland of Africa - not only due to the propensity of the Garamantes and the Berbers to demand exorbitant bribes for crossing their territory, but also because of the thousands of miles of bandit-infested wasteland that needs to be negotiated before struggling through jungles inhabited by creatures straight from Hades", he added, and took another swallow of wine.

Then Bassus's gaze settled on the goblet in his hand. "Where are my manners?" he said with a warm smile, as if addressing a guest at a banquet. "May I offer you a goblet of falernian?"

I shook my head.

"Are you sure?" he asked. "One never knows when it may be one's last."

He took my silence as an answer in the negative.

Then his eyes turned as cold as a viper's. "Suit yourself", he sneered, and barked a command at the Nokarian. "Cut him to pieces!"

Never before had I faced a man who was a master of the short stabbing spear, a weapon unknown in the Empire. I expected him to wield it in the same way that the Germani tribes use the spear, but I was almost immediately proven wrong.

With both hands on the haft, Obba executed a cut like one would with a sword, the blade of his spear moving horizontally from left to right. I had expected the unexpected and skipped back to avoid the strike. The blade narrowly missed, but rather than to retreat he stepped in, reversing the path of the double-edged weapon, this time leading with the other edge. Again I retreated and his weapon found only air.

He shifted his weight to his back foot and, anticipating a retreat, I stepped in to execute a thrust of my own. The Nokarian stepped back, but in the same movement he thrust with his spear, this time a one-handed move aimed at my helmetless head. I was sure that the thrust would fall short, but he surprised me by allowing the haft of the spear to slide through his fingers, thereby increasing his reach by more than a foot.

I twisted my body to the side and jerked my head from the path of the blade, but the edge of his iron scored a bloody line along my cheek. Wishing to push his advantage, he stepped in and cut from low to high across my body. I parried the spear with the flat of my sword, stepped in as well, and landed a blow to the side of his head with my left elbow that rocked him on his feet and he stumbled backward.

I moved with him, disengaged my blade and managed to draw the edge across his upper arm while deflecting his counterstrike with my iron-studded vambrace.

Ignoring the pain of the bleeding wound Obba set his jaw and went on the offensive. Using a single-handed grip he drew back his weapon over his shoulder and brought the blade of the spear around. I had no choice but to parry, and met him blade to blade, but it was a feint and the iron butt of his spear flicked around and landed a numbing blow against my right forearm, almost causing me to lose my grip on my sword.

He moved in for the kill, but as he stepped in I grabbed the haft of the spear with my left hand and brought my own blade to bear.

In turn he adroitly caught my forearm before my blade bit.

Like two bulls wrestling for dominance, we ended up locked in a stalemate.

From across the Nokarian's shoulder I noticed that Bassus was speaking with his other guard. The man issued a sneer, hefted his war axe, and started to move in our direction. There was little doubt in my mind what his orders were.

In that moment Arash came to me and whispered into my ear.

"Why do you do his bidding?" I growled under my breath.

"The old devil holds my woman", Obba replied in broken Latin, and tried to throw me over his hip - a move which I countered by shifting my weight.

"I have the power to remedy that", I said, and slackened my grip to show my peaceful intent. "Help me extinguish this evil and tomorrow when the sun rises you will leave Rome a free man with your woman at your side and a purse bulging with gold."

"Swear it on your god", he replied.

"I swear it by Arash the Avenger, the lord of the field of blood", I said.

"I, too, serve the god of war", Obba growled, relinquished his grip on my arm, spun around, and cast his spear deep into the chest of the approaching guard. The man clutched the protruding haft with both hands and toppled sideways onto the floor.

I indicated Bassus's fellow traitors. "Watch them while I speak with your master", I said, gesturing for Obba to retrieve his spear.

Bassus must have realised that the tide had turned, and in a sudden panic he jumped up from the couch. "In Rome we have laws", he screeched as I made my way towards him. "But you, lowborn, came to confront us with your arrogance and your blade. You are no better suited to the position of emperor than Claudius Gothicus was, or for that matter, Gallienus."

I came to a halt a pace in front of the head of the snake.

"My father was a man of honour who could trace his lineage back to the men of wisdom appointed by Romulus himself", I said. "Yet, what made him a great man was his courage and his sense of honour, not his birthright."

"Then you must take after your mother, the Scythian whore he took as a woman", Bassus spat.

"You once advised me to use iron and I will heed your words", I said, and thrust my blade deep into his gut.

He gasped and collapsed forward, his eyes wide open in surprise. I caught him by the toga and kept him upright with my blade.

"I give you iron as repayment for the murder of my friend, Marcus", I whispered, and kicked the body from my sword.

I heard a shout from behind and twisted my neck just in time to see the blade of a dagger descend towards my neck. But Obba was true to his word and a stabbing spear slammed into the skull of the senator. The impact flung the corpse across a low table, food scattering onto the priceless rugs.

The others must have realised that their fate was sealed, and drew their daggers. Within the space of four heartbeats seven corpses decorated the gold and ivory inlaid couches.

I stared at the dead traitors without remorse, and felt a great weight lift from my shoulders.

"Let us leave this place before we are tainted with the evil of these men", Obba growled.

Just then the room shook with the power of heavy blows from the way I had entered. Moments later, the portcullis shattered into kindling to reveal Hostilius wielding a heavy smiths' hammer. Behind him Gordas stood with a battle-axe in a fist and Diocles with his sword drawn.

The Primus Pilus took a moment to take in the carnage in the room. "We wanted to lend a hand", he said, lowering the hammer. "But it seems like you've done most of the dirty work already."

Chapter 33 – Peace

It was early in the afternoon when we returned to the legionary camp. I had had no rest for many watches, and went to the furs without removing my armour. None dared to disturb me - well, almost no one dared.

Sometime during the last watch of the afternoon, I heard someone fiddling with the flap of the tent. I turned onto my other side and half opened my eyes, just in time to see a man ducking through the door. As he entered, the sun that was low in the sky, blinded me for a heartbeat. With the yellow rays behind him, I could not discern his features other than that he was dressed in a simple undyed tunic.

I made to get to my feet, but he stalled me with an open palm. His manner somehow served to comfort me and I did not reach for the blade I kept close at all time.

As he sat down on the bed, I recognised him. "You have had a long day, Lucius", he said. "Don't get up, you need the rest."

"Marcus?" I gasped.

"I have come to say goodbye", he said, failing to hide the sorrow in his eyes. "And to thank you."

"But why are you sad then?" I asked.

"All I ever wanted was to see the Empire strong and united", he replied. "And for a short time, I believed that I would accomplish it. It was not my fate, but now I have left you with an almost impossible task."

I must have frowned, which caused Marcus to grin. "I am not sorrowful for myself, Lucius", he said. "But for your sake."

I chuckled. "Surely you are no longer blinded by the veil of the flesh", I said. "You must know how it ends?"

Marcus laid a comforting hand on my armoured shoulder. "There is much to be done, my friend", he said. "Keep your eye on the prize and remember to trust in the gods."

I woke with Segelinde's hand on my shoulder. "You were laughing in your sleep", she said.

"Marcus came to say goodbye", I said.

"I thought that it would happen now that his shade is at peace", my wife replied. "It has been appeased by the blood of his murderers. You have done well to honour your friend, husband. You will not see Marcus again until you cross the river."

Her words made me think of a man that once had been as close as a brother to me. "Sometimes, Kniva comes to me in the middle hour of the night", I confessed. "The gods know, I have tried to avenge him but I have failed time and again."

She squeezed my shoulder so hard, I felt it through the layers of felt and iron. "He comes to me too", she said. "Fear not, Arash the Avenger will give you a chance to do your duty to your sword brother."

"Now I must go", she said.

"Why?" I asked, concerned that she, too, was a vision in a dream.

"Because I have ordered the slaves to pour you a bath", she replied, and scrunched her nose. "You smell."

* * *

After I had washed the blood and grime from my body and slaves had massaged my tired muscles with olive oil and lavender, I strolled to the *praetorium*.

"About bloody time", Hostilius said with a grin, and waved me to a seat.

I could not help but notice that the Primus Pilus exuded a pleasant aroma. I sniffed the air. "Do I smell cedarwood or is it myrrh?" I asked.

Hostilius suddenly appeared decidedly uncomfortable. "I don't use women's stuff", he scowled, and indicated Diocles, who also appeared clean and refreshed. "It's the Greek that's reeking like a Sasanian whore."

Before Diocles could reply, Placidianus was escorted into the tent. I had been expecting him to report on the situation in the city.

"Tell us", I said.

"Rome is still in chaos", he replied. "Word on the street is that the praetorian prefect fell on his sword after he learned of the demise of the traitors."

"Without the instigators stoking the fire, the flames will soon dissipate", I replied.

"What are your orders, Lord Emperor?" he asked.

"I have prepared instructions for the praetorian prefect", I said, and indicated for Diocles to hand Placidianus written orders sealed with the mark of the emperor.

A frown of confusion appeared on his face.

"By imperial decree you have been promoted to praetorian prefect, Julius Placidianus", Diocles said, and passed him the scroll.

"Lord", the new prefect said, and saluted in the way of the legions.

"Your first mission is to restore order in the city", I said.

"I understand, Lord Emperor", he said. "And I will obey."

* * *

It took almost seven days for the violence to abate.

On Diocles's recommendation I closed the mint located at the Temple of Juno on the Capitoline Hill. I also took away the authority of the Senate to issue coins, which did not ingratiate me with the city fathers, but the stories of the fate of Bassus and his fellow conspirators put so much fear into the hearts of the senators that they kept their counsel.

But an emperor who rules by fear alone cannot endure. For that reason, I sent Fonteius and his men into the city for a night of sponsored debauchery. Their only orders were to report back to me the next day on the mood of the men of the *head count*.

* * *

"Sorry to say it, lord", Fonteius said, "but the mob hates you. Don't get me wrong, the ones who served under the standard know what you're about, but the common men despise you."

"Why?" I asked. "I have done them no disservice."

"I think the incident at the mint was the last straw", he said. "When them senator's guards laid into the workers. The last few years the rich got a lot richer and the poor poorer. Many men don't have enough to eat, never mind something to drink."

"Is there anything to be done to improve my public image?" I asked no one in particular.

"Mayhap you should amend some of the harsher laws that oppress the common people", Diocles suggested. "It will send a message that you are a benevolent ruler."

Hostilius choked on his falernian. "The Greek has lost his mind", the Primus Pilus said. "If you want them to love you, give them free wine for a while. Mark my words, they will sing your praises in the streets. Drunk men are never disgruntled."

I raised an eyebrow, impressed with Hostilius's grasp of the common man's needs. "How much gold have we gained by expropriating the estates of the traitors?" I asked Diocles.

"The treasury is healthy", he replied, which told me that an enormous amount of coin was involved.

"Change the dole", I said. "Add rations of pork, salt, oil and wine to the normal distribution of bread."

"Once you have given it", my aide said, "they will riot if you take it away."

"If we do not, the dissent festering in the streets of Rome will spread like the plague to infect every part of the Empire", I said. "The purple will be taken up by someone like Bassus and the Empire will be lost forever."

Diocles thought on my words for twenty heartbeats. "Should we issue fresh or smoked pork?" he asked, and reached for his stylus to begin drafting the orders.

Ten days later, two days before I planned to formally enter the city, I sent out Fonteius and Hostilius to gauge the waters in the drinking holes of the Subura.

"I recommend that you double the guard tomorrow", Hostilius said the following morning when he strolled into the *praetorium* with a palm pressed to his temple.

I issued a sigh, as I had harboured doubts whether the dole would succeed to expunge my tainted reputation.

"Because the people love you so much they will clamber over each other just to touch the hem of your robes", the Primus Pilus added with a grin. "Without sufficient guards you may suffocate."

"That is good news", I said. "We cannot fight a war on two fronts."

"What war?" Hostilius asked, suddenly alert. "Have the Germani breached the borders again?"

"No tribune", I replied. "This time we will be the aggressor. As soon as spring arrives, we will take the legions east to liberate the provinces that Zenobia has claimed while we were under siege from the tribes."

"Good", he replied, poured himself cup of wine and chugged the contents. "I have a score to settle with that bitch."

* * *

To be continued.

Historical Note – Main characters

Main characters of the series

Eochar - Lucius Domitius Aurelianus, or Aurelian, as he is better known, I believe, was the most accomplished Roman to ever walk this earth. Some would disagree, which is their right.

In time, all will be revealed, but for now I will leave you with a few quotes from the surviving records.

From the English Translation of the (much-disputed) *Historia Augusta Volume III*:

"Aurelian, born of humble parents and from his earliest years very quick of mind and famous for his strength, never let a day go by, even though a feast-day or a day of leisure, on which he did not practise with the spear, the bow and arrow, and other exercises in arms."

"... he was a comely man, good to look upon because of his manly grace, rather tall in stature, and very strong in his muscles; he was a little too fond of wine and food, but he indulged his passions rarely; he exercised the greatest severity and a discipline that had no equal, being extremely ready to draw his sword."

"..."Aurelian Sword-in-hand," and so he would be identified."

"... in the war against the Sarmatians, Aurelian with his own hand slew forty-eight men in a single day and that in the course of several days he slew over nine hundred and fifty, so that the boys even composed in his honour the following jingles and dance-ditties, to which they would dance on holidays in soldier fashion:

"Thousand, thousand, thousand we've beheaded now.

One alone, a thousand we've beheaded now.

He shall drink a thousand who a thousand slew.

So much wine is owned by no one as the blood which he has shed."

Marcus - Marcus Aurelius Claudius was an actual person, famous in history, and I believe a close friend of Lucius Domitius.

Cai is a figment of my imagination. The Roman Empire had contact with China, or Serica, as it was called then. His origins, training methods and fighting style I have researched in detail. Cai, to me, represents the seldom written about influence of China on the Roman Empire.

Primus Pilus Hostilius Proculus is a fictional character. He represents the core of the legions. The hardened plebeian officer.

Gordas – The fictional Hun/Urugundi general. Otto J Maenschen-Helfen writes in his book, The World of the Huns, that he believes the Urugundi to be a Hunnic tribe. Zosimus, the ancient Byzantine writer, mentions the Urugundi in an alliance with the Goths and the Scythians during the mid-third century AD. (Maenchen-Helfen's book is fascinating. He could read Russian, Persian, Greek and Chinese, enabling him to interpret the original primary texts.)

Vibius Marcellinus was an actual person. He will feature more later.

Segelinde – the Gothic princess, is an invention. However, Ulpia Severina, the woman who was married to Aurelian, is not.

Lucius's Contubernia – Ursa, Silentus, Pumilio and Felix. They were not actual people, but represent the common soldiers within the Roman Legions.

Diocles – was an actual man. The son of a freedman who became one of the great men in history.

King Bradakos of the Roxolani never lived.

Characters that make a guest appearance.

Postumus was a Roman legate of Batavian descent who emerged as the dominant figure on the Rhine during Valerian's reign.

Aurelius **Felicissimus** is believed to have been the *Procurator Summarum Rationum*, or for lack of a better description, the master of the Roman mint. His first name is not known but north of Rome an inscription has been found that makes mention of a certain Aurelius Felicissimus, a procurator that lived in the time of Aurelian.

Senator **Pomponius Bassus** is famous for apparently advising Aurelian to use gold and iron. Gold for the friends of the Empire and iron for its enemies. Apparently Bassus tasted the iron of his own advice when Aurelian suppressed the revolt of the mint workers.

Julius **Placidianus** was the prefect of the *vigiles* in Rome. Some believe that Claudius Gothicus promoted him to praetorian prefect while others are convinced that **Heraclianus** was still prefect during the start of Aurelian's rein.

Historical Note – Avenger storyline

State of the Roman Empire at the time of this book (October 270 AD to August 271 AD)

With the Danubian border secured, Aurelian departed for Rome.

A delegation of the Senate met the emperor in Ravenna where he receives the news that the Alemanni/Semnones (aka Juthungi) has invaded.

Aurelian cleverly crossed the Danube with a part of his force and ambushed the invaders on the northern bank, where they were encircled.

While besieging the Semnones, Aurelian was called away to the Danubian frontier due to an emergency that some associate with a renewed invasion of the Vandali. After dealing with the immediate threat, the emperor received the unsettling news that the Semnones invaders somehow managed to escape their encirclement and were heading south towards Italia through the Alpine Passes.

Aurelian immediately rushed south, catching up with the Germani near Placentia. A great battle (Battle of the Trebia) was fought where the Semnones concealed a large part of their force within the forest bordering the plain. The Romans were ambushed and suffered a crushing defeat. It is recorded that the emperor rallied his forces, avoiding a total rout of the Roman army. The setback was so severe that some feared the total collapse of the Empire.

Fearing the arrival of the Germani horde at the gates of Rome, the Senate, at first unwilling, agreed to consult the Sibylline Books. The sacred texts were opened and the rites observed. It is recorded that after the battle of Ticinum (Pavia), the Germani survivors claimed that an army of spectres fought on Aurelian's side. This is attributed to the intervention of the gods of Rome, who had been placated by the sacred rites. A surviving ancient inscription near Ticinum by the official overseeing the walls, compares Aurelian to Hercules while another refers to him as 'of eternal victory'.

Some invaders managed to escape the rout, but Aurelian pursued them through the passes and annihilated them.

Having crushed the Germani, the emperor travelled to Rome - not only to cement his reign, but also to confront the senators and functionaries who were defrauding the treasury.

Felicissimus, one of the ringleaders behind the corruption, died early on. The circumstances surrounding his demise remain unclear.

Being a military man, Aurelian quelled the uprising of the mint workers mercilessly and dealt with the instigators quickly and decisively. According to the records, seven thousand lost their lives in the ensuing violence.

Historical Note – Random items

- The mint in ancient Rome abutted the Temple of Juno Moneta.
- The *libra*, or Roman pound, weighs 328.9 grams.
- Roman silver ingots weighed one *libra*.
- During the third century, the eight-day week was still officially in use in the Roman Empire. The seven-day week, which originates from the ancient Babylonians, was adopted early in the fourth century AD. The eighth day of the week was traditionally a market day - a close relative of the modern weekend.
- The measurement of the double ditches surrounding Carnuntum is based on excavations at the Roman fort at Sorviodurum.
- Pike and redfish (huchen) are two of the most common fish species in the Danube. Mayhap it was different in times of old.
- The Romans believed that the three spinners of fate, the *Parcae*, were even more powerful than the gods.
- One of the largest and oldest trees in Europe is the *Heeder Linde*, a large leaf linden tree near Heeder,

Germany. I envisioned the spinners of fate sitting at the base of such a gnarled, thousand-year-old trunk.
- *Sabaia*, an ancient barley beer, was popular in Roman Pannonia.
- Ancient Pannonia was heavily forested. Later Emperors cleared much of the great forests to make way for farmland.
- Celtic nard, family of the better-known spikenard, used to be cultivated in ancient Roman Pannonia. The essential oil derived from the flowers of the plant was used in perfume or to spice wine.
- Beech tar is an excellent lure to attract wild boar over long distances.
- Secundus, 'the madman' whom I introduced in the previous book in the series, was inspired by an inscription on a gravestone in Bolzano, on the Via Claudia Augusta. Secundus Reguntus is the oldest known inhabitant of the town. He passed away early in the fourth century at the age of fifty-five.
- Moccus was the boar-god of the ancient Celts. He was a protector of hunters and associated with war.
- When conditions are favourable, a northerly wind causes orographic lift on the windward side of the

Alps. The phenomena that causes intense snowstorms is called the *Nordstau*.

- Cetium was situated less than a day's march south of the Danube. The town's purpose was to supply the six auxiliary forts along the *limes*. A stone inscription mentions Aelius Flavius who had risen to high secular offices during the third century. The town was surrounded by forests.

- The favoured route from Iuvavum (Salzburg) in Raetia to Italia was via the Radstädter Tauern Pass. From there, the route led south to the town of Sanctium (Villach), east to Tarvis, down the Isonzo Valley and then across the Pontebba Pass and along the Ferra Valley to Udine. I imagine that this would have been the route taken by the Semnones after they broke out of the siege of the Romans.

- The alternative route that Lucius took begins near Lauriacum and crosses the Pyhrn Pass near Selzthal. From there it continues south across the Solkscharte Pass to Klagenfurt. From Klagenfurt one could travel west to Sanctium (Villach) which is situated on the 'Salzburg to Aquileia' route.

- The oldest wagon wheel and axle discovered to date is from a bog in Ljubljana (Emona). The wheel is a solid disk crafted from ash while the axle was made of oak. It is older than five thousand years. Iron-rimmed wheels have been in use for two and a half thousand ears.

- The Sibylline Books were a compilation of ancient verses written by Greek and Roman oracles. They were only consulted when Rome was in great peril. According to legend, the last king of Rome was offered nine books of prophecy by the Cumaean Sibyl at a very high price. Twice Tarquinius refused the old woman's offer and twice she committed three books to the flames. With only three books remaining, the king consulted the augers, relented on their advice, and purchased the remaining three at the original exorbitant price.

- *Latifundia*, large, slave-based, industrial farms became more common during the later years of the Empire. These estates usually included a luxurious villa for when the wealthy owner wished to visit.

- The exact site of the Battle of Fano remains unknown. We do know that it took place on the banks of the Metaurus River near Fanum Fortunae (Fano).

- Although the ancient people of the steppes had access to cow and sheep milk, they preferred mare's milk.

Mare's milk is high in vitamin C which would, theoretically, compensate for a diet lacking in fruits and vegetables.
- A major focus of Roman religion was to interpret the signs of the gods to establish which actions would succeed and which ones were doomed to failure.
- The Celtic god Poeninos (the one who rules from the peaks) is linked to the name of the Apennine Mountains.
- The Etruscans, the ancient people who inhabited central Italy, apparently referred to themselves as the Rasenna. During the fourth century BC, the Senones, a Celtic tribe, displaced the Etruscans in Central Italy. Senones is believed to mean 'ancient ones' in old Celtic.
- Three classes of soldiers kept order in ancient Rome. The praetorian guard was the elite guard to the emperor. The urban cohorts reported to the urban prefect and was comparable to a modern police force. The city watchmen (*vigiles*) reported to the prefect of the *vigiles*. Their duties involved fighting fires, patrolling the streets at night and keeping order in the city.

- No archaeological trace remains of the Temple of Jupiter Apenninus which stood in the shade of Monte Catria near Scheggia in Central Italy.
- The House of Sallust is a famous *hospitia* (ancient hotel) unearthed in Pompeii. It used to be a residential house before it was converted into a hotel.
- Aurelius Heraclianus was the praetorian prefect under Gallienus. Some say that he was involved in Gallienus's assassination and died shortly after, while others believe that he served under Claudius Gothicus and committed suicide at some later date.
- Julius Placidianus became praetorian prefect under Aurelian, being promoted from his position as prefect of the city watchmen. It is unlikely that the promotion was done as a reward for assisting Aurelian to quell the revolt, but possible.
- The Aqua Appia was the first Roman Aqueduct. Most of its length it ran underground until it emerged somewhere at the base of the Caelian Hill. By the first century AD, some sections had been repurposed as a sewer.
- The Macellum Magnum was a large indoor market located on the Caelian Hill. Here, I assume, the very

wealthy spent their abundance of coin on exotic meat, fish and delicacies.

- The Nok culture/empire existed in the area that is today known as Nigeria. Various Roman missions to West Africa are documented, most of them during the first century AD. The Ife Empire is believed to have develop from the Nok culture.
- I based Obba's appearance, specifically his facial scars, on that of the more recent Yoruba tribal markings and the bust of an ancient Ife king that showed the same scarring. The Nok peoples' weapons are unknown so I based Obba's spear on the Zulu (South African tribe) short stabbing spear made famous by Shaka Zulu.

Historical Note – Place names

Castra Regina – Regensburg, Germany.

Carnuntum on the Danube – Near Petronell-Carnuntum, Austria.

Brigetio – Szony, Hungary.

Gerulata, the Roman fort east of Carnuntum – Rusovce, Slovakia.

Babylon – Qsar el Shamee, Egypt.

Aquincum – Budapest, Hungary.

Vindobona – Vienna, Austria.

Virinum – Magdalensburg, Austria.

Arelape – Pöchlarn, Austria.

Lauriacum – Enns, Austria.

Ovilava – Wells, Austria.

Tergolape – Schwanenstadt, Austria.

Isonta River – Salzach River.

Iuvavum – Salzburg, Austria.

Sanctium – Villach, Austria.

Aesontius River – Isonzo River, Northeastern Italy.

Placentia – Piacenza, Northern Italy.

Nura River – Nure River, near Piacenza.

Genua – Genoa, Italy.

Camillomagus – Redavalle, a few miles west of Piacenza on the road to Genoa.

Forum Cornelii – Imola, Northern Italy.

Ticinum – Pavia, Northern Italy.

Posterior Rhine – Hinterrhein River that runs along the Septimer Pass in Switzerland.

Pons Drusi – Bolzano, Northern Italy.

Author's Note

I trust that you have enjoyed the fifteenth book in the series.

In many instances, written history relating to this period has either been lost in the fog of time, or it might never have been recorded. That is especially applicable to most of the tribes which Rome referred to as barbarians. These peoples did not record history by writing it down. They only appear in the written histories of the Greeks, Romans, Persians and Chinese, who often regarded them as enemies.

In any event, my aim is to be as historically accurate as possible, but I am sure that I inadvertently miss the target from time to time, in which case I apologise to the purists among my readers.

Kindly take the time to provide a rating and/or a review.

I will keep you updated via my blog with regards to the progress on the sixteenth book in the series.

Feel free to contact me any time via my website. I will respond.

www.HectorMillerBooks.com

Printed in Great Britain
by Amazon